Sam smiled. "You really care about other people."

Did he care about her, too? Priscilla wondered. "I'm sure your father is sorry about what happened."

"I think so. At least that's what I told myself, or I would never have returned to Wisconsin." He slid his arm around her shoulder and turned her so that he could look down into her face. "We wouldn't be standing here in the moonlight if I hadn't come home."

Her pulse thrummed. "Then I'm glad you did."

"Me, too." His gaze seared her. "And I was lucky to find you again."

Time stood still, and Priscilla felt as if she could stay in this moment—in Sam's arms—forever.

She only wished that were true.

Dear Reader,

There are two of us writing as Lynn Patrick—Linda Sweeney and Patricia Rosemoor—and we're both horse crazy, so *The Long Road Home* was especially fun for us to write. In the past, we traveled to Kentucky to research horse farms for a story. And the Kentucky Derby, of course. Plus, on a trip to Ireland, we had a private tour of The Irish National Stud.

Linda grew up on a farm and often had to round up the cows on one of their horses. I (Patricia) rode for pleasure and competed both in Western and English. I got to round up cows, too, one time when doing research for a ranching series. My mount used to be the lead horse, and when the cows saw him, they ran like everything, with my horse right on their tails. The cows crossed the river as was planned, only a bit too soon, as they brought down some fencing.

We hope you'll enjoy a fun ride on the road to love with Priscilla and Sam.

Best,

Lynn Patrick

HEARTWARMING

The Long Road Home

Lynn Patrick

Recycling programs for this product may not exist in your area.

ISBN-13: 978-0-373-36720-7

The Long Road Home

This edition published by arrangement with Harlequin Books S.A.

For questions and comments about the quality of this book, please contact us at CustomerService@Harlequin.com.

Printed in U.S.A.

Lynn Patrick is the pseudonym for two best friends who started writing together a few decades ago. Linda is a professor with a reading specialty, and Patricia writes as Patricia Rosemoor. Together they enjoy creating worlds that are lightened by the unexpected, fun and sometimes wonderful vagaries of real life.

Books by Lynn Patrick

Harlequin Heartwarming

Shall We Dance
The Marriage Assignment
Home to Sparrow Lake
A Forever Home

Harlequin Superromance

Good Vibrations

Visit the Author Profile page
at Harlequin.com for more titles.

For all those dedicated people who have
given the wild mustangs at the
Black Hills Wild Horse Sanctuary in South Dakota
another chance at living free.

PROLOGUE

A SKITTER OF hoofbeats drummed through his subconscious, gradually awakening him. With a start, Sam Larson sat up in bed. No dream, the sound was coming from outside the cabin. A rush of hoofbeats and whinnies and snorts…

He shot out of bed and into his jeans, then hopped across the room while pulling on his boots. The door opened to a Wisconsin night swept by a warm breeze and silvered by moonlight. Before he could step outside, one of his horses whipped by the open doorway.

Sam whistled. "Cloud, whoa, girl." He whistled again.

The Pinto stopped, the skin along her spine quivering. When he called a second time, she turned and trotted back to him.

"What are you doing out here?"

She snorted in answer.

He threaded calloused fingers through the mare's black mane and coaxed her back toward the pasture, and from a distance saw that the grassy expanse was empty. The gate was open. Horses scattered, prancing nervously, spooked, one heading for the opening in the property fence that would take him directly onto the highway.

"Tomcat!" Letting go of Cloud, Sam moved toward the gelding, calling him with a sharp series of whistles.

Tomcat slowed and threw his head in Sam's direction. His eyes rolled and he still moved sideways toward the opening, as if he was trying to make up his mind whether or not to listen.

"C'mon, boy, you don't want to go out there." His heart thundered with dread at the idea of the horse getting onto the road where he could be run over...or, rather, run into, a thousand pounds of flesh versus a ton of metal. Sam stalked him. What the heck had gotten into his small herd? "C'mon back here where it's nice and safe."

Another sharp whistle convinced the horse. His big head hung low, Tomcat switched direction and lumbered toward Sam.

"Where did you think you were going?" He patted the horse's neck and looked back to see Cloud directly behind him. "You could have gotten killed out there."

Grabbing onto their manes, he spoke in a low soothing voice as he walked them to the pasture, saw them inside and closed the gate. A glance around told him the other horses were settling as if already forgetting whatever had riled them in the first place.

He rounded up the horses and got them back in the pasture one at a time: Chief, Acer, Lightning, Marengo, Rain Dancer.

They were calm now, but something—or someone—had spooked them.

That gate didn't open itself. And those horses didn't just calmly wander out of the pasture.

Sam ran a shaky hand through his hair. Back in town for less than a month and his new business could have been ruined before it even got revved up. But surely no one had reason to want that. No doubt it was some wild kid playing a trick on him. He'd been wild enough himself as a teenager, had gotten into more trouble than his father would stand.

He looked over to the farmhouse he'd grown up in and thought about the reasons for his return to Sparrow Lake. More trouble, and this time not of his own making. He shook his head and wondered if he'd made a huge mistake in coming home.

Wondered if he should report the incident to the authorities.

Even as he thought it, he knew he wouldn't. The horses were okay. And he didn't know how that gate got opened. Not to mention he'd rather deal with the situation himself. Bad run-ins with the authorities in the past meant he didn't exactly trust them in the present.

Some say the past can come back to haunt you, whether for good or ill.

Sam hoped his luck would finally change for the better.

CHAPTER ONE

ENTERING THE ONE-ROOM Sparrow Lake Library to collect her mother who'd given an early morning workshop for new readers, Priscilla Ryan paused just inside the door when a stack of brochures on a counter caught her eye: Larson Dude Ranch, Trail Rides and Riding Lessons.

Priscilla didn't know of any dude ranches in this part of Wisconsin and wondered if Dwayne Larson had really turned his dairy farm into a ranch. Didn't make sense. She picked up the brochure but didn't see anything about the owner. And then another thought occurred to her, but no, surely Sam hadn't come home after fifteen years.

Sam Larson, one of her big mistakes.

The day after the prom, the town's bad boy had simply gotten on his motorcycle and had left Sparrow Lake without saying goodbye. Her heart had been broken...but she'd gotten over it.

Why would Sam return now?

An ironic question considering she'd been elsewhere for years herself. First, college in Madison, then a lucrative job in Milwaukee. A year ago, she'd given up that life and had returned to Sparrow Lake to start her own small business, The Main Street Cheese Shoppe. Not long after, her latest boyfriend had decided he didn't really want to take the next step. Yep, that was her lot in life—always the bridesmaid, seven weddings so far. She'd figured if she was going to live single, she wanted to be closer to her aging parents.

Could Sam have the same idea?

"Oh, darling, I meant to be outside, really." Appearing frazzled as she'd been for months, her graying red hair frizzing around her plump face, Helen Ryan stopped in front of her daughter and punched her glasses back up her short nose. "I just got caught up with Maddie Hawkins, but I'm ready now."

"No problem, Mom." Her mother was always running on borrowed time lately. Priscilla shoved the brochure in her pocket. She didn't have the energy to think about the past. "Let's get going."

Her mother hurried along, looking even more petite in her oversize brown jacket that didn't quite match her brown pants. It was probably another purchase from a local church's resale shop. Mom didn't think clothes were all that important.

"When are they arriving?" her mother asked.

"Their plane is scheduled to land in an hour."

And while it would only take a half hour or so to get to Milwaukee, they had to navigate the airport, park and get to the gate.

They left the library, her mother practically singing with happiness. "Just think, we'll have the girls for half the summer!"

"Right."

Her nieces, sixteen-year-old Alyssa and twelve-year-old Mia, would be staying with Priscilla in her apartment above the cheese store. Aside from her office, she had a second bedroom that was used for guests on occasion. Her older brother Paul, a lawyer for an international firm in New York, was headed to the Middle East for six weeks, and he'd asked her to take his girls. He and his wife felt their daughters would be safer in Wisconsin. Priscilla had gladly agreed and was as excited as her parents. The last time they'd seen the girls had been more than three years ago, when Paul had brought his family in for

Christmas. Her parents had wanted to visit her brother and family in New York once, but Paul had begged off, insisting he was too busy and that it wasn't a good time.

They got into Priscilla's SUV, her mother grunting a little as she lifted her oversize purse into her lap. Priscilla bit her lip. That purse was like a magician's hat. Mom could find anything you needed in there. Priscilla had once suggested a smaller purse might be a good idea, but her mother's eyes had grown wide, her eyebrows had arched over her glasses and her mouth had gaped a little. Mom hadn't said a thing, just looked away, purse-lipped, obviously insulted, and Priscilla had never brought up the subject again.

As they headed out of town, Mom brought up her latest favorite subject.

"I told your father he'd better go buy that bathtub today. I want to be able to have the girls at least part of the time they're here."

"Right."

Though Priscilla knew that even if her father bought a new tub, it would probably take him the whole summer to replace the one he'd torn out months ago, the reason the girls would be staying with her. There was a gaping hole in the bathroom, and her mother didn't want her granddaughters having to take a jury-rigged shower in the unfinished basement.

"You would think that now that Roger is retired from the post office—" Mom hesitated and sniffed "—he would look forward to finishing all those home improvement projects he promised to take on."

"Right."

What else could she say? She didn't want to spur on more complaints. Her mother was doing a good enough job on her own.

"You know he spends most of his time asleep in front of the television."

"Right."

She'd heard it all before, and sadly, it was true. Priscilla only wished her dad would find something to bring him out of his slump. He'd changed since retiring, and not for the better. He used to be a vital man with tons of energy. Now he had a personal relationship with his old worn-in recliner.

"I fear the plumbing problems are never going to be fixed!"

"Right."

Her normally positive, always busy mother was only working part time at the library now, and spending so much time with her altered-state husband was driving her crazy.

And if Priscilla didn't change the subject, her mother would drive *her* crazy.

"Hey, did you see this brochure?" She pulled it out of her pocket and held it out. "I found it when I came into the library. Larson Dude Ranch?"

Mom took it. "Hmm. Dwayne Larson retired from farming."

"To start a new business?"

"Doesn't seem likely. He planned to sell the dairy farm acres to surrounding neighbors. Last I heard, Dwayne got himself hurt in a roofing accident. I don't think he'd be up to running a new business, certainly not one with horses, even if he thought it was a good idea. Which I doubt anyway, knowing that old sourpuss."

A thrill shot through Priscilla's stomach. If not Dwayne, then…

"So you haven't heard anything about this dude ranch?" she asked, knowing they would pass it once they were on the highway.

"Nope. Why the interest?"

Priscilla heard the suspicion in that tone. She quickly said, "I thought Alyssa and Mia might like to go riding." Right, she'd come up with it just that second. An excuse for her interest.

"Maybe the girls would, Priscilla. I think I remember they like animals. At least I hope Mia loves those Hello Kitty pajamas I sent her."

Priscilla tightened her jaw. Her mother *thought*, didn't know for sure, because she never got to spend any time with her grandkids. Her brother might be a successful lawyer working for an international company, but the least he could do was visit his own parents and let them see their grandchildren a couple of times a year. Mom rarely heard from them unless she called.

"Lots of young girls go through a horse-crazy period," Priscilla said. "If that's the case, then we have something fun for them to do." On the highway now, she added, "The property is right ahead."

At first there was nothing to see except a new dude ranch sign, a freshly painted barn and fences, plus a small herd of horses chomping on grass in a nearby pasture. Then a tanned, lithe rider appeared, heading toward the horses.

"Is that Sam?" Priscilla murmured.

"Not sure. Haven't seen him for a decade."

"More like fifteen years."

Mom was craning, but Priscilla had to keep her eyes on the road.

"Huh. Looks like it *could* be him."

Priscilla didn't say anything, but her heart beat faster and she gripped the steering wheel. Hard.

It didn't matter, she told herself. She was over him. Sam Larson didn't deserve another thought.

SAM HARDLY SLEPT all night. He'd been up at least once an hour, checking on the horses. Thankfully, they'd settled down and the gate had stayed locked. Even so, by morning, he wasn't any less disturbed by what had happened. His gut was knotted and would probably stay that way until he figured out what was what.

So when Logan Keller showed up for work, the twenty-year-old got the brunt of Sam's worry. He'd barely stepped out of his truck before Sam asked, "Hey, Logan, you locked the pasture gate before you left yesterday, right?"

The kid looked away from him over to the pasture. "The gate was open?"

"Wide. And the horses were scattered, all riled up."

"They look all right." Logan turned back to Sam. "What happened?"

"If I hadn't come out of the cabin in time, Tomcat would have made it onto the highway. You ought to see what happens when an animal that size is hit by a vehicle. Especially a truck." The highway was a main route for eighteen wheelers. "We would have been picking up pieces of horseflesh this morning." He scowled at the thought.

"So you're blaming me?"

Sam realized the lanky kid looked real uncomfortable. "I didn't say that."

"Sounded like it."

"I just want to make sure we're both careful. And I want you to keep an eye open for anything that doesn't look right."

"Yeah, sure." Logan started to move off, then stopped. "You know, if you had a cattle guard on the entrance, Tomcat wouldn't have been able to get to the highway."

A cattle guard being a depression in the road covered by a grid of metal bars and fixed to cement footings on either side. Ranches all over the west had them. Sam had seen some local farms using them, too. The gaps between the bars were wide enough to be an effective barrier to animals reluctant to walk on the grates. But it didn't stop vehicles or people from crossing over.

"I plan on installing a cattle guard in the near future," he said. "Just haven't gotten around to it yet."

He wanted to wait until the business got a good start. He'd spent most of his savings. Not only had he turned the old dairy barn into a horse barn and spiffed it up, he'd renovated an old shed near the barn into a first-rate tack room. Not to mention what it cost to buy horses and tack. So far, he'd given a couple of lessons, and Logan had taken a few groups out on trail rides. There was a trail ride going out that afternoon, too. It was a start, but he couldn't afford to put out a couple thousand more dollars until he was sure his business was viable and would bring in a decent amount of income. But if someone was messing with his business…

"Go ahead, get to work," he told Logan.

The kid didn't wait to get away from him.

Sam ran a hand through his hair. Someone messing with his business? He didn't want to believe it. Returning to Sparrow Lake—

coming back to his home and his father—had been difficult enough.

Kids. It *had* to be kids. A prank that could have turned serious but hadn't. That was all it had been, what he had to believe.

He'd just lived a six-month nightmare not of his own doing.

This was a do-over for him in more than one way.

He had to make this work.

"HERE'S THE DUDE ranch we were telling you about," Mom gushed as they passed the Larson farm while driving back from the airport. "Look at those horses!"

"Wow, nice!" Mia leaned closer to her grandmother in the backseat to glance at a pinto and a sorrel near the fence. "I've been riding English so I won't have any problem. Western is easier."

At twelve, Mia was small, though Priscilla wondered if she'd grow much more in the next few years. She seemed to have the same petite frame as her grandmother, along with the thick red hair that seemed to have a life of its own. Though it was pulled back in a ponytail, tendrils kept escaping to curl around Mia's small freckled face.

"What do you think, Alyssa?" Mom asked.

Deeply involved with her cell phone, which had just beeped, the teenager didn't answer as she texted furiously.

"Alyssa?" Priscilla prodded, earning only a grunt in reply. "Would you like to visit a dude ranch?"

Still texting, Alyssa muttered, "Umm, maybe..."

"Can we do it this afternoon?" asked Mia, sounding enthusiastic.

Priscilla smiled. "We'll see. First we need lunch."

As Mia went on, explaining tack and boots and other horsey details to her grandmother, Priscilla felt grateful that they'd at least hit a homerun with one of her nieces. She gave the older one another irritable glance from the corner of her eye. In the past two years, a time in which the Wisconsin Ryans had not seen hide nor hair of the New York branch of the family, Alyssa had become a very pretty and stylish young woman. At least Priscilla assumed the girl was stylish with her asymmetrical ombre hairdo—brunette roots lightening outward to blonde. Her makeup looked carefully applied and her black jeggings hugged her slim body. Too bad Alyssa didn't think a smile would look nice with her ensemble. The teenager seemed rather sullen.

"About that lunch," Mom chirped as they neared Sparrow Lake. "We could go to The Corner or there's a new pizza place that just opened up across town."

"Pizza sounds good to me," said Mia.

When no comment came from her older granddaughter, Mom tapped her shoulder. "Alyssa?"

Still no reply. The teenager seemed to be in her own world, one that contained only her and her smartphone, the fancy type with a screen like a small computer tablet.

Before her mother asked the question again, Priscilla raised her voice. "Alyssa! Excuse me, could you stop texting for a moment?"

The teenager looked up, brows raised.

"We're deciding on what you'd like for lunch," Priscilla explained.

Obviously having tuned out the conversation, Alyssa said, "Lunch? I don't know… Thai…or sushi is okay."

She should have guessed. "Sparrow Lake doesn't have a Thai restaurant." Though they did have a Chinese take-out place downtown. Priscilla didn't think that would appeal to her niece, though. Too common. "Sorry, no sushi place either. How about an artisan cheese board with crackers and gourmet salad at a swanky establishment?" She could whip up something with escarole and nuts and dried cherries.

"The Main Street Cheese Shoppe?" said Mom. "I didn't want to put you out, but that would be nice."

"I like cheese," Mia agreed with a grin.

"Alyssa?" said Priscilla loudly.

"Cheese is fine," Alyssa replied.

Though the girl didn't look up from her phone, which had beeped again.

In the rearview mirror, Priscilla saw Mom frown at Alyssa before turning to her younger sister. "Is something important going on? I mean, with your sister's phone messages?"

"Nah, just the usual stupid gossip with her friends." Mia gave a heavy, put-out sigh. "Alyssa's addicted to her phone. She can't even turn it off when she sleeps."

"Oh, my," Mom murmured.

Mia slipped a similar phone out of her pocket and showed it to her grandmother. "I have one, too, but I don't have my face glued to it all the time."

"That's because you have no friends," Alyssa told her sister with a withering glance.

She did listen sometimes, Priscilla guessed.

"Hey, take that back!" Mia leaned forward. "I have friends!"

"Just a few nerdy losers."

"They aren't losers!"

Mia looked as if she wanted to punch her sister, so Priscilla was happy that Mom grabbed the younger girl's shoulder and drew her back. "Now, now. I'm sure your friends are quite nice."

"I just don't want to text all the time," grumbled Mia as they pulled up in front of the cheese store. "I like to play games. Have you seen Furious Falcons Nightmare?"

"I have to admit I haven't even seen Furious Falcons," Mom told her.

As they entered the cheese store, Mia was happily explaining the ups and downs of the game to her grandmother.

Now if they could only get Alyssa halfway interested in something other than texting her friends.

They had barely claimed a table inside when Priscilla noticed Will Berger on the walkway outside the shop. In his early seventies, he had emphysema and so was pushing a portable oxygen tank on wheels. At the moment, he'd stopped and was swaying slightly as if he was having difficulties.

"Uh-oh, I think he's got a problem breathing," Priscilla muttered and raced outside. "Mr. Berger, are you okay?"

The man gave her a dark look in response.

"You can come inside my shop."

"I don't like cheese!"

"I meant you can sit for a while and can catch your breath."

He shook his head. "Women always think they know everything." With that he tottered on, pushing his oxygen tank and muttering, "And now they're taking over our businesses, too!"

Which left Priscilla gaping after him for a moment before going back inside.

"Is everything all right?" Mom asked.

"Apparently. All but his rudeness. I simply offered him some help."

"Berger is like that with everyone," Mom said. "Once he came in the library looking for some old book that we'd retired because it was falling apart. You wouldn't believe the way he insulted me, as if I'd personally made it impossible for him to get what he wanted."

"I guess he's always been like that."

"Over the years, he's gotten much worse.

I'm beginning to wonder if he doesn't have some kind of mental health problem in addition to his emphysema."

"That would be a real shame with him living alone and all."

Her father had changed, too, since he'd retired. Luckily, he had her mother to make sure he was all right. Mr. Berger had no one as far as she knew. His son Tim lived and worked in Racine.

Thinking she might interest her nieces in the kinds of cheeses and other foods she carried in the store, Priscilla realized her mistake as she looked at them—both were immersed in their cell phones. Great.

If she couldn't figure a way to get them interested in other things happening around town, it would be a very long summer.

CHAPTER TWO

IT WAS GOING to be a very long summer. Alyssa nibbled at a few kinds of cheese and tasted her salad as the others chowed down. Soon her phone buzzed again. She ignored the disapproving look from her aunt Priscilla and slipped the phone from her pocket to read the new text. It was from Tisha. Luke was getting together with that new girl they'd seen at the coffee shop, plus Brad was angry and not speaking to anyone. Everything was going on and here Alyssa was stuck in a stupid, boring, small town out in the middle of Wisconsin! She heaved a big sigh that earned another snarky look from Aunt Priscilla, then she texted Tisha in return.

After lunch, they went upstairs to change their clothes, since Mia, the silly twit, couldn't wait to ride the horses out on that farm they'd passed. In the bedroom she was sharing with her sister, Alyssa opened her suitcase but decided to wear the same jeggings. She removed her sandals, however, and slipped on a pair of over-the-knee high-heeled black suede boots. The day was a little warm so she also changed her T-shirt to a midriff-baring purple tank. She slashed on some bright lipstick and threw a beaded scarf around her neck, sighing anew at the idea of being isolated in Wisconsin. Why she and Mia couldn't stay by themselves, she had no idea. She was only a year or two younger than the NYU students who populated their neighborhood, and they were getting along without their parents.

"It's going to take her forever, you know," Mia was saying as Alyssa came out into the living space of the apartment. She was sitting on the couch, still showing Grams the Furious Falcons game.

Grams looked up. "Oh, not forever. Here she is." She rose to give Alyssa a hug. "You look so pretty!"

Alyssa hugged Grams in return. Grams and Gramps Ryan had always been nice to her. It wasn't that she didn't care about them. On the other hand, she hadn't been around Aunt Priscilla all that much, and, so far, she seemed plenty annoying.

Right now, she was giving Alyssa a studied

once-over. "Those boots are kind of fancy for riding, don't you think?"

"Mia is the one who wants to ride. I'm just coming along." No horse sweat for her! She suddenly wondered if she could get out of it. "Unless I can stay here…"

"No, no, I want to be with *both* my girls," exclaimed Grams.

Alyssa assumed they were ready to go then, but Mia came off the couch, only to scrabble around on the floor. "I just had it."

"What?" asked Aunt Priscilla.

"My stylus." Mia tried to find it under the couch. "I was using it for my game. It's got to be here somewhere. I don't want to lose it."

"A stylus?" Grams opened her large purse to rummage inside. "Don't waste any more time looking for it. I think I have one."

"Why would you have a stylus?" asked Aunt Priscilla. "You wouldn't let me buy you an eReader for Christmas. You said you wanted to read books the old-fashioned way."

"I always buy things when I see them on sale." Grams finally looked up from her search, a small green pen-like item in her hand. "I saw these little things were a dollar each at FamilyMart."

Aunt Priscilla laughed and shook her head.

"Honestly, you have everything. I just hope no one ever needs a hand grenade."

The two women and Mia continued talking as they went downstairs and left the store, Alyssa following. The dorky older guy Aunt Priscilla had introduced as her part-time employee told them to have a good time and continued sweeping the wide floorboards. The store's interior was meant to look kind of country, yet sophisticated, with light paneling and barrels with butcher block tops to display the many kinds of cheeses for sale, along with some locally made sausage and other products. There were a few small tables and chairs off to one side where customers could taste cheeses or sit down for lunch or snack. Alyssa had to admit the place presented a pleasant atmosphere and the cheese board with crackers and a salad they'd had for lunch had been good. Her aunt obviously knew more about merchandising than she did fashion. Dressed in beige pants with a beige T-shirt and nondescript shoes, her red hair pinned back simply, as if to get it out of the way, Priscilla could easily pass for being ten years older than Alyssa knew she actually was.

Alyssa's attention returned to her texts

as they got in the car, dropped Grams off for some meeting, and headed for the horse ranch. Tish said there was a really hot guy hanging around in the hallway of her building and she got him to say "hi" to her. How could she get him into a longer conversation?

Alyssa was about to text a suggestion as they pulled into the parking lot of the "ranch" with its big, old white barn. A matching farmhouse sat a short way down the road. Suddenly the phone indicated there was no service. "Unbelievable!" Were the hills on either side cutting off reception?

"Wow, look at those horses!" Mia nearly burst out of the car in her enthusiasm.

But it was the young man saddling the mounts in the corral that drew Alyssa's attention away from her useless phone. Slim but muscular, blondish hair feathering from beneath his straw cowboy hat, the guy had a killer smile and a square jaw. Alyssa *loved* square jaws.

Alyssa slipped the phone into the case she wore on a chain around her neck. At the moment she didn't care about reception. Tish could take care of herself. She had her own encounter to enjoy.

"Which one of these horses is most spirited? I want to ride fast," Mia was saying to the young guy as Alyssa approached.

"Hey, chill out. We're just going on a trail ride this afternoon," the guy told her, laughing. Then his smile seemed to freeze as he caught sight of Alyssa.

"Hi." Alyssa adjusted her sunglasses. She wished she'd had time to freshen her lipstick. She put her hand out for a shake. "I'm Alyssa."

"My sister," added Mia with a disgust that Alyssa ignored.

"Logan." The cute guy took Alyssa's hand then released it more quickly than she would like. "Sisters. Hey, uh, great...you can both go on the trail ride."

Alyssa posed carefully, hand on one hip, hoping her big city glamour would affect Logan. "I'm just here to hang out."

"We don't really have a hang-out spot around here but you're welcome to wait until we get back," Logan told her before turning to Mia. "I think you'll like Cloud, the Pinto. She's got a sweet temperament, along with some spice."

Alyssa asked him, "You're going on the trail ride, too?"

"I'm leading the group." Then he walked

away to introduce Mia to the spotted horse nearby.

Drat! Alyssa looked down at her beautiful boots. Guess she'd have to take the chance on getting them sweaty after all. "I've changed my mind. I need a horse, too."

She'd had riding lessons for a short time when she was Mia's age, before she'd lost interest. She could look pretty good on the back of a horse if she wanted to.

If that's what she had to do to get next to a cute cowboy.

AT LEAST ALYSSA was enjoying something, Priscilla thought, hanging on to Gold Mine, the pretty Palomino Logan had saddled for her. She could let go of the tension she'd been feeling since the drive to her place from the airport. Her niece might be flirting with the young hand, but Alyssa was little more than a kid, and he was several years too old for her. Thankfully, she noted that Logan remained friendly but professional, nothing more.

Also thankfully, Sam was nowhere around, so she didn't have to worry about running into him, after all.

"Aren't you going to get on your horse,

Aunt Priscilla?" Mia asked from atop a little Pinto mare named Cloud.

"I'm just waiting until the last minute," Priscilla hedged. "We'll be in the saddle long enough as it is."

Besides, which, she'd only been riding a few times and not since she was a teenager. A far more experienced rider than she, Mia was already walking her mount around the corral adjacent to the barn, turning Cloud this way and that. A few other riders, strangers to Priscilla, were doing the same.

When Alyssa asked Logan, "Aren't you going to give me a leg up?" Priscilla whipped around to see what was going on.

Logan gave her niece a friendly grin. "If you can't get off the ground on your own, we do have a mounting block—"

Alyssa made a sound of exasperation. "Never mind!" Then put a foot in the stirrup and bounced right up into the saddle.

Logan looked at Priscilla. "Do you need help, ma'am?"

Priscilla flushed. She couldn't let her nieces outdo her. She placed her left foot into the stirrup and said, "I've got it."

"Okay." Logan moved back, probably to get his own horse.

The other riders were all looking at her. Waiting for her to mount Gold Mine. Hanging on to the reins and the horn on the saddle, Priscilla tried to hike herself up. But the saddle seemed to move and her stomach did a flip as she slammed back down on one foot.

"C'mon!" Mia yelled. "You can do it!"

Hands now sweating, face burning, Priscilla tried again and almost made it. Almost. On the third try, a strong pair of hands at her waist gave her a boost. The hands didn't let go. They felt…too personal. Standing in one stirrup, she turned to ask Logan to let go. But Logan wasn't hanging on to her. Sam was. Her eyes locked with his familiar gray ones, and her mouth gaped a bit as she got off balance again.

Keeping her from falling back into his arms, Sam grinned at her. "Well, some things don't change. You're looking *good*, Prissy!"

Hearing him call her by her high school nickname, Priscilla was struck nearly speechless. She'd hoped she would be prepared for this meeting, but she couldn't keep from reacting to him. Yes, Sam was back in Sparrow Lake and still had the same effect on her. He'd been gorgeous as a youth and was equally gorgeous as a man, his handsome face tanned, his dark hair poking out from beneath his black Western hat to brush the collar of the work shirt that showed off some impressive muscles.

She tore her gaze away from him, muttering, “I’m not very athletic.”

“You’re on an easygoing horse, so you don’t have to worry.”

It wasn’t really the horse she was worried about. Heart pounding, she threw her right leg over the saddle and plopped into it.

“Not going to say a proper hello, Prissy?”

She frowned at him. “Sure I’m going to say hello. Why wouldn’t I?”

His grin widened. “Well?”

“Hello, Sam. Nice to see you after all these years! And my name is Priscilla, not Prissy.” She looked around wildly, saw the others lining up behind Logan, who was opening the corral gate. “Gotta go or I’ll get left behind.”

He grinned harder. “Right. Go.” He swatted her mare’s rump.

Gold Mine jerked forward and moved to the end of the line. Priscilla thump-thump-thumped in the saddle and hung on to the horn. Several riders ahead of her, Mia looked back, grinned and gave her a thumbs-up.

Just when Priscilla was regaining her

breath, she realized she hadn't left Sam behind, after all. He rode up next to her on a big dark bay so close she could see the small lines around his eyes. They gave his face a new maturity and added to his good looks, as did an air of world-weariness.

Weary or wary?

Priscilla wasn't sure which.

"A little tip about getting on a horse," he said, his familiar if more mature whiskey-smooth voice making her stomach curl. "Hold on to the reins in your left hand, then grab the horse's mane instead of the saddle horn. That way you don't pull the saddle over."

Apparently the reason she'd had so much trouble getting up, Priscilla thought, as they followed Logan's lead through a stand of trees. "Won't that hurt the horse?"

"Nope, no pain involved. No nerve endings."

"Oh."

"I wouldn't have expected you to know that," he assured her.

"Same here. Last I remember, you rode a motorcycle out of town twelve years ago, not a horse."

"Twelve years is a long time, Prissy, enough time for a man to learn all kinds of things."

Prissy. Priscilla clenched her jaw. She'd thought she was done with that nickname. Obviously, Sam wasn't going to let her forget it. But if she made a big deal of it, he undoubtedly would do the same just to tease her. Since they were entering a pretty, hilly area she'd never seen before, she decided to just relax and enjoy the ride as best as she could.

HAPPY TO SEE the only person he'd regretted leaving behind when he'd fled Sparrow Lake, Sam smiled as he watched Prissy thump-thump in the saddle as Logan picked up the pace of the ride. They settled into a slow jog along the trail that Sam had created through several pastures and alongside a big patch of woods. Compared to a mountainside, the rolling, sometimes timbered hills were gentle, yet Priscilla was trying real hard to keep her seat. But she made no complaint. Just like old times. She rode out whatever might be bothering her. A quiet do-gooder, she'd been nice to everyone, but he remembered the guys on the football team making fun of her because she wasn't one of the "cool" girls. She'd never seemed to care about fancy clothes or new hairstyles, she hadn't worn eye makeup under those big, thick glasses she'd worn back then. She might not have heard the comments behind her back, but Sam was certain she'd known. He remembered how she'd always held her head up high when she'd passed them in the school hallway. He'd always given her credit that she'd had the guts to be herself.

And he remembered the night that had changed the way he'd felt about Priscilla Ryan, too. He'd asked the bespectacled, mousy librarian's daughter to the prom on a bet with some of the guys on the team. Not that he hadn't liked her, but she'd been quiet and hard to get to know. Truth be told, he'd felt sorry that his friends had been ragging on about a girl who'd never done anything or said a mean word to anyone, and he'd taken the bet knowing that, if he didn't ask her to the prom, no other boy would.

What a surprise he'd had when she'd opened the door on prom night. He still remembered feeling gutshot just looking at her, all gussied up and without her thick glasses. Her long, bright red hair released from her usual ponytail swirled around surprisingly pretty green eyes and brushed the delicate green fabric surrounding her slim, silky shoulders. What a bigger surprise she'd been on the dance floor. It was as if the music had freed her, had allowed her to blossom. She'd simply glowed with happiness. He remembered joking with her. And laughing. And smiling more than he ever had with anyone. He hadn't been sorry he'd taken that bet, not one bit.

It had been the best night of his teenage life.

A sappy smile curving his lips when he glanced over at her, he asked, "So how has life been treating you, Prissy? Do you have a house filled with kids?" He hadn't missed that she'd brought a couple of girls with her. "Or is it just the two?"

Her brow puckered. "Two?"

Sunlight squeaking through the trees dappled the area they rode with bits of brightness, making her red hair glow as if on fire. Mesmerized, he simply stared at her.

"What are you talking about?" she asked, jerking him out of the moment.

He indicated the mounted girls both ahead of them, the older one in the crazy boots practically pressing her horse against Logan's. "Those two. Your daughters."

Appearing thunderstruck, she snorted. "Those are my nieces! They just flew in from

New York this morning, and I brought them out here because Mia is horse crazy."

Hmm. The little one had the same red hair, the reason he'd drawn that conclusion. "But you do have kids, right?"

"Uh, no."

"Why not?" Interest he couldn't quite define shot through him. "Did that biological clock of yours get stuck or something?"

Now she gave him an intent look that made the flesh skitter down his spine when she said, "Doesn't matter when I'm not married."

"Not married," he echoed softly. *"Really?"*

"Really."

Hard to believe no man had ever snapped her up. He eyed her tan jeans and T-shirt. She might not be flashy on the outside, but, as he remembered so well, she had hidden depths.

"Why ever not?" he asked.

"Maybe I never met a man I could stand long enough to take on full time." She arched an eyebrow as if that included him.

His turn to snort. "Didn't remember you had such a way with words."

She simply shrugged.

He wanted to ask if there was *any* man in her life other than her father, but he figured he'd better stop being so direct or he might offend her. Besides she might not want to talk to him at all. Still, he really wanted to know more about her.

"So what have you been doing all these years if not starting a family?"

"I went to college, studied American Literature, then got a job in the big city that had nothing to do with my degree." She shrugged. "Pretty much like most everyone else I knew."

Sam frowned. Of course she was educated. He'd been in too much of a hurry to get away from his old man to worry about finishing high school. He'd gotten his GED a few years back, but college…that would have been a luxury when he'd been breaking his back just to scrape by.

"But you returned to Sparrow Lake."

She flushed a little, and looked straight ahead rather than at him. "Our parents aren't getting any younger, are they?"

And in his own case, not any less judgmental. "So you live with them?"

"No, not with them, just close by if they need me. I have an apartment above The Main Street Cheese Shoppe."

"I would have figured you for a pretty little house with a white picket fence."

"Maybe someday if the cheese shop really takes off. I, um, own it."

Surprised, Sam stared at her. "So you started your own business, too." They had something in common, after all.

"Last year," Priscilla said. "I learned enough working at Milwaukee Cheese Mart to start my own mini version of the business. But Sparrow Lake is small potatoes, even with the visitors we get. I'll have to expand selling on the internet like the Mart does if I want to go big."

"You're ambitious."

"Not so much. But I am realistic. I don't have anyone looking out for me, so I have to do it myself."

So, no man in her life, either. Sam couldn't quite say why, but as they circled a large field where cows grazed and headed back to the barn, he couldn't stop grinning.

CHAPTER THREE

WHY IN THE WORLD was Sam grinning like a fool? Remembering how the town boys used to make fun of her, Priscilla sat straighter in her saddle. She probably looked ridiculous, since she had never been a horseback rider. But Sam wasn't like that. He'd never been, she reminded herself. He might have teased her some, but he'd never treated her with disrespect.

Before she could ask him what was so amusing, she realized Mia had hung back to join them. Uh-oh, her niece was frowning.

"Mia, is something wrong? Aren't you having fun?"

"It's okay...well, a little boring. I'd have more fun if we could gallop our horses."

"We have no reason to gallop them," Sam told her. "We're not rounding up stray cattle."

"Now that would be fun!" A hopeful-looking Mia looked over to the grazing cows. "Can we?"

"We might scare the milk out of 'em," Sam said. "What do you think?"

The girl looked crestfallen. "I suppose not. Couldn't we at least canter?"

"You mean lope. You're riding with Western gear now. We jog and lope, not trot and canter," Sam told her. "And we hold both reins in one hand. I assume you're right-handed, so use your left hand to rein your horse."

Mia immediately switched. "Like that?"

"Pretty much. Maybe a little higher and looser."

"How do you control direction like this? I mean, if you want to turn the horse?"

"A simple rein on the horse's neck and pressure from your opposite leg."

Mia tried it and flashed them a big grin. "Awesome!"

Sam laughed. "I give Western lessons if you want to learn more."

Mia jumped on that one. "Can I take them, Aunt Priscilla? Dad gave us enough money to do whatever we want this summer. Can we come back tomorrow?"

Her niece looked excited enough to burst, but Priscilla wasn't ready to commit herself before they talked it through. After all, Alyssa would have a say in what they were going to do every day. Though she didn't think the teenager would object to coming out here again, not the way she'd kept her horse practically glued to Logan's.

"We'll talk about it tonight. Maybe we can arrange a lesson for later in the week."

"What's wrong with tomorrow?"

Fighting to keep her cool despite the whiny tone Mia was now using, Priscilla repeated, "We'll discuss it tonight."

With an exaggerated huff, Mia moved her horse forward, away from her and Sam.

"Hmm, seems like she expects to get what she wants when she wants it," Sam observed.

Right. It seemed as if Alyssa wasn't the only spoiled one in the family. "My brother gives them no boundaries at times. I suppose it's hard not to give your kids everything they want."

"I wouldn't know."

"You don't have kids?" she asked.

"Not without a wife."

Realizing they'd practically repeated their earlier conversation about her, Priscilla laughed with him.

Then Sam said, "The truth is, I never had time to think about starting a family."

"Too busy working?"

"You could say that."

Obviously Sam had gone a long way from being a farm boy used to dealing with dairy cows. Priscilla asked, "So how did you become such an expert on Western horsemanship?"

"When I left here, I headed west. Ended up in Wyoming. And Montana. And Idaho. And the Dakotas."

"Doing…?"

"Working the rodeo circuit."

"Rodeo!"

Though why she was so surprised, Priscilla didn't know. Sam had always been a wild kid, a wilder teenager. He'd always taken chances with himself. And unfortunately with others. There had been a time that last winter that hadn't ended too well. He'd given classmate Tim Berger a ride on his motorcycle, and he'd been hotdogging it on the highway despite the bitter cold. They'd hit a patch of black ice and the cycle had gone over. Sam had been bruised and cut, but Tim had been badly hurt. His leg had been broken in several places. He'd had a long recovery and even all these years later walked with a limp.

"Took to rodeo like a duck takes to water," Sam was saying. His voice resigned, he added, "But rodeo is a young man's game."

"If I remember correctly, you're thirty-two."

"But you don't rodeo without getting hurt at times. My body is a heck of a lot older than I like to consider."

His body looked a heck of a lot better than most of the local young men, but she guessed he might have taken some bad falls. Old injuries weren't always apparent, but they could be a continuing problem.

She said, "So you quit the circuit to start a ranch on your dad's property."

Sam looked away from her and cleared his throat. "Something like that. Pop had that accident falling off the roof, too. Broken leg or not, he's staying put in his own place."

"So you wanted to make sure he was okay." Which only made sense. Priscilla had panicked when she'd heard Mom had taken a fall on the ice and had broken her arm the winter before she'd returned to Sparrow Lake.

"Since he'd given up dairy farming, Pop talked about selling the land. But I convinced him to let me have a go at a different kind of business first."

"It seems like you've got a good start."

Priscilla checked out the other riders. Everyone but Mia seemed to be pretty happy. Especially Alyssa, still glued to Logan's side.

"Not really a good start," Sam said. "A few lessons a week added to a daily trail ride with a half dozen customers won't pay the bills."

"You've got to give the business some time to build."

"Like you did."

"Not to mention figuring out ways to promote it to get new customers."

Looking thoughtful, Sam said, "I'd like to talk to you about what it takes to make a new business successful."

"Sure. I can do a little brainstorming with you."

"I'm booked up getting this place in order the next couple of days, but after that, I'll give you a call."

"Anytime," Priscilla said.

The idea of spending time with Sam, even if it was just business, sent such warmth shooting through her that nothing could spoil her good mood.

PRISCILLA'S MOOD WAS soon tested on the ride back to town.

"Alyssa and Logan, sittin' in a tree, k-i-s-s-i-n-g…" Mia sing-songed from the backseat.

"Shut up, Mia! That's dumb!"

"Make me!"

Alyssa unsnapped her seat belt and turned toward her little sister so fast that a startled Priscilla swerved the car.

"Sit down!" she yelled, her heart pounding. "Now! And put that seat belt back on!"

Alyssa huffed but did as she said, while Mia snickered from the backseat.

"And you, Mia, stop instigating trouble if you want to come back out here to ride!"

"Well, it's true!"

"I didn't kiss him," grumbled Alyssa. She tossed her head. "But maybe I will."

"No, you won't," Priscilla said.

Her niece gave her a dirty look. "Why not? I can kiss him. He's really cute."

"And too old for you."

"I'm not a baby!"

"You're sixteen, Alyssa. A teenager. Logan is a young man. Probably twenty, maybe older."

"So what? Back in New York, I date older men."

Mia snorted and widened her eyes. "Oh, yeah? When? Who? Where?"

"Shut up!"

"I'm gonna tell Dad!"

When Alyssa started to turn toward the

backseat again, Priscilla raised her voice, "All right, enough, both of you!"

Thankful that they both went silent for the moment, Priscilla took a big breath. Surely they wouldn't snipe at each other the whole time they stayed with her. More than anything, she hated confrontation. Hated the fact that she'd yelled at the nieces she loved. She'd avoided mean-spirited sniping since she was a kid. As unbelievable as it seemed, she wished one of Alyssa's friends would text her so the girls would leave each other alone. Checking the rearview mirror, she realized that Mia had pulled out her cell phone and was already involved in playing some game.

"So what is it with you and that guy?" Alyssa suddenly asked.

"That guy…Sam? What do you mean?"

"You were into him on the whole ride."

Priscilla squirmed a bit. That might be true, but how had Alyssa even noticed when she'd been so into Logan?

"Sam and I went to high school together. We were just catching up."

"On what?"

"On what we've been doing with our lives."

"You live in the same town."

"We do now, but Sam was gone for a lot of

years. He just moved back recently. I didn't even know he was here."

"But you're glad to see him, right?"

"Well, sure. It's always nice to see old friends."

"Looked like he was more than a friend, Aunt Priscilla. Was he your boyfriend?"

Priscilla felt her face grow warm. How ridiculous. "No…well, we had one date, but that was fifteen years ago." And she didn't have to explain it to a sixteen-year old.

Though she couldn't help but remember that toe-tingling kiss they'd shared after the prom. And Sam's declaration that he wanted her to be his girl.

"Then you broke up?" Alyssa probed.

"Uh, we weren't exactly…together. He left town."

"Just like that?"

"Uh-huh." The day after the date, Sam had been gone. Hadn't even said goodbye. Worse, she'd learned that the only reason Sam had asked her was because a couple of his football player friends bet he couldn't get her to venture out from behind her thick glasses and give him a good time.

"I wouldn't let some guy like that get away," Alyssa said.

"I didn't exactly have a choice."

"He's pretty cool," Mia said, leaning forward. "A real cowboy. You are going to let me take those lessons with him, aren't you?"

"I said we would talk about it. I want to make sure we do things that both of you enjoy. And your grandmother may have some ideas about your activities. She wants to see a lot of you while you're here."

"I want to go back to the ranch, too," Alyssa said. "I *love* riding."

Mia snorted. "Since when? You said it was boring."

"I was bored doing the same thing all the time. But going out to the ranch is different."

Right, Priscilla thought. The ranch had Logan. That fact, as well as going back into Sam's territory made her more than a little nervous. Logan had been friendly, but not too friendly. Surely he realized Alyssa was too young for him. She couldn't fault him for her niece's new crush. She could still fault Sam… but she could handle anything, including him.

She hoped.

"Well, Grams and Gramps will want to spend all day tomorrow with the two of you," Priscilla said. "But I'll see about making arrangements for later in the week."

"Yay!" Mia said.

Alyssa simply grinned.

Making Priscilla want to roll her eyes. Whatever made her think having a teenager as her responsibility for half the summer was going to be a piece of cake?

CHAPTER FOUR

SAM'S CELL BUZZED in his back pocket. It was after supper and he was alone doing dishes and thinking about how nice it had been to see Priscilla again. Maybe it was someone calling about lessons or rides for the next day, so he pulled the phone free with some excitement.

Pop.

He answered, "Yeah, Pop, what's up?"

"You need to get over here, right away."

"Are you okay?" Sam's pulse rushed. "You didn't fall again?"

"Don't worry, I'm still on my feet. I got a bone to pick with you, Sam."

Sam let out a breath. He didn't know why he bothered worrying about the old man. So Pop had a bone to pick with him. Well, when didn't he?

"Yeah, I'll come by as soon as I'm done here."

"Now, boy!"

That familiar, imperious tone made Sam's gut clench. He took a really deep breath and told himself to stay calm. "All right. Be there in a few."

"You'd better be!"

What was wrong this time?

Leaving the cabin, Sam climbed into the truck and headed for the main house a half mile down the road. Pop was always demanding his presence, never to have his company, rather to chide him about something. Just like in the bad old days. The reason he'd left and hadn't looked back for so many years. It had taken something he didn't even want to think about to make him consider coming home.

When Priscilla assumed Pop was his reason for returning to Sparrow Lake, he'd let her. Despite his reservations, he *had* wanted to check on the old man, but he had other reasons, too. He couldn't go back to rodeoing, not after what had happened to him. Something he would never forget. But he didn't owe Priscilla big explanations. Not about that. Not about the past. He'd always done what he'd thought he had to. Now he was starting over. And he'd known Pop had retired and was done with the land. He'd had to find a new way to make a living, but he was no dairy farmer.

He pulled up in front of the farmhouse, a white two-story with a wide porch, and parked in front of the steps. Not knowing what to expect, he entered the front vestibule with a sense of trepidation.

"Pop?"

"In here."

Though nearly seventy, Dwayne Larson had a voice that was as deep and strong as it had ever been. Sam followed it into the dingy front parlor that looked exactly like it had fifteen years ago. Too crowded with old furniture, most of which was stacked with newspapers and magazines that his father refused to throw away. Why he still wanted to read *Midwest Dairyman* and keep years of back copies when he was retired was a mystery to Sam.

Ensconced in his favorite recliner, the casted leg up, Pop grumbled, "About time. What took you so long?"

Sam refused to respond to the bait. "What do you need, Pop?"

"For you to be responsible."

Uh-oh. What new crime had he committed in his father's eyes now?

"You'll have to be a little more direct."

"The boards you left lying around the parking area!"

"What boards?"

"The ones with big nails in them. Do you want to ruin your client's tires?"

"This afternoon, the parking lot was fine. No boards with nails or otherwise."

"You calling me a liar, boy?"

"No, of course not."

Though Sam wondered about his father's medication. If he was taking those pain killers he said he wouldn't touch, they could be making him imagine things. How would he have seen the parking lot anyway in his condition? Or had someone put this particular idea in his head?

Sam tried to cool down the confrontation. "When I leave here, I'll swing by the parking lot on my way back to the cabin."

But Pop wasn't having any conciliation. "A horse ranch in Wisconsin is a silly idea anyhow."

Not a new sentiment. Sam knew his father didn't approve, even if he had rented the land to Sam and had signed a contract agreeing to the business.

"It's not the only ranch in Wisconsin, Pop.

There are several west and north of here. It's just the only one in this area, which gives me an edge in making it work."

That's what he was counting on, that people who weren't dedicated riders with their own horse properties or who couldn't afford to go to fancy riding schools, would like a less expensive, less demanding alternative.

"Met up with Will Berger at the bank this afternoon, and he gloated about the stupidity of my letting you start a dude ranch here."

Berger being an old rival of his father's, he would say anything to make Pop mad. "Wait a minute. You went out? Who drove you?"

"Drove myself. A broken leg's not going to stop me."

Pop couldn't drive his truck with a broken leg, not with its clutch, but he could drive the old Chevy one-footed, since it was automatic. A broken leg *should* stop the old man, at least until the cast was off, but Sam wasn't going to start yet another argument. To no surprise, his father did it for him.

"Why can't you just get a normal job?"

"I'm good with horses. Great with horses." Pop had no idea of how great—he'd never seen Sam rodeo. "That's all I've been doing for fifteen years."

"Not for the last six months, you haven't."

Pop never wasted an opportunity to remind him of how his life had gone off the rails. Again, he refused the bait. "If anyone can make a go of a dude ranch around here, it'll be me. Just believe in me for once, would you?"

Pop waved a dismissive hand. "You might be good with horses. Doesn't mean people around here are interested in riding 'em."

"This whole area between Kenosha and Milwaukee gets a lot of tourism. A whole other potential for more clients."

He knew it was useless to try to convince Pop, however. No matter what he did, the old man would disapprove. Being retired and getting around on crutches wasn't improving his habitually cantankerous personality.

"I'm going to go check out that parking lot. Before I go, do you want me to get you anything?"

"I got a broken leg—I'm not an invalid!"

Sam started to say something, then clamped his mouth shut and turned on his heel to leave. He wasn't out the door before he heard Pop yell something negative after him, but Sam just closed his ears to the probable insult.

Throwing himself into the truck, he headed for the barn and the parking area beyond. Why did the old man have to be so mean? He hadn't always been like this. Sam remembered a time when he'd thought Pop was the best father in the world. That had all ended on his thirteenth birthday.

He didn't want to think about that again, so he was relieved on arriving at the modest visitors' parking area that could hold a dozen or more vehicles. Cutting the engine, he left the truck and scanned the area. Sure enough, there were some loose boards with protruding nails. Looked as if someone had pulled down a building or shed and this was the product. But why toss them here? On closer inspection, he realized boards weren't the only things dumped here. Scattered throughout the lot were dozens of nails and screws.

Where on earth…?

The midnight visitor again?

The thought came to him unbidden: What if it hadn't been a kid? What if it had been someone trying to hurt his business before he even got it off the ground?

But who?

He'd been a reckless teenager, had made enemies in high school, had gotten into more trouble than any other kid in Sparrow Lake, but that had all been small potatoes. And that had been a long, long time ago. Time usually tempered bad memories. People he'd run into in town when buying supplies for the ranch had been friendly enough. Even Cooper Peterson, his most bitter rival who'd hated him for being the better, faster rider when he'd challenged Sam to motorcycle races that Sam had won every time.

Had Peterson been playing him? Or someone else who held a grudge?

The idea threatened the possibility of him making a fresh start here. He couldn't let it happen. He had to make it work. Had to make things right if his past misadventures had caught up to him.

He couldn't fail.

Couldn't start over again.

He had no place else to go.

TO PRISCILLA'S RELIEF, her nieces seemed to settle down when they returned to her apartment. At least for a while. After a light supper of chicken and leftover salad, they watched some television—well, she and Mia watched television. Alyssa was back to texting as she lounged in a chair.

Mia yawned for the third or fourth time. "I feel tired. And it's not even late."

"Your body clock is one hour ahead of central standard time," Priscilla pointed out. "Plus the fresh air and exercise could have done you in." She rose from the couch. "Let's check out your bedroom and make sure you've got enough pillows and blankets." When the apartment air-conditioning was on, the guest bedroom could run cold.

Mia nodded toward Alyssa as they left the living room. "We're not sleeping in the same bed, you know."

No, Priscilla didn't know. "Why not?" There was only one queen-size bed in the second bedroom.

"Ugh. Sleep with *her*? I toss and turn a lot. And Alyssa's on her phone all night. It would keep me awake. I can sleep on the couch in your office."

"It's only a love seat." And the room was small, too, her building being from the turn of the century when spacious quarters weren't considered necessary.

"I'll make do," said Mia, yawning again. "In case you didn't notice, I'm not that tall."

But Priscilla objected, "I can't have you cramped up on a love seat." She thought quickly. “There’s a folding cot in the front closet. It’ll fit in the bedroom and you girls can take turns sleeping in the bed.”

“That’s still in the same room. Alyssa’s on her phone all night.”

Priscilla raised her brows. “What?”

“I told you she’s addicted to that thing. I don’t know what she and her crazy friends have to text about at 2:00 a.m. but Alyssa sleeps with her phone under her pillow. She just *has* to answer.”

No matter how many times she heard about the phone, Priscilla still had trouble believing. “And your parents allow this?”

Mia shrugged.

“But your sister will be tired from waking up all night. You are sisters and I don’t have the space, you two need to share the same room.” She didn’t think she was being demanding. “We have to make do. That’s life, sometimes.” And she had to use her office to email some orders.

Mia sighed. “Talk to Alyssa.”

Priscilla went back to the living room, deciding she’d deal with the separate beds first, then the phone. She got the reluctant teenager to help her and Mia wheel the cot into the guest bedroom, but Alyssa was adamant about not turning off her phone.

"It's bad for your rest!" Priscilla insisted. "You can't sleep if you keep waking up to text."

"I'm fine. And everybody does it." Alyssa snapped, "My dad and mom bought me this phone and they think it's okay."

Was she going to have to call her brother? Priscilla wondered. She was sick of the debate and they'd only been going at it for a few minutes.

"If I have to stay in here with you, you'll keep me awake," complained Mia, sounding even more grouchy. She put her hands on her hips and faced her sister.

Alyssa gave the younger girl an evil stare. "Oh, okay, I'll put my phone on vibrate, nerd. You won't hear anything." She looked at her aunt. "I *have* to know what's going on. I can't be out of the loop."

Honestly, what on earth could be so important? Priscilla made the cot up with sheets and a pillow. "It's not like the Department of Homeland Security will be calling you."

Alyssa caught the sarcasm. Her eyes flashed. "My life is super important to me! I'm young and I don't want to miss out. We already had to come to this stupid small town out in the middle of nowhere for the summer. Dad said…"

"Okay, okay," Priscilla interrupted, trying not to feel insulted. The girl was only a teenager. And she simply didn't want to make an international call over texting, for Pete's sake. "Make sure you keep the phone on vibrate."

"Yeah, you'd better," grumbled Mia. "Or I'm going to be getting up and ramming the stupid thing down your throat!"

"Oh, you're so tough!" Alyssa came back, looking ready to lunge.

"Whoa, whoa." Priscilla grabbed Alyssa's arm to intervene. She told Mia. "Your sister has promised to be quiet. You're tired. Why don't you get into your pajamas and climb into bed?"

Alyssa grumbled something before walking away and Mia went to her suitcase where she opened it on top of the dresser, rummaged around, and pulled out pink Hello Kitty pajamas. Priscilla would have to assure her mother that the garments were indeed being used.

After that, Priscilla returned to the living room but she wasn't interested in TV. Disgruntled and out of sorts with all the upheaval, she went to her office to listen to some soothing music on headphones and play some computer solitaire until she felt calmer. Then she was able to place the orders she had planned and go over some invoices. When she decided it was time for bed, she came out to find that the TV was off and Alyssa was in the bathroom, a sliver of light seeping out from under the closed door.

Priscilla went to her own bedroom to change into her nightshirt. Then she peeped out into the hall, noting the apartment's one bathroom was still closed. It might be closed for quite a while, too. She guessed she would have to grab her keys and go downstairs to use the bathroom in the store. With a teenager around, it would probably not be the first time. She only wished bathroom use would be the only problem her nieces presented. If they didn't drive her crazy this summer, she would be lucky.

CHAPTER FIVE

"COME ON, AUNT PRISCILLA," called Mia, heading for the car. "I can't wait to get on the back of a horse again!"

"You are the back of..." started Alyssa before a dirty look from Priscilla stopped her from completing the sentence.

The teenager clamped her mouth shut and got into the front seat, while Priscilla slid behind the steering wheel.

They were heading out to Sam's ranch again, after a couple of days' break while Mom had kept the girls busy running around Sparrow Lake. Though she felt guilty for admitting it, Priscilla had enjoyed taking time off from her nieces and working at the cheese shop. It was peaceful in comparison to the chaos upstairs. She was glad she had the business since the place had become her second home, especially at night, when the apartment's bathroom was too often occupied and her office commandeered as a third bedroom.

The cot in the guest bedroom hadn't worked out, since Alyssa's phone had been too noisy for Mia, even on vibrate. After the first night sleeping on the love seat—luckily, the sisters hadn't come to blows—Mia had asked Priscilla if they could move the cot to the office. Priscilla had complied, but now there was no space left to use the computer or the desk in that room.

Today she was taking the girls back to the Larson Dude Ranch for that promised Western lesson. She felt on edge, though she wasn't sure what made her more nervous, the possibility of her nieces getting into another argument or seeing Sam again.

She needn't have worried about Sam, however. Once they got to the ranch and were saddling up horses, he barely seemed to notice her. He merely gave her a quick nod before turning his attention to Mia and Alyssa, and she couldn't help feeling a little hurt. Then, watching him work with the girls, she realized he wasn't acting like the Sam she knew at all today. Though he appeared totally professional and gave one hundred percent to the girls, he didn't do so with that easy charm that had won her young heart.

Charm he hadn't lost if measured by their meeting the other day.

Something must be wrong.

"Where's Logan?" asked Alyssa.

"He'll be around later."

"Okay." With a look of resignation, Alyssa mounted her horse, not making too much of a fuss over the real reason she had probably come out to the dude ranch. At least the lack of reception for her phone meant she had to do something else besides text.

Sitting on the fence, her legs dangling into the corral, Priscilla watched the riding lesson closely. When it ended, Sam instructed the girls to remove tack, to brush down their horses' backs with towels to dry them, then to check their feet and clean their hooves if necessary before bringing them out to the pasture.

As the girls got busy, he seemed as if he was trying to make up his mind as to what to do next—leave or stay. In the end, he walked over to Priscilla and climbed up on the fence to sit next to her. His arm brushed hers, making her catch her breath. She steeled herself against the sensation.

Clearing her throat, she asked, "You're going to let them work on their own?"

"I can see them from here. Besides, they're not beginners. They know what they're doing."

"They seem to," Priscilla agreed, surprised that Alyssa took as much care with her horse as Mia did.

And Sam was still in that down mood. His brow was drawn and his mouth was pulled into a straight line instead of the teasing smile that always got to her. She wondered what was going on with him, but she wasn't about to ask. She didn't have to. Apparently he needed someone to talk to.

"I only wish I knew what *I* was doing," Sam said.

"In what respect?"

"I'm worried about the future of the farm."

Apparently, he was taking all the responsibility for the land on his shoulders despite the fact that his father had intended to sell the place.

"You're just getting started, Sam. Take it easy. You just need a little patience."

She felt like patting his hand or something for encouragement, but, not wanting to touch him, she kept her distance.

Sam sounded even more depressed when he said, "What I need is luck. I nearly lost some horses the other night when they mysteriously got out of the pasture."

The way he said that made her ask, "And you think someone did it on purpose?"

"Logan swore the gate was locked when he finished. And the horses didn't just wander out calmly. They were a little freaked, like someone purposely spooked them."

"Oh, Sam, that's terrible."

"It could have been worse if one of them had wandered onto the highway. And that's not all."

"What else happened?" This didn't sound good.

"The other day, after the ride, while I was at my cabin having supper, someone scattered boards with big nails in the parking lot. Loose nails and screws, too. If I hadn't cleaned it up, some of my customers would have had ruined tires. That probably would have been it for them. They wouldn't have come back."

Priscilla frowned. "I haven't heard about any kids messing around on people's property, not since Brian Lange and his buddies were caught playing pranks and straightened out doing some community service. That happened a couple of summers ago. I wasn't here at the time, but I heard all about it from his sister Kristen. You remember her, right? My best friend in high school?"

"Vaguely. Smart. Ambitious. Couldn't wait to graduate to get out of Dodge."

"She did that, but she came home to Sparrow Lake, too. Now she manages her aunt's quilting shop."

"You'd think there was some magic about this area, pulling us all back."

"Not everyone. My brother doesn't even visit more than once every couple of years."

"A big-shot lawyer has innumerable choices about what to do with his life."

Though obviously not enough time to discipline teenagers, Priscilla thought glumly, thinking again about the problems with Alyssa.

But she was being selfish. Sam's woes were far more pressing. Furthermore, she had the feeling that his mood had to do with more than loose horses and boards with nails. With more than fearing his business would fail. He'd said rodeo was a young man's game, but she was pretty certain many competitors were in their forties and even fifties. Maybe there was another reason he couldn't or didn't want to go back. And maybe he'd been doing one thing for so long, he didn't think he had any other viable choices. She wished she knew more so she could be supportive, but she hesitated asking him more directly. If he wanted her to know what had happened, surely he would tell her.

He suddenly asked, “You haven’t heard about anyone in Sparrow Lake having it in for me, have you?”

“No. I didn’t even know you were back in town until we showed up for the trail ride. I’ll keep an ear open and ask around, though. Mom seems to know what’s going on with everyone.”

“Thanks. I appreciate it.” His grim expression lightened a bit, as if having her on his side made a difference. “I asked around about the Main Street Cheese Shop. I hear you’re all the rage these days.”

“I’m doing okay. It usually takes a business about three years to really succeed, but I’m making pretty encouraging progress.”

“You’ll have to tell me how you did it.”

“Sure. It’s not a secret. Just a lot of hard work.”

“I’ve never been afraid of hard work. Maybe we can have dinner and talk about what you did more specifically. I could use some pointers.”

Despite her reservations about getting too involved with Sam, Priscilla agreed. “Right. I told you I thought that was a good idea.”

She sympathized with him having such trouble getting his business off the ground. From experience, she knew it was difficult enough to get a new business going successfully without the kind of setbacks he was having. But she didn’t just have herself to think about this summer.

“My parents want to take the girls to Lake Geneva for a day.” A beautiful little resort town with mansions facing a lake, boutiques for Alyssa and boat rides for Mia. “I’m not sure when they plan to do that, not as yet. Sometime in the next few days, I think. I’ll find out.”

He nodded. “Sounds good. Thanks, Prissy.” He covered her hand with his calloused one.

Despite her pulse fluttering at his touch, she would have to be cautious, not fool herself into thinking they could have something more personal going simply because she still felt attracted to him. After all, she didn’t know if she could trust Sam Larson with more than friendship after the way he’d simply left town right after he’d kissed her and told her he wanted her to be his girl.

No one knew why he'd left. That still bothered her. Not that she was going to ask. She didn't want to get into an uncomfortable discussion. Anything to avoid that kind of tension. She remembered in high school, Sam was voted the most likely to end up dead by 30. Had he done something terrible? Was that why he'd left? Was whatever he had done somehow reflecting back on him now? If he had some big secret he was hiding, he wasn't exactly being honest with her.

Again.

She'd gotten over him once—at least she'd convinced herself she had—and she didn't need to go back there. They'd been just kids, then, really. Still, it had obviously had a lasting influence on her. Could it be that Sam's disappointing her the way he had was part of the reason she'd never given herself fully to any other man? She'd had a serious boyfriend in Madison and a couple more in Milwaukee, but those relationships had never worked out. Always the bridesmaid, never the bride—that was the running joke she had with her girlfriends.

A joke based on the disappointing truth.

PRISCILLA TRIED NOT to think about Sam that evening. Mom had invited them for a barbeque, but when they arrived at her parents' backyard, Mom was fuming.

"Supper will be a little late." Mom's eyes were narrowed behind her glasses. "Your father forgot to light the coals."

He muttered, "I was distracted."

"And then he fell asleep. You're always sleeping, Roger."

Priscilla didn't say a word. Though her mother had a point, she wasn't about to get in the middle of their ongoing argument.

"Didn't you sleep last night, Gramps?" Mia asked.

"Oh, a little."

Mia furrowed her brows. "Does Grams text, too?"

"Text?" he asked.

Mom laughed. "No, honey, old people like us don't text all that much, though you've explained so much about it, I may take it up."

"Text?" he repeated.

"You type on a little keyboard," explained Priscilla, "on a phone."

Dad merely grunted but Mom told Mia, "Gramps just likes to get some rest in his recliner before he comes to bed. You know, in front of the TV, with his eyes closed. Last night he did about six hours of 'resting' before he came to bed."

"I wasn't asleep," Dad objected. "I was watching a program."

"Watching what program?" Mom asked.

"Uh, well…something about history."

Mom snorted. "Looked like an old basketball game to me, on the classic sports channel. You'd have remembered if you hadn't been resting so hard." She gestured toward the grill. "Let's get those burgers on."

"Okay, okay."

Shutting out the bickering, which tended to get on her nerves, Priscilla stared around her at the pretty flowerbeds. Mom was some gardener. Too bad the big patio didn't look as neat and pretty. Grass and weeds poked out between the irregular stones. One of the legs on the table loaded with platters of uncooked burgers and corn on the cob was held together with duct tape. And the chairs around it could use a new coat of paint. The patio was one of those projects Dad wasn't doing that Mom kept complaining about.

"Aren't those coals ready yet?"

"I don't know, Helen." Dad sounded down, like he didn't really care. He looked as if he didn't care about much. Sweat trickled down his balding head into his face, but he didn't even bother to wipe it off. His shirttail hung out of his pants and the button holding it together at his waist looked ready to pop. "Fifteen, maybe twenty minutes."

Mom made a sound of frustration and spun on her heel. "I'll be inside."

Priscilla followed her. "I'll come with you."

First she glanced over at the girls to see if they would come after her. Mia was standing by the grill next to Dad, her arm around his thick waist. His expression brightened a bit, and he gave her a one-armed hug. A tuned-out Alyssa was sprawled out in one of the lounge chairs, texting, as usual.

Sighing, Priscilla entered the kitchen where her mother was digging in the refrigerator. "Let me help you, Mom."

She took a giant container of potato salad from her mother and then searched for a place to set it down. Every flat surface in the cramped, outdated kitchen seemed to be filled with something. Wow, this was worse than usual. Priscilla swept a bunch of Dad's sports magazines to one side on the kitchen table and put the bowl down. Mom set a container of coleslaw next to it.

"Bad enough your father couldn't get to

fixing up the patio before the girls came from New York."

"Right."

"But not even lighting the coals today?" Mom shook her head, then punched her glasses back up her nose. "He's not paying attention."

"Right."

Mom's voice went up a notch. "He's been like this ever since he retired from the Post Office."

"Right."

"If you ask me, he needs to see a counselor."

"Right..." Priscilla started. "Uh, do you think he would?"

Her mother sighed and shook her head. "I don't know. He doesn't listen to me anymore. Maybe if you talked to him about it."

The last thing Priscilla wanted to do was get in the middle of this ongoing battle between her parents. Their lifelong bickering had always bothered her, and the only way she could deal with it was to stay out of their fights. But this sounded more serious than usual, and if Dad needed her help...

"Doesn't Dad have any interests anymore?"

"Just watching television with that remote going, changing channels till he falls asleep."

Which reminded her of Alyssa texting and Mia playing games on their phones. "Maybe the girls inherited gadget fever from their grandfather."

Mom looked confused. "Gadget fever?"

"They both like to work with their phones. Play games, text."

"Oh, right. I noticed."

"But, if you ask me, Alyssa is carrying it too far." Priscilla felt she had to confide in someone. "Do you know she won't even turn her phone off when she goes to sleep? She keeps it under her pillow and replies to text messages from her friends all night. If anyone is lacking sleep, it's her."

"My, my." Mom shook her head. "Kids these days."

"I had to put a cot in the office for Mia. She says the vibrations from her sister's phone bothers her." Priscilla admitted, "It's been a mess. I don't know whether to discipline her or go easy…"

Mom interrupted, "Oh, I wouldn't be disciplining her, dear. At least not for something that isn't so serious. They're not in school."

"But it can't be good for a girl to be up all

night with her phone on. I've almost been tempted to call Paul."

"Overseas?" Mom looked concerned. "Now I wouldn't do that, Prissy."

"I know. I don't want to bother him."

"And my grandkids may never come see me if things get too unpleasant for them."

Priscilla sighed. "I know that, too. I just don't want to be an...irresponsible aunt."

Mom came closer and gave her a hug. "You're not irresponsible. Don't even think that. Kids are technology-crazy nowadays. In fact, we all have too much technology for our own good."

"We sure do," Priscilla agreed, hugging her mother back. "Too bad we can't get updated along with our computers." She had to ask one more question, "Do you think it's normal for Alyssa and Mia to fight so much?"

Mom laughed. "Oh, honey, I thought you and Paul were going to start World War III when he was in high school."

"That was because he was so many years older than me." In comparison to Alyssa and Mia, who were closer in age. "He thought you were a little pest. One time he locked you in a closet."

Priscilla nodded grimly. "I remember that."

"However, I don't think he would have done that if you hadn't thrown his sneakers out the window or spied on him and his friends."

Priscilla didn't remember *that*. She objected, "I was a good little girl!"

"Well, you were never aggressive in an openly hostile way."

Her mother certainly had a different view of things. "I wasn't aggressive at all!"

Mom laughed. "Sweetheart, all kids are naughty at one time or another. You're only human. Kids will be kids. They outgrow their stages."

"I'll have to keep that in mind." And she knew no one was perfect, including herself. She'd just forgotten about the sneakers, she guessed. As they put condiments out on a tray to take outside, Priscilla decided to bring the conversation back to her father. "Maybe Dad will outgrow his behavior, too." Though she intended to keep an eye on him. "Maybe he has something like post-traumatic retirement syndrome."

Mom smiled. "Well, we can hope so anyway."

"Say, what about Dad's bowling? He used to go every week."

"He's not doing it anymore. Some younger guy insisted on keeping score, which your dad used to do. Roger says he's not useful anymore there, either, so he quit the league. Of course he could be useful around here, but—"

"Let me think about this, Mom," Priscilla said, cutting her off before she could go another round. She'd been hoping for a nice relaxing evening with the whole family together. "Maybe I can come up with a way to get Dad in a better mood."

"Someone has to!"

To distract Mom, she changed the subject. "People can have worse problems. Sam was pretty down this afternoon, too. It seems someone around here doesn't like him."

"What happened? Did he get into another fight?"

"Mom, that was when he was a teenager. He told me that, last week, someone opened the pasture gate and spooked his horses. And the other evening, someone spread boards with big nails around his parking lot. That could have caused a lot of damage to customers' tires."

"Oh, that doesn't sound good."

"No, and he's worried that the culprit is out to ruin his business."

"How terrible!" Mom pulled a pitcher of lemonade from the fridge, set it on the counter between a mixer and a blender. "Sam is just getting started."

"You haven't heard any kind of rumors about Sam or the ranch, have you?"

Mom shook her head. "No. Nothing. At the library, some of the kids said they were excited because their parents were going to let them try a trail ride."

"So you've only heard positive stuff."

"So far. Maybe you should go over to the hardware store and talk to old Bob Kinney. Everyone winds up in his place, so if there's any gossip going around town, he's probably heard it."

"Good idea. If you don't mind having the girls to yourself again, I might head over there after supper."

Mom's expression lit at the suggestion. "Mind? I would love it. I can't get enough time with those girls."

"Even Alyssa?"

Mom grinned. "I'll just ask her to shut off her phone."

"And you think that will work?"

"The power of a grandmother..."

They both smiled and headed back outside to see if the coals were finally ready.

PRISCILLA WALKED INTO Kinney's Hardware an hour before closing. There were still quite a few customers in the aisles, browsing the goods. Some homes in the area were a century old and older, and when they needed to be repaired, Kinney's was the place to look for parts. The shelves were packed with everything anyone could possibly require for home maintenance.

Old Bob Kinney was ringing up purchases for a woman nearly as elderly as he was. People called him Old Bob because he'd been a town fixture forever. And he looked it. His short hair was white, his face wrinkled with time. Although when she was a kid, he'd been a tall man who could fill a doorway, now he was a bit stooped and had little flesh left on his bones. He had to be in his early nineties, but he'd never considered retiring that she knew. Good for him. She saw for herself how being forced into retiring had made Dad miserable. And Mom.

While she was waiting, Priscilla chose a half dozen color identifiers for keys to her shop and to her apartment. And when Old Bob handed the customer her bag and she left, Priscilla stepped right up to the old-fashioned register and set the colorful rubber rings on the counter.

"Priscilla." Old Bob smiled at her, revealing a missing tooth. "Haven't seen you in a cow's age."

Though she had no idea of how long a "cow's age" might be, she merely said, "I've been lucky that I didn't have anything I needed to fix lately. How are you, Bob?"

"Can't say I'm as spry as I used to be, but I'm still getting along." He picked up the key identifiers and dropped them in a bag, then rang them up. "I hear your brother Paul's girls are in town."

Terrific. He just gave her the perfect in to the real reason she was here. "They are, for a good part of the summer." She handed him money. "I've taken them out to the new Larson Dude Ranch a couple of times."

Old Bob grunted.

Uh-oh, didn't sound like he approved. She said, "Sam is doing a great job with the place."

"Putting his old man out of business."

Priscilla didn't miss the note of disapproval in his tone as he handed her the change.

In case he wasn't aware of the fact, she told him, "Dwayne retired before Sam came back."

Old Bob just grunted again. He probably identified with Dwayne Larson, even though the man had chosen to retire.

"Are you angry with Sam for some reason?" she asked.

"Personally? I haven't had any bad dealings with him since he got back in town. But you wait…just give him a chance."

That's what she was trying to do—give Sam a chance to *succeed*—but Old Bob meant it in a negative way. "Why? Did someone say something bad about him?"

"Didn't have to. Sam Larson's reputation precedes him. He was always trouble with a capital T."

"When he was a teenager," she agreed.

"No one can forget what he did to Will Berger's kid."

Priscilla took a deep breath. Sam hadn't had that motorcycle accident on an icy road with Tim on purpose, but the boy's father had blamed him anyway. And Tim might have come away with a limp, but other than that, she was pretty sure he was okay.

"That happened fifteen years ago. I thought maybe you heard a customer say something bad about Sam now."

"Sam? You talkin' about Sam Larson?"

The familiar smoke-roughened voice grated on her. Priscilla turned to see Cooper Peterson, an old rival and sometimes pal of Sam's, directly behind her. He was holding packets of screws and a couple of strange-looking tools. His hands were streaked with black grease—he worked as a mechanic for one of the local gas and repair stations. And he belonged to a stock car club whose latest exploit was driving into mud holes and racing out of them.

"Cooper."

"Priscilla."

His grin showed off shiny white teeth, the best-looking part of him as far as Priscilla was concerned. His long hair was stringy, he sported one of those little chin beards she disliked, and he smelled like cigarette smoke. He was from a whole family that a lot of people disliked, partially because they were unpleasant and partially because they were often up to no good. But what she liked least about

Coop was that he was still the low-life he'd been in high school, especially when it came to using women. He sported a different one on his arm every other month. She couldn't believe so many foolish females lived in one area, but he was romancing them younger and younger, apparently to keep up the supply.

"So are you and Sam back together?" he asked.

"We never were together in the first place."

"I remember prom night…oh, that's right." Coop's gaze narrowed on her. "You scared him off so that he left town the next day."

Priscilla stared hard at him and Old Bob asked, "What can I get you, Coop?"

Coop set the boxes and tools he was holding on the counter in front of the elderly man, but his gaze remained on her. He flicked an eyebrow at her and said, "You know, you and I never had a chance to get to know one another better."

Good grief, was he really flirting with her? She gave him a careless shrug. "Must not be destiny, Coop."

He leaned in a little closer. "We could defy destiny."

That would be the day. Not that she would say so. For one, her telling him what she really thought could lead to an uncomfortable confrontation with him, something she wanted to avoid at all costs. Plus, Coop might know of anyone bad-mouthing Sam.

"That'll be fourteen dollars and twenty-one cents," Old Bob said.

Coop handed him a twenty and asked, "So what's going on with Sam?"

Her pulse jumped. "I don't know. Neither does he. A couple of things have happened that seem to be aimed at stopping him from building his new business."

"Hunh." Coop appeared thoughtful.

"What? Have you heard something?" Priscilla asked.

"Not exactly."

"What, then?"

"Sam talked his old man out of selling the land to Walworth Builders. They want to turn farmland around here into another bedroom town for people who work in Kenosha, Racine and even in Milwaukee."

Old Bob snorted. "Hah! I heard they were gonna build a retirement village."

"Maybe they want to develop both," Coop said.

"Then we'd have a bunch of old coots doing nothing but sitting around and complaining about their rheumatism and lumbago." Old Bob shook his head. "Some of them developers would do anything to make money."

Anything? "You don't think they might do something illegal to get the land they want to develop," Priscilla said.

"Why not?" Coop shrugged. "Business is business."

She was shocked. When Priscilla had worked for Milwaukee Cheese Mart for a half dozen years, there had never been any hint of impropriety. Then, again, the Cheese Mart was a century-old family-owned company with values handed down through generations of owners. For all she knew, Walworth Builders could be family-owned and honest, too. She'd never even heard of the company before. But maybe she should ask around, see if anyone else had the lowdown on the land developers.

As a matter of fact, she knew exactly who to ask—Police Chief Alex Novak. She was sure her best friend's husband could find out if there were any complaints against Walworth Builders.

But if so…

How could they prove the company had anything to do with the problems on the ranch? More importantly, if the company was involved, how could they stop Sam's new business from being wrecked?

CHAPTER SIX

PRISCILLA'S NERVES WERE on edge as she made a last check in the mirror. The gray wide-legged trousers and sheer gray blouse over a matching cami was a little fancy for Pompeii Pizza—actually a little fancy for anywhere in Sparrow Lake—but she'd changed three times and had finally settled on the outfit she hadn't worn since leaving her job in Milwaukee. She didn't know why she was so worried about looking nice, when she was simply having a business meeting with Sam over dinner at the new pizza restaurant that had opened a few weeks back, just in time for tourist season. It was his idea to try it out. He thought they should support a new business in hopes that, in turn, the owner would support theirs. Good thinking.

While swiping on a little lip gloss, she heard Sam's knock. Her pulse fluttered and refused to settle.

Grabbing her bag, she opened the door, oddly a little breathless. “I’m ready.”

“And looking real good, Prissy.”

His tone made her flush, and for a moment, she felt as tongue-tied as she had the day he’d asked her to the prom. “Uh, thanks. You, too.”

Sam had taken as much care with his appearance as she had with hers. Khakis instead of jeans. A collared shirt open at the throat instead of a work shirt. Cleanly shaven, he smelled as if he’d splashed on some guy-fragrance. Something woodsy. Subtle. Nice.

“Shall we?” he asked.

Locking the door, she led the way down the stairs, too aware of Sam directly behind her. Did he always wear that aftershave or had he splashed some on just for her? This was not a date, she reminded herself. Sam was simply treating her to dinner in payment for being able to pick her brain about how to grow his business. It only made sense that he’d shed the dude ranch image for the evening.

As they headed for the restaurant, he asked, “So have you gotten an update on how your nieces are liking Lake Geneva?”

“Not from them. Mom called a while ago, though. Apparently Alyssa had to go into every shop in town and buy something, while Mia insisted on taking the boat ride around the lake to see all the estates. Twice."

"Sounds like they can be a handful."

Thinking about her own experience with the girls, Priscilla didn't disagree. "My brother and his wife spoil them rotten. Paul gives his kids everything they ask for and even stuff they don't know that they want. He says that's in response to our being so poor growing up."

"Wait, you weren't poor. Your Dad worked for the post office and your Mom was a librarian. So what made your brother think you were poor?"

"We didn't have all the extras kids have today, I guess. We had nice clothes, but Mom liked to raid secondhand stores. Said we grew too fast to spend a lot of money on any one outfit. Then again, she still likes shopping in them. Also, we were expected to go outside and play and use our imaginations. No fancy electronic toys. No personal computers. No cable television."

"And that was before everyone had a cell phone or tablet." They'd arrived at the restaurant. Sam got the door and held it open for her. "Expectations change, I guess."

Heading inside, Priscilla said, "Even so, you don't have to buy kids every single thing they ask for. How are they going to be prepared for adult life if they don't have to save to get what they want or earn anything on their own?"

"Good point."

The hostess seated them and left them with menus. Priscilla looked around at the warm brown walls and big potted plants. Tables were covered with colorful print cloths and topped with white butcher paper. Each table was decorated with a small flowering plant in its center.

Impressed, she said, "This isn't a typical pizza joint."

"Pretty nice."

Too bad only half the tables were occupied, and those by couples or larger groups of adults. No kids. While it was nice to be able to eat in peace, she wondered why this wasn't more of a family place. When she opened her menu, she guessed the food itself might have something to do with it. The first thing she saw was bread sticks with goat cheese. She loved goat cheese, but unfortunately it didn't sell well in her shop—lots of customers were hesitant to try something they weren't familiar with—so she had discontinued all but one line.

The selection of pizza ingredients was mostly what she would deem upscale. Veggies and sauces that kids would deem "yucky." She was pretty happy with the selection, and they were able to get individual pizzas so they could each have the ingredients they preferred. While Sam went for blackened chicken, bacon, red onions, mozzarella, cheddar and barbecue sauce, Priscilla chose Portabella mushrooms, sun-dried tomatoes, goat cheese and a spinach-ricotta sauce.

Their efficient waitress took their orders and delivered their beers a few minutes later, at which point Sam became all business.

"So when you opened the cheese shop last year, can you think of one specific thing you did to help grow it? You know, give me someplace to start."

Priscilla didn't even have to think about it. "As soon as I opened my doors for business, I invited the town to the shop on a Friday evening. You know, a grand opening. Potential customers got to sample the best cheeses and wines and other snacks I was selling while having a good time in a party atmosphere.

So they wanted to come back. And the cost to me was tax deductible."

"Hmm, a grand opening." His brow furrowed. "I'm not selling food, though."

"No, but you could still lure people with the promise of something tasty but inexpensive. Nachos, chili, pork sliders. Whatever. You're selling the ranch, so you could have tours of the place and let everyone meet the horses."

She could see Sam warming up to the idea. His lips curled into a smile that made her heart beat a little faster.

"Maybe some demonstrations, like how to tack up a horse," he said. "And we could give the kids short rides around the corral."

"There you go."

They brainstormed the open house idea until their food arrived. In addition to the pizza, they shared a salad of spinach with grapefruit, dried cranberries and candied walnuts. And as they ate, more customers arrived until only a few tables remained empty. Despite the unusual menu, the food was great, and Priscilla hoped the restaurant would be a success.

"So did this place have a grand opening?" Sam asked.

"Not that I remember, but this is one of the few restaurants in Sparrow Lake, and it is in the middle of town, so everyone sees it all the time."

Sam frowned. "By comparison, the only people who see the ranch are the people who drive the highway to Milwaukee and back."

"Word of mouth is really important, too. If all these people here today like the food and tell their friends, this place will be packed in no time. Same with the ranch." She reached over and put her hand on his for support, not expecting the wave of something she couldn't name that swept through her at the contact. "Get enough people out there for an open house and the word will spread."

"Get people where?" came a familiar voice.

Gloria Vega was standing over them, her dark dancing gaze pinned to their joined hands. One eyebrow lifted and Goria's red lips curved. Oh, no. Though a generous, sweet person, Gloria loved romantic gossip and probably thought they were on a date. Priscilla jerked her hand away. She hadn't seen the woman in the restaurant, so she must have just come in. Now Gloria was giving Sam a thorough once-over.

Suddenly on edge, Priscilla began talking

a little too fast. "Gloria, how are you? This is Sam Larson, who recently moved back to Sparrow Lake. He started a dude ranch on his father's farm. Sam, Gloria works at Sew Fine. That's the quilting shop Kristen manages."

"Nice to meet you, Gloria."

"You, too, Sam. So you're the dude ranch guy. Yeah, I heard about it."

Something in Gloria's tone broke through Priscilla's nerves. "Have people been…you know…saying things about it?"

"Saying things?"

"Gossiping. About the business? About Sam?"

Gloria pulled out an empty chair, sat and slid closer to the table. "What am I missing?"

Priscilla met Sam's gaze. He sat back in his chair and indicated she was free to say whatever she wanted. So, lowering her voice, making the other woman promise to keep things quiet, Priscilla let Gloria in on the two incidents that had Sam so upset.

"Oh, that's terrible. No, haven't heard anything like that."

"Like what then?" Priscilla asked.

"Well, some people expected Dwayne to sell to Walworth Builders. They were kind of counting on it happening."

"Counting on it? Why?"

"Jobs. Profits on supplies. More consumers when the development opened and people moved in. The economy might be picking up, but a development as big as the one Walworth was planning would have given Sparrow Lake a real financial boost."

"How loud is everyone complaining?" Sam asked, voice gruff.

"Not everyone. There are those who don't want a golf course that close to town."

"Golf course." Sam looked surprised. "That's the first I heard of any golf course."

"Yeah, something about that hilly area behind your place making a challenging place to play."

Priscilla said, "Cooper Peterson thinks they're planning a bedroom town, but Old Bob Kinney was sure it was supposed to be a retirement community. Now a golf course?"

"Maybe all of that," Gloria said. "I hear the owner is real pushy and unpleasant. Someone said he'd do whatever it took to get his way."

"Anything more specific?" Sam asked.

Gloria shook her head. "Nah, just speculation."

Noting he was on edge, Priscilla asked Sam. "What did your father have to say about it?"

"Just that he got an offer from someone who wanted land on the highway. He didn't specify what they were going to do with it. He was determined to sell until I talked him out of it. I convinced him to give me a chance to start a new business. I agreed to pay taxes and insurance and anything else he wanted if he would hold off selling to see if I could make it work."

And now Sam obviously feared that it wasn't going to work, that someone was going to wreck his dream. It hit Priscilla that he'd put so much more money into the place than she could have guessed.

Gloria waved to someone across the room and got to her feet. "Listen, it was nice meeting you, Sam. I hope business picks up. I'll tell all my friends about it. Horseback riding would be great for their kids."

"Thanks. I appreciate it. And nice meeting you, too." Sam's voice sounded strained, and as Gloria walked away from the table, he muttered, "Could this development company really be that low to try to ruin me?"

"Maybe...but it just doesn't seem likely," Priscilla said.

"Why not?"

"Because I talked to Kristen's husband

about it. Alex is the police chief here. I told him what happened with horses being let loose and the nails spread around the lot and asked him about Walworth Builders. He looked into it and got back to me earlier. It's a fairly new company with no complaints that he could dig up." She realized Sam was staring at her, seeming displeased. She finished in a rush. "Of course, Alex admitted that could mean they haven't been caught at anything."

"You contacted the authorities about what happened on my property? Without asking me first?"

The timbre of his voice knotted her stomach. "I—I contacted a friend—"

"Who happens to be the police chief!"

Priscilla was stunned at Sam's reaction. He'd raised his voice with her and now was actually glaring at her as if she'd done something wrong. "Okay, so why didn't you make a complaint?"

"Because I don't want anything to do with the authorities! Let's just leave it at that."

Priscilla sat there saying nothing as Sam called the waitress over for the check and paid it. What had started as a nice evening had just ended on a discordant note. Not wanting more of the same, she couldn't wait to get away from him.

SAM REGRETTED SNAPPING at Priscilla. By the time he'd paid the check, he'd cooled down, and now that they were leaving the restaurant, he was reluctant to take her right home before mending fences. But the distance between them was fraught with tension.

Clearing his throat, he said, "Why don't we take a walk down to the lake."

Priscilla already had a foot in the opposite direction. "Um, I don't know—"

"Look, I'm sorry for how I spoke to you earlier." That she continued to be uncomfortable was obvious. "I know you were just trying to help." When she didn't immediately answer, he said, "Please, let's just walk a bit."

"A-all right."

Not that she looked all right. Or that he felt all right. He hated that he'd upset Priscilla, who had gone out of her way to help him, but the last thing he needed was to be under the scrutiny of the top cop in Sparrow Lake.

They walked away from Main Street, down toward the lake. A comfortable breeze was blowing, and Priscilla's bright red hair whipped across her cheek. He had to make fists so that he wouldn't reach out and tuck the errant strands back behind her ear. He was tempted to touch her, all right, not that she would appreciate it after his flare of temper. He was more attracted to Priscilla now than he had been when he'd picked her up for the prom. She was a sweet woman, not a mean bone in her body, unlike the aggressive and sometimes not-so-nice types he'd met while rodeoing. And she was part of a warm, happy family, even if those nieces of hers were a little spoiled and demanding. He envied that. He'd like to get to know her better.

Too bad he was too much trouble for any woman. He had nothing to offer anyone. After not working while he spent six months in prison and then paying his high-priced lawyer to get him out, his savings had been sorely depleted. And now what had been left was nearly gone, invested in a fledgling business that might never get off the ground.

Not that he could tell Priscilla any of that.

He'd returned to Sparrow Lake because he'd been at odds about his future, because he had nightmares over what had happened to land him in prison, and now he didn't want her to know the sordid details of how the rodeo life had lost its luster for him.

They were nearly to the walking path around the lake when he said, "We never did finish talking about what you did to get your cheese shop going. Other than the grand opening."

"I had some help getting the store publicity."

"What kind of publicity?"

"An article in one of the area newspapers. And another in the southern Wisconsin travel guide."

"How?"

She wouldn't look at him. "Kristen. She did the same for Sew Fine before she took it over. She might be willing to help you."

Ask the police chief's wife for help? Sam took a big breath and decided to be agreeable. "I'll keep that in mind."

They walked together in silence for a moment until someone yelled, "Priscilla!" Standing on the McClintock Boat, Bait and Tackle patio—or so the sign told him because he didn't remember the business—the older woman with obviously dyed bright red hair was waving them over.

"That's Kristen's Aunt Margaret."

"I thought I recognized her." He knew she

was the owner of Sew Fine, the shop Kristen now managed.

"Do you mind if we stop to say hello?"

"Of course not." Anything to make Priscilla happy.

Smiling, she waved back and rushed toward the patio, Sam following. By the time they got there, Margaret had been joined by a man with thick salt-and-pepper hair and a lightly lined face. Sam didn't remember him. Priscilla gave the other woman a quick hug and then made introductions. John McClintock, owner of the business and Margaret's beau, had only moved to Sparrow Lake and opened the shop a few years back.

"You're Dwayne's son." Margaret raised an eyebrow. "I remember you."

Sam waited for her to say more about those memories, but Margaret simply invited them to sit and have some fresh lemonade.

The sun was setting, casting a warm glow over the water. They got comfortable at a table with a big umbrella and chairs with thick cushions. John poured the lemonade, while the women chatted for a few minutes, catching up. Margaret and John had just come back from a trip down the Intercoastal to Florida and back in his boat. Sam thought the older couple were in love if the glances they exchanged were any indication.

"Sam and I were just having a brainstorming session about his business," Priscilla said. "Trying to come up with ideas to get his dude ranch going."

"I saw your brochure," Margaret said, then turned to John. "Maybe we should sign up for riding lessons."

John laughed. "Get on a horse at my age? I don't think so, sweetheart. Never rode, never will. Riding in a wagon would be more my speed."

"A hayride!" Margaret sipped at her lemonade and nodded. "That sounds like a lot of fun." She asked Sam, "Do you have a wagon?"

"There's an old one on the property. Not sure what kind of shape it's in, though."

Priscilla said, "Hayrides would be a great way to get a bunch of people involved at the ranch in one evening. You could take photos and put them up on your website to lure more people there. Especially tourists."

"Um, that would be a problem, since I don't have a website."

"Which is something else you need to do to spread the word."

"I'm not a technical person."

"Kristen is," Margaret said. "You could hire her to put a website together for you. She's a marketing genius."

And the police chief's wife.

Sam had a feeling he would have to get over this fact. Either that or lose Priscilla's friendship.

Something he wasn't willing to do.

CHAPTER SEVEN

SAM AWOKE WITH a start to the sound of loud pounding on his door. Only half-awake, he threw back the covers and stumbled to his feet, knocking the alarm clock off the bedside table. From the floor it glowed 7:32 a.m. He was usually up by six. But there was no room for worrying about time with the racket going on outside.

The pounding continued. “Sam! Sam, you gotta get out here!”

It was Logan’s voice but why the kid was nearly beating the cabin’s door down was a mystery.

Sam grabbed his jeans off the floor and nearly jumped into them. He was still yanking a T-shirt down over his head when he threw open the door.

“Sam!” Logan’s eyes were bugged out and his tanned face nearly white. “It’s the horses!”

Sam panicked. “What? Did they get out again?”

"They're sick! I'm afraid Gold Mine's gonna die!"

Sliding his feet into the beat-up moccasins he used as slippers, Sam took off after Logan as the kid ran toward the barn. Both Gold Mine and Tomcat had been put inside the night before, the mare because she had a sore foot and the mischievous gelding because he'd been running the other horses around in the pasture. Tomcat was young and new to the small herd, obviously needing to learn his place.

But how had both of the horses gotten sick? And what was wrong?

Plunging through the open barn doorway, Sam felt his blood freeze. In the enclosure he'd set up as Gold Mine's stall, the palomino was on her back, rolling in the straw, feet pawing at her midsection. Colic? Sam didn't have time to mull over what the horse might have eaten to make her sick. In the opposite stall, Tomcat stood stiff-legged, his head down, a sheen of sweat on his flanks.

Definitely colic…which could be deadly.

"We gotta walk them," he told Logan. "Now! Get a long line and take Tomcat out of the barn. I'll get Goldie up."

He was so busy working with the mare,

coaxing her to her feet, he barely noticed Logan sliding the corral-side door open to take Tomcat outside. Sun flooded the barn's interior but Sam's core still felt like ice. Colic was dangerous, could twist a horse's intestines, make a horse founder and ruin his feet, even kill the animal outright. He sighed with relief as Gold Mine, with some effort, managed to stand up, then take a shaky step. He let her lean against him.

"Come on, girl, you can do it."

Outside, Logan had Tomcat walking in a circle. Another long line clipped to her halter, Gold Mine plodded along with Sam as he walked some feet parallel with the fence. When the horse groaned and stumbled, her insides no doubt quaking, Sam reached over to touch her, chirping encouragingly, "Let's keep it up, girl. Come on, baby."

Sam had no idea how long they were moving, horses and men, but he wished his dad would notice something was up from his house some yards away. Somebody needed to call the vet and he didn't want to stop and do it himself. He hadn't even thought about bringing his cell phone with him. He had no idea what he'd done with the thing the night before. He'd plunged into the day headfirst.

He had Gold Mine halfway down the fence line when a car pulled in from the highway. It was a gray subcompact that looked familiar… Priscilla. Her startled face came into view as she arrived with her nieces. Oh, right, Sam suddenly remembered the youngest was supposed to start her Western riding lessons early this morning.

As soon as the car rolled to a stop, Priscilla and Mia came flying toward the fence, Alyssa a few paces behind.

"Sam, what on earth?" gasped Priscilla.

As Sam kept walking, they followed him and the horse along on the other side of the fence. "Colic. Got to keep them moving. Can you call the vet?"

Priscilla glanced around. "My phone is in my purse. What's his number?"

"I don't know." Sam heaved a sigh. He hadn't called the man enough times to have it memorized. "Do you think you can walk this horse? I'll call."

"I can do it," Mia was already scrambling over the top of the fence. She landed with a soft thud and reached for the long line.

The girl was small but competent from what Sam had seen. "Okay. Just keep her moving. Don't stop. Don't let her have any water if she tries to drink from the trough."

"Right."

"Encourage her. She's real sick."

"I sure will." Mia swiped one hand over Gold Mine's sweaty neck. "Poor girl! We'll get you better. Come on."

Meanwhile, Sam hoisted himself over the fence and headed for his dad's house, Priscilla hurrying along beside him.

The old man already stood outside on the porch, a disgusted look on his face. He raked Sam over with his gaze, taking in the ragged T-shirt and wild hair. He showed no visible concern or sympathy, which was no surprise. "What's going on now? Horse rustlers?"

Priscilla greeted him, "Hello, Mr. Larson."

In answer, Pop grunted, nodding in her direction.

Sam just walked on, heading for the phone.

Pop followed the pair inside. "Hey, I asked what's going on?"

"I need to use your phone. I've got some sick animals."

"You want the vet?" Pop rattled off a phone number.

As Sam punched in the number, he could

hear his dad muttering about responsibility or lack thereof.

"He never could take care of cows," growled Pop. "Why would he be better with horses?"

Priscilla frowned.

Sam wanted to say something to the old man about being polite around visitors but when the vet suddenly picked up the phone on the other end, he concentrated and rattled off his information. Thankfully, Dr. Isaacs was available. "In ten minutes? Okay, we'll be in the corral."

Still ignoring Pop, Sam grabbed Priscilla's elbow and ushered her outside.

"Your dad calls you irresponsible when you're in a crisis?" She sounded appalled.

Sam didn't want to get into explanations. "It's just his way. He's a charmer."

As they headed back to the corral, Priscilla asked, "What happened to the horses anyway?"

"I don't know. Logan got me up and I've been dealing with this as best I can."

Priscilla gazed down at his moccasins. "Do you want me to get you some shoes? Those can't be too comfortable on gravel."

"Nah, I've got along so far." At least he had something on his feet. He'd been so freaked he could have ended up barefoot. "Thanks for offering, though." She always wanted to help.

Once inside the corral, he saw that Alyssa was walking Tomcat now and the horse seemed a bit better. At least his head was up and his ears moving. Sam glanced around. "Where's Logan?"

"I don't know," said the girl. "He had to leave."

Left in the middle of a crisis? Sam bit back his anger. At least Alyssa was pitching in. He and Logan were going to have some words, though, when he got hold of the kid again. He noticed that the old beater Logan drove was not in its usual parking spot under a tree.

"Come on, let's take care of things until the vet gets here," he said to himself as much as to Priscilla.

"Just tell me what to do."

Sam could count on her and it looked as if he could count on her nieces, too, at least at the moment. He was thankful some sort of help and kindness were available. That hadn't always been true in the past.

PRISCILLA AND SAM split up when he suggested she help Alyssa while he caught up with Mia and the palomino. Priscilla watched him stride away before turning to her older niece. “Do you want me to walk Tomcat for a while?”

“We’re doing okay.”

Alyssa’s voice sounded tight and Priscilla thought the girl looked as if she had tear streaks on her cheeks. Was she that upset over the situation? Priscilla fell into step beside her.

“I didn’t know you were so knowledgeable about horses.”

“I told you I took riding lessons. I heard about colic.”

“Well, the vet’s coming any moment.”

The teenager didn’t say anything and Priscilla gazed at her with sympathy, growing even more certain that Alyssa had been crying. However, her instincts told her sick horses weren’t the issue. Had something happened between her and Logan?

“Are you doing all right?”

That brought an angry ‘don’t you dare inquire’ stare from the teenager. “I’m fine!” snapped Alyssa, raising her chin. “I can walk this horse. Why don’t you help Mia and Sam?”

Well, okay. Sam had told her to stick with Alyssa but Priscilla was definitely being told to mind her own business. "Let me know if you get tired or anything," she offered before walking away.

As Priscilla headed toward Sam and Mia, she saw Sam had taken the lead from the younger girl. He patted her shoulder. "You're doing a great job."

"She tried to lay down a couple of minutes ago, but I wouldn't let her."

"Good. You're some horsewoman."

"If I had to, I would've propped her up."

Despite the tense situation, Sam managed a guffaw. "I bet you would."

Priscilla joined them. "How'd the horses get colic anyway?"

Sam took a deep breath. "I have no idea."

"Did they have some bad feed?" asked Mia.

"I checked the hay when I bought it and I didn't see any mold. That's all they've had, plus a little grain after trail rides," Sam explained. "They mainly graze. They've been eating the pasture down." He glanced back at Alyssa and the bay. "What happened to Logan?" he asked Priscilla.

"Alyssa just said he had to leave."

"Fine time for him to take off."

That's what Priscilla thought, too. Her heart went out to Sam. He looked haggard. Before she could offer any consoling words, however, the vet pulled in the drive and parked his truck beside the corral. Dr. Isaacs was a slight middle-aged man with a business-like, if friendly, manner. Carrying a big case, he came through the gate and immediately took over. Priscilla watched as Isaacs checked Tomcat's vital signs and used a stethoscope to listen to his belly.

"He's not doing too bad. It's good that you got to him when you did," the vet told Sam, who'd brought Gold Mine over.

"They had a little hay last night but it was fine," said Sam. "No mold. I don't see how they got into anything that would be bad for them."

"Well, they found something," said Isaacs, moving on to examine Gold Mine.

The vet spent more time with the mare, looking her over carefully. Finally, he turned to Sam. "You're lucky. I don't think either of these horses needs surgery. I'm going to give this one a shot of painkiller." Then he gestured to Tomcat. "Maybe him, too. That fellow either didn't eat as much of whatever it was or he's stronger."

Isaacs opened the case again to take out some syringes, then administered the medication. Next, he walked toward the barn. "Let's take a look at that feed."

Leaving the girls to keep walking the horses, Sam and Priscilla accompanied the veterinarian as he inspected the hay in the barn, as well as the horses' feed tubs. He frowned and fingered something from one of the tubs. He held it up to look at it more closely. "This seems to be a pellet for feeder cattle."

"A pellet? I don't give the horses pellets of any sort," said Sam.

"Well, they definitely have been eating some." Isaacs moved to the next stall and leaned down to pick another pellet off the floor. "Feeder cattle get all kinds of supplements in their food. It's rich, meant to fatten them up faster and protect them from disease when they're confined."

"And that feed would make horses sick," said Sam.

"Sure would. Enough of it could kill them."

"I wouldn't give my horses any kind of cattle feed."

"Then how did they get it?" Priscilla wondered aloud.

"How about that Keller kid you have working for you?" Isaacs asked.

"He wouldn't poison horses."

Sam sounded certain about that, Priscilla noted, even though Logan had taken off.

"Well, somebody did...wanted to kill them or make them real sick anyway," said Isaacs.

Priscilla was shocked. "Someone tried to kill these horses?" As the reality sank in, she slipped her hand inside Sam's calloused one. "Oh, Sam!"

He squeezed her hand in return.

"See anybody around who shouldn't be here?" the vet asked.

Sam shook his head. "No, but I didn't get up until 7:30."

"For the horses to react to the food, they would have to have eaten it much earlier," said Isaacs.

"Last night? Early this morning? I'm guess I'm going to have to keep a closer watch."

Though how he was going to do that, he didn't say.

"Poisoning horses...that's terrible." Priscilla was shocked.

Sam shook his head. "They're like my family."

"You should probably notify the cops." Isaacs went outside and picked up his case. "I have to be going. Your animals should be all right. Check for any more of those pellets before you bring them back inside."

"And I'll call you if anything gets worse."

"It shouldn't, but you do that," said Isaacs. "If I don't answer, you can leave a message with my emergency service and they'll find me."

The veterinarian headed for his vehicle. "I'll drop by tomorrow and see how the horses are doing."

"Great."

After Isaacs drove away, Sam told Mia to take a break while he took over walking Gold Mine. The mare seemed to be recovering. At least Priscilla thought so. Her eyes seemed to be brighter and she wasn't stumbling.

"I guess we're not having riding lessons today," Sam told Mia.

"It doesn't matter," said the girl. "I would rather help sick animals."

Alyssa stopped Tomcat near her aunt. "Go ahead and walk him if you want. I need a break, too."

Priscilla took the line and marched in the direction Sam had taken, soon catching up. Tomcat was indeed recovering, she thought, though she wasn't an expert on horses. He tossed his head, snorted and seemed almost perky.

"Someone would deliberately poison horses?" She still couldn't understand how anyone could do that.

"Looks like it."

"That's way more serious than leaving a gate open or scattering boards and nails in your lot."

"Sure is."

"Someone really must have it in for you."

"Yeah, but who?" Sam scowled. "I draw the line at harming innocent animals. If somebody has a problem with me, they can deal with me personally."

Priscilla thought about Walworth Builders. "Surely some company that wanted your land wouldn't go that far."

"Who knows? I intend to find out."

"By reporting this incident to the police?"

Sam didn't answer.

"You could call Alex Novak and tell him about it."

"Yeah, I could."

But she had the feeling he wouldn't. What was his problem with police?

He patted her arm. "Don't you be telling him about this either, okay? I need to think about things. It's enough that you…that we told that woman about what we thought were pranks the other evening."

Priscilla wondered if his reluctance to be open could stem from his suspicions about who might actually be involved. Logan? "Could Logan have fed the horses something different for some reason? Accidentally? Maybe he got confused."

"I don't have any cattle around. He would have had to go out and buy the feed." Sam added, "And he knows the difference in commercial feeds. He grew up on a farm and has lived here all his life."

Still, Priscilla couldn't be so sure about Logan herself.

As if he knew what she was thinking, Sam told her, "Logan was more freaked today than I've ever seen the kid. No one would feed horses something like cattle pellets, then stick around to watch what happened."

"But it's odd he left."

"I'll deal with him," Sam said, his tone final. Then he changed the subject, "You know, Prissy, I really appreciate all you've done today." He moved closer to slip an arm around her shoulders.

The warmth of his touch made her catch

her breath. "It—it wasn't much," she managed to stutter. "I'm not as good with horses as Mia."

"You were plenty good today. I don't know what I would have done without you."

His face was so close, Priscilla thought he might kiss her. Her stomach fluttered and she had trouble taking a normal breath. But Sam let her go when Gold Mine snorted and came to a stop.

"What's the matter, girl?" He stroked the mare's neck and examined her closely. "I think you're definitely better. Ready to go back to the barn?"

Priscilla told herself that she was not disappointed that he hadn't kissed her. Her imagination had simply been working overtime.

A short while later, Sam tied both horses near the barn door. "I'm going over their stalls before I put them back in, just to make sure I find all the feed pellets."

"We can help," offered Mia, who had joined her aunt.

"You've done enough for today. Go on home," Sam said, then paused as if he remembered something else. "Hey, about that riding lesson. Want to come out here again tomorrow?"

"They have plans," Priscilla cut in before Mia answered.

Mia looked annoyed. If it was up to her, she'd probably live at the ranch. "Such as what?"

"Your grandmother wants you to do that workshop with her." Something taking place at Sew Fine, the quilting store in downtown Sparrow Lake. "We can come back out here the day after."

"Okay." Mia looked satisfied with that.

Sam nodded. "The next day's good, too. We're not swarming with customers."

"Yet," added Priscilla, newly determined she would do what she could to drum up business. If only Sam would let her help him figure out how to stop the person who was trying to shut it down.

AFTER PRISCILLA AND the girls left, Sam thoroughly cleaned out the stalls and found a few more pellets. He put them in his pocket with the others Isaacs had found, deciding he would visit the feed stores in Sparrow Lake to see where someone might have purchased them.

He brought the horses into the barn and settled them, though he fully intended to return with a bedroll for the night. He hadn't been exaggerating when he'd said he loved his animals like family. He would protect his animals like family, too, if he had to sleep in the barn from now on.

Though, the horses would be back in the pasture in a couple of days, not the barn, and Sam couldn't be aware of what was going down on every acre. He'd need an army for that.

At least he'd had Priscilla and her nieces to help out today. He'd give the girls a couple of extra riding lessons to pay them back, he decided.

Feeling drained, he strode back to his cabin, kicking a small rock out of his way. The impact hurt his toes through the thin moccasins, making him furious, and he yelped in pain. He wanted to yell a lot more to let out his frustration, but Pop would probably stick his head out of the farmhouse to ask what was going on.

What *was* going on? Who had sneaked onto the ranch in the middle of the night to mess with his horses?

He'd never had the chance to ask Logan if he'd seen anything before the kid had taken off. He absolutely did not believe Logan would do anything to the horses, but he had to admit the young man was acting strange. He planned to find out why, and the kid had better have a good reason.

As soon as he got to the cabin, Sam found his cell and punched in Logan's number. No answer. He tried the number again with the same result. Fine, he'd call him later and then again after that. There was no question in his mind that he'd do whatever it would take to get to the bottom of this mess.

Sam changed his clothes and threw some old blankets into a pile to use as a bedroll. He took the handful of feed pellets from the pair of discarded jeans and slipped them into a plastic bag he found in the kitchen. Then he pulled on his boots to return to the barn. He was going to go over the place again with a fine-tooth comb.

Security cameras might be the answer. Sam thought about where he might install some as he strode along. He'd heard they weren't that expensive to buy. No telling how expensive they'd be to put up in the first place, though. Sam wasn't handy with electronics.

When he'd started the dude ranch, he'd hoped to at least break even for the first two years. After that, he'd hoped to not only take care of himself, but contribute to Pop's retirement. Instead, it seemed he was trying to climb a slippery hill in a rainstorm, with some unknown enemy deliberately trying to send him sliding back to the bottom. The feed incident proved he wasn't just having bad luck. Someone actually had it in for him. He had to make it stop, but how?

He didn't want to complain too loudly, however, because he'd drag in Priscilla again. He knew she'd always be supportive. But, like most people, she had immediately suggested involving the cops, and Sam wasn't ready for that confrontation.

CHAPTER EIGHT

"I DON'T LIKE to sew." Alyssa sounded as peevish as her expression.

Priscilla gave the teenager a warning look, but she didn't think Alyssa noticed as they drove to Sew Fine for the workshop their grandmother had gone to a lot of trouble to set up for them. Mom would meet them there.

"You said you weren't interested in riding either, but you liked the dude ranch just fine once we got there," came Mia from the backseat. "Of course, there was a cute guy to flirt with." She met her aunt's eyes in the rearview mirror. "I suppose there won't be any boys at a quilting workshop."

"Probably not," said Priscilla. "Though some could probably sew if they tried."

Quilting had been a traditional pastime in this area of Wisconsin for more than a century. Mom wanted the girls to have some idea about local heritage since their ancestors had lived in the state for more than a hundred years.

"It's supposed to be more about designing a quilt block than it is sewing a whole quilt." Priscilla herself had also been roped into the Block Party workshop, so she'd looked over the flyer advertising it, and had decided it could be fun. "It's only a couple of hours. You'll meet some other people, maybe even girls your age."

Block Party was supposed to be a family event, especially for mothers and daughters or, in their case, grandmother and grandchildren or aunt and nieces.

Priscilla glanced over at Alyssa, who didn't look any less unenthusiastic. She seemed distant and a little sad, although the teenager had felt well enough to tint the lighter ends of her hair magenta last night. It was the only spot of color against the funereal black of her clothing, as usual, a midriff-baring top and jeggings. Alyssa was staring at her cell phone, as if willing someone, anyone, to text her. Priscilla still wondered what had happened the day before at the dude ranch.

As soon as they reached the quilting store, they ran into Mom outside. Mia immediately and proudly gave her a rundown of what they'd done the day before, working with the sick horses. "We saved their lives, Grams."

"My, my," said Mom, her eyes wide. "That's wonderful! But what happened to them anyway?"

"They had some bad feed…cattle pellets, the veterinarian said," Priscilla cut in, not wanting to get into a big discussion about whoever might be trying to sabotage Sam.

He obviously didn't feel comfortable about other people knowing his business. At least not discussing it because of what Priscilla and her nieces had said. Small town gossip would probably pick up on events, no matter what, since who knew whom Dr. Isaacs would talk to. But Priscilla had asked the girls to keep a lid on things before they headed for the quilting store that morning.

"Let's not talk about the horses at the workshop, okay?" she reiterated again. "Sam wants to keep it quiet, deal with the situation himself."

She had called Sam that morning to see if the horses had fully recovered and was relieved to hear they were nearly back to normal. He hadn't said anything else about the mystery of the cattle pellets and he hadn't mentioned Logan. In fact, though he thanked her again for their help, he'd said he had to get off the phone at the moment. Just like yesterday, he seemed kind of uptight.

Well, Priscilla wouldn't bring up the topic if she could help it, but she still planned to do some discreet investigating of her own wherever and whenever she got the chance.

Inside the shop, on the other side of the bins and shelves of quilting supplies and bolts of cloth, was an area where classes were held. Today, two big tables had been pushed together and several participants were already examining the supplies Gloria Vega was laying down.

"Helen," Gloria said warmly, grasping Mom's hand. "So nice you could come." She smiled and turned to Priscilla. "You, too, Priscilla. Welcome to Sew Fine. And who are the two gorgeous young ladies with you?"

Mom introduced Alyssa and Mia, while Gloria stared at Alyssa's hair. "I lo-ove your hair style," she told the teenager. "I wish I could wear something like that but I'm too old."

Alyssa actually managed a tight smile. "You're not too old."

"I want you to meet my daughters." Gloria drew Mia and Alyssa to the other side of the table to meet an attractive dark-haired girl about Alyssa's age. "This is Sabrina, my oldest." Then she gestured to a round-faced younger girl with glasses. "And this is Jackie."

The girls chatted as the rest of the workshop participants arrived and found places to sit. There were a couple of mother/daughter pairs, a grandmother and granddaughter, plus Nellie, the older lady who ran the consignment shop in Sparrow Lake. She had her gray hair pulled back tightly and huge black glasses balanced on her nose. She was busy arranging thread and other supplies in a tray.

"Nellie's going to help out," Gloria told the group. "If you have questions, you can also ask her."

"And I'm going to man the store while you're all busy," said Kristen Lange-Novak, who had just entered with a jingle of the front door. Smiling, she came over to hug Priscilla. "Great to see you."

Priscilla hugged her back, always glad to see a close friend. She was going to have to call Kristen one of these days to catch up… and also ask her about advertising ideas for the dude ranch, such as where and how flyers could be made cheaply or how to get featured in an article for the local newspaper. Sam couldn't object to that.

Kristen glanced at Alyssa whose appearance couldn't help but make her stand out. "Wow, that's some hair you've got there."

Gloria's dark eyes sparkled. "I was telling her I wished I could wear mine that way."

"I don't know what your husband would say." Kristen laughed. "But Alex would kill me if I came home with a 'do like that."

And Priscilla really didn't think Kristen would want such wild hair. She was too conservative. Today, she had her blonde hair pulled back in a loose ponytail clasped with a faux pearl barrette. She wore matching single pearl earrings, crisp white linen pants and a jersey navy top. As usual, she looked beautifully put-together. Priscilla always felt a bit shabby standing next to her. She stared down at her second-to-best jeans and plain beige and white striped blouse.

"I don't think Kristen has met the Ryans' summer visitors," Mom said, making Priscilla realize she needed to do some introductions.

Kristen warmly greeted Alyssa and Mia, then the other participants for the workshop. She seemed to know everyone but one mother and daughter. About the time they'd exchanged names, a customer came in, and Kristen headed for the store's front counter.

Gloria started the workshop by handing out material, squares of batting, same-size squares of patterned cotton, and prepared, iron-on appliqués. Each participant was to choose some appliqués for her square, use an iron set up nearby to adhere them, and then stitch or quilt everything together. It didn't seem too hard. Priscilla noted that Mia chose appliqués of running horses. Not a surprise. Alyssa seemed more interested in talking to Sabrina than picking out materials, but she finally settled on some fabrics with metallic accents.

As time went on, Priscilla had to admit the workshop was fun. While she sewed her own messy version of a quilt block, they gossiped about happenings around town with a camaraderie that included everyone but Alyssa and Sabrina. The two teenagers seemed to be involved in a private, amusing conversation, probably about boys. At least Alyssa was talking to someone, Priscilla thought with relief. She really hated to think either one of her nieces would go home to New York saying they'd had a bad time in Wisconsin.

Mia seemed to always have a good time.

She was chatting with everyone. Thankfully, as Priscilla had asked, Mia did not bring up the sick horses. Instead, she shared her plan for Western riding lessons out at the dude ranch, wondering if Sam could teach her barrel racing.

"Whoa, barrel racing is kind of advanced, isn't it?" asked Priscilla, thinking of her niece's safety.

"Aunt Priscilla, I was almost ready for show jumping in New York. I already know something about dressage," stated Mia. "Why not barrel racing?"

"I'm sure you can do whatever you set your mind to, dear," Mom put in encouragingly. "My granddaughters are very accomplished."

The mention of riding and lessons brought up the dude ranch, several of the women saying they'd never heard of the place.

"Where is this dude ranch?" asked Nellie, pushing her glasses higher on her nose. Her eyes, slightly magnified, gave her an owlish expression.

"It's the Larson Dude Ranch," said Gloria. "Dwayne's son came back from out west and he's got a bunch of horses."

"Hmm, wasn't the Larson farm one piece

of land that Walworth Builders was trying to buy?" Nellie asked.

"I heard they were interested," said Gloria, exchanging knowing glances with Priscilla, "but I don't think the Larsons will sell." She cut off a thread and laid her scissors down.

"And it wasn't just the Larson place the company was scouting," put in Mrs. Stanley, one of the mothers in a mother/daughter pair. "They've been approaching several farmers with land near Sparrow Lake."

"It's sad to see farmland go," said Nellie.

"Not necessarily," Gloria put in. "There are a lot of farms around here and no 'green' communities. That's what Walworth Builders is planning. Maybe it'll be good for the town."

That launched a discussion of what a 'green' community might be. Gloria had obviously heard something new since she and Priscilla had last spoken.

Nellie asked, "You mean they'll use solar energy?"

Gloria nodded. "Alternative forms of energy should be on the agenda, along with building with sustainable materials and recycling."

Kristen had heard the discussion and approached the tables. "The Hubers intend to do more than use clean energy. They want to develop a community that unites inhabitants and environment, including the town of Sparrow Lake, as is. Grace Huber is very positive about that."

Obviously Kristen knew someone at Walworth Builders, Priscilla noted, before putting in her two cents. "That sounds very politically correct in today's world, good in theory. But that doesn't mean the company doesn't intend to make a profit." Or push aside anyone who got in their way.

"Making a profit isn't a bad goal," said Kristen. "You and I, as business owners, should understand that."

True. When another customer came in, an older woman with tightly pulled-back silver hair, Kristen left to see what she wanted. Priscilla recognized the woman, Emily Auerbach, the mayor's eccentric wife.

Everyone got back to work when Gloria announced they only had a half hour left of the workshop. Though Priscilla wasn't exactly pleased with the results of her project—it was slightly crooked and not the best design—she sewed down the rest of her appliques and gave the block a final pressing.

Helen was waiting by the ironing board

for her turn. "Roger and I want to take the girls out for a fish fry in Spencer tonight," Mom said, referring to a town nearby. "Then they can stay overnight. Would you like to go, Priscilla?"

Priscilla considered the invitation but decided, "No thanks." She'd had enough of groups of people and would appreciate some time on her own. "I need to get back to the cheese shop and see what's going on."

"Certainly, dear. I know the girls keep you busy."

"But I'm enjoying it," Priscilla said hurriedly, only fibbing a little. Her time with her nieces was sometimes taxing, but she truly wanted to get to know them.

As Gloria and Nellie cleaned up, sweeping up colorful fabric fragments and thread, putting supplies away, the workshop participants got ready to leave. Priscilla noticed that Kristen was leaning on the counter and didn't seem to be busy. Mrs. Auerbach was in the back, rummaging through material.

She decided to take advantage of an idle moment and sidled up to the counter. "You seem to know a lot about Walworth Builders, Kristen. Who's Grace Huber?"

"Grace and her father, Henry Huber, are

heading Walworth Builders. I talked to her. Very nice."

"Really? Where did you meet?"

Kristen looked at her quizzically, probably wondering why Priscilla was so interested.

"I ran into Grace at a town council meeting." Which Priscilla knew that Kristen sometimes attended. "She introduced herself to the group and I talked to her afterward. She was very pleasant…unlike her dad, sometimes, I guess. She said he could be a grump and she was handling the community outreach for the company. She struck me as very dedicated to 'green' values. She said she wants their plan to fit in with Sparrow Lake's future."

"That sounds admirable."

"I thought so. I was expecting a pushy developer whose goal was to build a commuter community for people who work in Milwaukee. Or a gated, high-class golf course type of thing for those who can afford to live well once they retire from the city. Instead, it sounds like something else entirely. You might be interested in talking to her yourself as a local merchant."

"Maybe I would." Priscilla knew she could be wrong, but Walworth Builders didn't sound like the sort who were pushy and insistent on buying up land.

As if Kristen read her mind, she said, "I heard about the incidents out at Sam Larson's dude ranch."

"You did?" Priscilla wondered if gossip had gone this far already.

Kristen nodded. "Horses let loose. Nails in the parking lot. I just can't see a company like Grace Huber's doing any such thing. Sam ought to talk to Alex about pranks like that."

"I agree." Priscilla frowned. At least no one was talking about the sick horses yet. "But Sam doesn't want to do that at the moment..."

"Whyever not? Is he still having trouble with authority?" Kristen broke in. "I remember he was such a rebel in high school. But he's a grown man now."

"Who's a rebel?" Mrs. Auerbach asked, suddenly arriving at the counter to drop three big bolts of cloth with a thud.

"Oh, we were just chatting. Nothing in particular," Kristen told her, obviously thinking it best to not go into detail.

The mayor's wife was known to be a bit strange and sometimes even hostile. She poked at the top bolt of cloth. "I'll take four yards of this and two yards of each of the others."

"Of course," said Kristen. "How's the mayor anyway?"

"He's nearly overcome with worry about the future of this town, that's how he is."

Which Priscilla was sure was an exaggeration. "I'm sure everything will be okay," she said soothingly as Kristen measured out the yards of fabric, cut them, and folded them into a bag for the older woman.

Mrs. Auerbach wasn't in the least relieved. "Walworth Builders is going to ruin Sparrow Lake and build some sort of monstrosity with a huge fence around it." She nodded toward the workshop tables. "I heard the quilting group over there talking about it. Phillip has been talking about it, too."

Though the mayor probably wasn't claiming there'd be a monstrosity, Priscilla was certain. His wife was known to embroider truths a bit. He'd been elected in spite of her.

"And if it's not horrible buildings going up, the farms are being ruined anyway." Mrs. Auerbach said with a sniff. "Larson's dairy farm is some sort of ranch now, with horse rides for children."

"What's wrong with kids riding horses?"

asked Kristen, as Mrs. Auerbach handed her a credit card.

"Horses are dangerous. Children can fall off. Or be trampled."

Priscilla came to the ranch's defense. "Sam Larson is careful. And very professional."

"Plus I'm sure he has insurance," put in Kristen as she finished the transaction and gave Mrs. Auerbach a pen to use in signing the receipt.

"Careful? Professional?" Mrs. Auerbach wasn't going to be dissuaded from negativity. "I've heard that Keller boy is working out there. He's a juvenile delinquent. His parents even kicked him out for his escapades."

To that, Kristen said, "Well, you never know. Maybe giving him a chance to work at something interesting will change him."

"Change like your brother?" Mrs. Auerbach said. "Brian Lange was a juvenile delinquent, too."

Now Kristen looked irritated. "Brian wasn't that bad. He got into trouble when he first came to Sparrow Lake but he was mixed up. He's doing well in college now and is quite responsible."

The small crowd of workshop participants surging toward the front of the store interrupted the rest of the conversation. Looking startled, Mrs. Auerbach glanced around, grabbed her bag and headed for the door with the others.

Kristen said nothing more about the woman's accusations, but for Priscilla, the mention of Logan stood out. She had no idea why Sam seemed to want to believe the best of him but, if nothing else, he had certainly been irresponsible the day before. How bad were the things he'd done in the past? She intended to find out.

SAM CAME OUT of Homestead and Farm Supply feeling just as frustrated as when he'd gone in. Homestead and Farm was the fourth place he'd visited looking for feeder cattle pellets and it was also the fourth place that sold that type of feed. Whoever had given the feed to his horses could have gotten it anywhere in Sparrow Lake, including local farms that raised cattle. There was no way Sam could check out every possibility.

Walking back to his pickup, a gray car slowed down and beeped. He looked up to spy Priscilla at the wheel. And she was alone. On his way to find Logan—at least he hoped to locate the kid where he'd been staying at a cousin's house—Sam hesitated, but only for a moment. When she rolled down the window, he went over to talk to her.

"Know anything new?" Priscilla asked, her expression sympathetic.

"Not a thing. All the merchants that sell feed carry the kind of cattle pellets the horses ate." He had spoken with her this morning but he told her again, "They're doing a lot better. Tomcat is next to normal and Goldie seems interested in going back to the pasture." He added, "I didn't mean to be short on the phone today, but Dr. Isaacs was there. Thankfully, he gave the horses a clean bill of health."

"I completely understand. I bet you're relieved."

"For the time being." He told her, "Pop is watching the place this afternoon." To his surprise without more than a grumble, as if Pop finally approved of something. "But I'm thinking about getting security cameras for the long haul."

"That's a good idea. I have a couple installed in my store. I know someone who could probably put some in for you at a reasonable price."

"You do?" Now that would be helpful.

"His name is Rick Scofield. He's my friend Heather Clark's guy. I'll get his phone number for you."

"I would appreciate that. Maybe you can give it to me tomorrow when you come out again for riding lessons with your nieces."

"Right." She frowned as if remembering something. "Oops. Change of plans. My mom is bringing the girls out tomorrow. I forgot I have to work brunch at my shop."

"Okay." Too bad. Sam always wanted to see more of her, especially when he wasn't dealing with a mess.

He longed for things to settle down so that he and Priscilla could reconnect a bit, for one thing. He needed someone positive and supportive in his life.

As if she read his mind, Priscilla said, "You know we don't have to wait until I call you with that phone number. I have it on my computer at the cheese shop. I was just heading over there. Why don't you come with me? You look like you could use a time-out from all the stress. And some cold lemonade."

Sam figured he probably shouldn't agree—he needed to find Logan and figure out what was going on with the kid—but he could use a friendly ear right now. "Cold lemonade. And I get to see your cheese shop. How could I say no?"

Priscilla grinned at him, and Sam couldn't resist grinning at her in return. They paused, their gazes connecting, his chest tightening, as he leaned against the car.

Then she said, "Follow me," put the car in gear, and started off down the street.

Letting out the breath he hadn't known he was holding, Sam got into his truck and followed. Waiting for him in front of the Cheese Shop, Priscilla seemed to be in a better mood than she'd been since she'd first brought her nieces out to ride. She radiated positive energy. She was smiling freely, walking with a bounce in her step. Sam fought the urge to put an arm around her waist as they went inside. For some reason, he imagined touching her would make the positive energy contagious. Unfortunately, they didn't have that kind of relationship.

But what if they did?

As they entered the shop, the interior was light and airy, with wide floorboards, light paneling and barrels with butcher block tops set with product displays. Priscilla had done a great job of making the place look inviting.

The nerdy-looking guy behind the counter

quickly set down the book he was reading. "Hey, boss. Didn't know you were coming in."

"I have a few things to do. This is Sam Larson. He's running the new dude ranch."

"So you have horses, right?" the guy asked.

Sam bit back a laugh. "Horses are what a dude ranch is all about."

"Like many things, I've read a lot about horses but never tried one."

Priscilla asked, "Steve, would you get us a couple of lemonades. And maybe a plate of cheese and crackers."

"Absolutely."

Priscilla indicated the area that held a few small tables and chairs off to one side. "Have a seat, and I'll look up Rick's phone number for you."

While she did that, Sam checked his phone for any calls or texts or emails he might have missed. Nothing. Which meant Logan hadn't tried to reach him. What was going on with the kid?

Priscilla set down a piece of paper with Rick's name and number, then slipped into the seat opposite him. Her knees jarred into his. She swallowed a laugh and adjusted. "Sorry. Tiny tables."

"*Cozy* tables." And Sam hadn't minded the contact.

"Good spin." She glanced at the cell phone in his hand. "Were you going to call Rick now?"

"No, actually I was just checking to see if Logan tried to contact me." He shook his head. "Nothing."

"I can't believe you still haven't heard from him."

"When I leave here, I'm going to track him down and find out what's going on with him."

Priscilla frowned. "Maybe he felt guilty about the horses getting sick."

"He was plenty worried, all right. If he couldn't stand seeing them sick, though, I don't know if I can count on him."

"But you're going to talk to him anyway?"

"I believe everyone deserves a second chance to prove himself."

"As do I."

The conversation was interrupted by Steve delivering the refreshments. "I brought you some triple cream brie."

"Great. Thanks." She turned to Sam. "Help yourself."

Priscilla spread some cheese on a cracker and Sam followed suit. He took a bite and washed it down with lemonade. "Mmm, tasty."

"Thanks. This is one of my favorites." She bit into her cracker. Swallowing, she said, "You know, speaking of second chances, I guess your starting a business here in Sparrow Lake is that second chance for you."

"It is. But it's looking like someone wants me to fail. I just hope no one tries anything with the horses while I'm gone. Pop said he would keep an eye on the place and call me if he sees anything suspicious."

"Sounds like he's calmed down some. Maybe your asking him for help was a good thing."

"Why do you say that?"

"Because he's retired," Priscilla answered. "Maybe that's it. He gave up the dairy farm he ran for decades, and now what does he have to do? The life he knew is gone. That could be why he's so testy with you. I know that now that Dad is retired, he's driving Mom crazy. He mopes around, falls asleep watching television, even though he could work on projects around the house. Maybe without his job—without contact with the outside world—he feels like he's not needed anymore. It's like he doesn't have a reason to get up in the morning. Perhaps your father feels the same, just has a different way of showing it. Think about what it would be like to suddenly have an open agenda."

"Actually, it sounds good," Sam admitted. "I could use a few of days of having nothing to do."

"But what if that 'nothing' stretched on for the rest of your life? What if you realized it was your job that had been making you feel useful?"

"Hmm." Could it be? Sam wondered. Pop had been pretty crummy to him since his mother's death, but he'd reached an all-time low since Sam had come home. "Maybe you have something there," he admitted. "Could be why he's so cantankerous. But what can I do about it now? He gave up the business, sold off the cows and the equipment."

"There is a new business on his property he could get involved in."

Sam started at the suggestion. "You mean mine? He hates the idea of a dude ranch."

"Maybe he wouldn't hate it so much if he thought you needed him. You said he's keeping an eye out on the place while you're gone."

"Right."

"Did he argue with you about doing so?"

"No. Actually, he groused a little but said okay pretty easily."

"There you are, then. You're having trouble getting your business going. You could use some advice from someone who stayed in business all his life. Keeping a private dairy farm going has had its own challenges the last couple of decades."

"That's a fact."

"I want to show you something," Priscilla said, rising from her chair. "I'll be right back."

"Sure," Sam said distractedly.

If Pop would agree to help him, Sam was willing to try it. He would do anything to forge a better relationship with his old man. He didn't believe in miracles, though. Didn't think getting Pop to work with him would fix things between them. But maybe Pop would calm down enough that Sam wouldn't constantly want to avoid him. He'd returned to Sparrow Lake not only to start his own business, but to make sure his father had someone to help him when needed. Giving Pop a reason to get up in the morning would be one way he could do that.

Interesting that he and Priscilla were dealing with similar situations in their personal lives. They really had more in common than simply starting their own businesses. Certain there was more to discover, he wanted to get to know her better. Wanted to ask her out despite the reasons why he shouldn't. He had nothing to offer a woman like her, what with his new venture on the edge of failing, while hers was thriving.

Not to mention she'd always followed the rules, while he'd always been trouble. And even though it wasn't his fault this time, it seemed that trouble was continuing to nip at his heels. He was simply too much trouble for any woman who wanted a serious relationship.

And he couldn't see Priscilla Ryan wanting any other kind.

CHAPTER NINE

"Here it is," Priscilla said as she arrived back at the table. She set a colorful flyer down in front of Sam.

"An Ice Cream Festival?"

"Right, over at the park this evening. Every summer, there's a contest to see who makes the best homemade ice cream. People love it. They get to vote for their favorite ice cream and flavor. And the South Wisconsin Dairymen's Association sponsors the event and gives out a nice little trophy to the winner. It's a popular event that's always well-attended. I wanted you to see the flyer because you could use something like this to promote the dude ranch. You know, hold some kind of event and then create a flyer that would attract a lot of people who would like to see what's going on."

Sam frowned. "I wouldn't know where to start."

"Start by figuring out what kind of event."

Looking thoughtful, he said, "Like that hayride Margaret suggested."

"That would probably attract people."

"We could take them out to someplace in the woods and have a bonfire."

Hearing a new spark of what sounded like enthusiasm in his voice, Priscilla added, "And roast marshmallows."

Sam nodded. "But who could design a flyer like this? I don't have any artistic talent."

"I've got a friend at school who's an art student," Steve volunteered from behind the counter. "She could create an even cooler flyer than that one, and she would be less expensive than a professional. She needs samples for her portfolio."

"Sounds good," Priscilla said.

"Let me think about it. I have to check that wagon and see how much work it needs. If it's usable without too much of a time investment, it might be a good idea." Sam asked, "Would you check with your artist friend about whether she would do the flyer? And how much she would charge?"

"You got it."

"It's settled, then." Priscilla grinned at Sam, who actually looked…hopeful, maybe. "We ought to celebrate with some ice cream."

"You want to go to the festival?"

Her stomach twirled a little as she quickly said, "I'd been planning on taking the girls but they're with my parents visiting friends in a nearby town. I wouldn't mind going over to the park, along with some friendly company."

She held her breath until he said, "And I wouldn't mind trying some homemade ice cream. What time shall we go?"

"I was thinking about seven." Her words came out in a relieved whoosh.

"Okay." Sam stood. "I'll meet you back here at seven, then. In the meantime, I need to get going. I want to check on Logan."

"All right. See you at seven."

Priscilla's lips curved into a big smile and her pulse fluttered as she watched Sam leave the store. She told herself to calm down. They weren't going on a date. Just two friends trying out homemade ice cream.

As if he'd read her mind, Steve said, "Wow, you got yourself a date. Good going."

Though she tried to give him a stern look, she couldn't quite manage it. "Don't you have work to do?"

"Right." He picked up his book and ploughed back into it.

Priscilla rolled her eyes but didn't complain.

Wiry, quiet, and a studious bookworm, Steve Welch worked part-time at the cheese shop while finishing his graduate studies in nearby Milwaukee. He spent his time reading when he wasn't helping customers. He was a perfect employee for Priscilla's purposes. This summer, he'd gladly increased his hours because of her visiting nieces and also recommended a friend to fill in when he wasn't available.

Priscilla rose and stretched. The lemonade and snack had given her new energy. She'd been wishing for some personal space while finishing up at the Block Party, since she had some work to do at the shop. However, she certainly couldn't pass up an evening alone with Sam—didn't want to pass it up—so she would hurry and do what she could before going out with him later.

Since it was nearly closing time, Steve was putting items away and getting ready to cash out the register. He pulled a couple of library books from the shelves beneath the register and put them on the counter, obviously so he wouldn't forget them.

"I'm going to work on the online orders as

soon as I get the chance," Priscilla told him. "We're a bit backlogged. Has anyone called about their order?"

He adjusted his wire-rim glasses. "No phone calls today. We had quite a bit of foot traffic, though. Everybody wanted a salad or a cheese board for Saturday lunch."

"Locals?" she asked. He'd lived in Sparrow Lake all his life. "Or tourists?"

"I think it was mainly tourists. I didn't recognize anyone."

"Good, news about this place is getting around."

"Someday you'll have to hire a full-time employee year-round."

Which probably wouldn't be him, unfortunately, since he would graduate with an advanced degree in another year or two. Then again, he might be able to use evening or weekend work. Steve knew a lot about cheeses, including which ones went with which wines. He also knew a lot of people in the town.

"Do you know Logan Keller?" she asked. Still a question in her mind. One that she hadn't wanted to ask Sam himself.

"Logan Keller?" He looked thoughtful. "He

was a couple of years behind my brother in school. I know something of him."

"Did he get into trouble a lot as a kid?"

"Hmm. I know he got arrested for having beer in a car and being underage. He wasn't the only one, though."

"How about stealing?"

He shook his head. "Not unless it was shop-lifting. Logan was just one of those wild kids with a bad attitude. You know, he cut school, got in trouble for some vandalism, that kind of thing. Why do you ask?"

"Just curious. Someone told me Logan was a juvenile delinquent."

"I never heard of him being sent to juvenile detention or anything. I believe someone said he did some community service. I think he comes from a messed-up family—seven kids, a drunk of a father."

"Did his family throw him out?"

"That I don't know. Do you want me to ask my brother?"

"No, that's okay."

If Logan's family was so problematic, it might be better if he didn't live with them. Though it didn't sound as if he was a serious law-breaker. Emily Auerbach had exaggerated again.

Steve locked up. After he left, Priscilla kept the lights on behind the counter so she could use the computer. She drew up a stool and had printed out a couple of new orders for cheese and wine gift baskets when she heard a tapping on glass beside the front door. She looked up to see a familiar face peering in. Heather Clarke. Heather waved and gestured, obviously wanting to talk to her.

As soon as Priscilla unlocked the door, the two women hugged.

"Hey, good to see you," she told Heather. "What have you been doing with yourself?"

"Oh, you know, just taking care of two growing girls, a dog, a fiancé, a yard full of plants, and working full-time for EPI." Which stood for Environmental Partners, Inc.

"You haven't been doing much, then," Priscilla teased, thinking Heather looked very happy rather than overwhelmed. In addition to being perky, she was fit and lightly tanned from working in the landscaping business.

"I've heard you've been busy, too," said Heather. "Kristen told me about your nieces from New York." She glanced around. "Are they upstairs?"

"They went to a fish fry with their grandparents and won't be back until tomorrow."

"Aunt's night out then…or in." Heather gestured to the printed-out orders. "I see you're busy. I don't want to interrupt you."

"Oh, don't worry. I can take a little interruption. I've been thinking about giving you a call anyway," said Priscilla. "Just to catch up and, well, ask you about security cameras."

"I thought Rick already installed them for you."

"He did install them at the Cheese Shoppe. I think I might have another customer for him, though." In consideration of Sam's finances, Priscilla asked, "Can someone…um, make payments for Rick's services?"

"A friend of yours?"

"Yes." Definitely a friend, if not more, though she was afraid to hope.

"I'm sure Rick could work something out. Give him a call." Heather grinned. "And, now, to the main reason I wanted to talk to you today…" She paused, as if getting ready to reveal a big secret.

Priscilla was intrigued. "Go on."

"Rick and I are getting married in October."

"Congratulations!"

"And I need a bridesmaid. Will you stand up for me?"

"Me?" In the past year, Priscilla had become good friends with her best friend Kristen's younger sister. Still, the seven bridesmaid dresses hanging in her upstairs closet flashed through her mind.

"I know you stood up for Kristen, too," Heather said, "but I'd be so honored to have you."

"Well…sure."

Heather cautioned, "Don't worry about the expense of yet another dress. We're having a recycled type of wedding."

"Recycled?" Priscilla knew Heather was dedicated to environmental causes.

"I'm simply asking my bridesmaids to wear a nice dress or pants outfit in a shade of green."

"Cocktail length?"

Heather nodded. "I'll provide accessories, mainly flowers. Don't you think that's appropriate for a gardener and her second wedding?"

"That sounds great actually," Priscilla had to admit. And Heather had been widowed so young, left with young twins to raise, that Priscilla was all in on this wedding. Whatever Heather wanted. "My bridesmaid's dress for Kristen's wedding was a shade of green." They'd all worn different colors.

Heather quirked her brows. "Right, so yours was."

"It's floor-length but can be shortened."

"It'll be perfect."

"Recycled—that's admirable, actually." Since Priscilla had paid quite a bit for dresses she had never worn again. "Not that you don't want your wedding to be special."

"I'll have a new dress," Heather said, "though it will be something simple. Just exchanging vows with my groom will make the wedding special." She grinned.

"Rick is definitely a good guy, one of the best," Priscilla admitted. A former military man, he was a straight arrow who would always look out for his family.

"It's the people who make life special, not fancy dresses and country club banquets. Most weddings cost an obscene amount. I want my friends and family to have a wonderful time but in a meaningful way."

"True." Priscilla admitted, "I'd rather use the money for something else." Like starting a business or buying another house. But she was practical at heart.

She and Heather hugged again.

"You deserve a lifetime of happiness, Heather." Especially after being widowed by war. "And your girls deserve a guy who will do everything for them."

Heather grinned. "They do. Thanks, Priscilla. I should get going."

As her friend left the shop, Priscilla thought about the new life in store for Heather and the twins.

Everyone deserved to be happy, Priscilla thought. Even her. She was going to be a bridesmaid again. For the eighth time.

Would she ever be a bride?

Not that it mattered, she told herself, getting busy with those orders.

Even so, she couldn't help but wonder what might happen between her and Sam.

IT ONLY TOOK about fifteen minutes for Sam to find the run-down place where Logan had been staying. He thought nobody was home when his knock went unanswered at the screen door, but, after a few minutes, about the time Sam decided to leave, Logan himself appeared. The kid looked as if he was headed for a firing squad.

"Feeling better?" Sam asked through the screen.

Logan cleared his throat. "What do you mean?"

"I figure you must have been deadly sick yourself to go off and leave sick horses." Having said that to give Logan an easy out for being so negligent, Sam gestured to the door. "Can I come in?"

"I'll come out. My cousin says she doesn't want anyone seeing the mess this house is in."

On the porch, with thumbs looped nonchalantly in his belt loops, Logan appeared sheepish as he stared at his feet.

"What happened?" Sam insisted, knowing something was really wrong with the kid. "How could you go off and leave me in that kind of situation?"

"The girls were helping."

"Yeah, they were, but it wasn't their job. I hired you because I heard you did such a good job at the animal shelter." Where Logan had worked off some community service, then stayed on. "You said you loved horses, dogs, animals in general. You said you loved to ride."

And Logan was good at the job, Sam had to admit.

"I do love animals. I love working with them," asserted Logan, then blinked. "It was…

it's just that I couldn't stand seeing what had happened to Gold Mine and Tomcat. I was afraid they'd die." He looked stricken. "They didn't, did they?"

"They're okay. No thanks to you."

Logan blinked again and cleared his throat. Sam realized the kid was fighting back tears.

"Animals are innocent," said Logan, "unlike some people we know."

Though Logan had been convicted of minor crimes such as shoplifting and vandalism as a teenager, he had never been guilty of deliberate cruelty, Sam was sure, to either beast or man. He had hired the kid because of his good heart. And he wanted to give him another chance to prove himself.

"I'm really happy the horses are okay," Logan stated, then tried to explain, "I know it doesn't make sense to you, but I was just freaked out." He took a deep breath. "I couldn't stand it. I saw the girls were doing okay and I—I took off. For what it's worth I'm really, truly sorry. And I won't do it again." His shoulders seemed to sag. "Unless you want to fire me. If you do, I understand."

His gut told Sam to believe Logan, though some mystery still surrounded the situation. But obviously he wasn't going to get whatever it was out of him right now. "If you get upset again, don't take off, okay? A horse can get into a bad state of affairs. You have to put your emotions aside even if it's a mess you want to run away from."

"Then I can come back out to the ranch?"

Thinking that Logan should get that opportunity, Sam nodded. "I need the help. For one thing, we've got to keep an eye on the horses and make sure nothing like this happens again." Then he asked, "Did you see anyone yesterday morning? Anything out of the ordinary?"

"I only wish I had. I just got there and found the horses, then woke you up."

"Too bad. Somebody would have had to drive to the place."

"Maybe they parked down the road and walked in," said Logan. "It's easy for some people to sneak around. Even with the yard light on all night. They wouldn't be able to do that so easily if you had more security."

"That's what I've been thinking." He had to do something to stop his business from being destroyed. "I'm looking into getting some cameras."

"If you need help putting them up, I wasn't too bad in shop in high school."

Another plus for the kid.

Though Sam had been angry with Logan for leaving, he'd also been worried about him. He knew from experience how difficult it was to straighten out when you took a wrong turn in life. He was glad Logan would be coming back. Maybe if he took the time to get to know the kid better, Logan would open up with whatever was troubling him and Sam could be of help.

"IT'S NOT A DATE."

That's what Priscilla told herself as she stood in front of a mirror and frowned at her own reflection. She thought she looked nice enough in a pale green sundress that bared her shoulders, but the humidity made her hair a little wild around her pale face. Sighing, she pulled the mass back into a ponytail and secured it with a scrunchie. A swipe of lip gloss and she was ready to go.

Even though this wasn't a date, as she hurried down the stairs, she felt a flush of anticipation at seeing Sam that had nothing to do with their businesses. She still was attracted to Sam, but her practical side told her falling for him again was a no-win situation. She might be willing to help him with his business, but as friends. She hadn't forgotten how he'd told her he wanted her to be his girl and that the very next morning, he'd left town without even saying goodbye.

Waiting for her outside the shop, Sam had his back to her when she reached the sidewalk. She grinned when she saw he was dressed in a short-sleeved black Western shirt with embroidery along the yoke. The way he was standing, his back so straight, he seemed a little tense. Had things not gone well with Logan?

"Hey, Sam."

The moment he turned toward her, he seemed to relax. His gray eyes softened when they lit on her, and his face creased in a big smile. "Evening, Prissy."

She didn't bother objecting to the nickname. She was starting to like it. From him, anyway. "Did you find Logan?"

He nodded. "I think we worked things out."

"Did he say why he left you with sick horses?"

"Said seeing them like that freaked him out."

"And you believe him?"

"Partly. I just have this gut instinct that tells me something more is going on with him. He's not in a good situation personally. He's living with some cousin, but he didn't even want me coming inside the house. Who knows why. Or what set him off."

Priscilla sighed. "I hope it works out. For both your sakes."

"Let's concentrate on something more pleasant." Sam held out his arm. "And delicious."

The way he was looking at her—as if *he couldn't be happier*—made Priscilla blink in surprise. This wasn't a date. Was it? Uncertain of his intentions, she gingerly took his offered arm. Set near the water, Sparrow Lake Park was about a five-minute walk. Nearly five minutes to hold on to Sam, to speculate how *he* viewed their evening together.

Sliding her hand along his tightly muscled upper arm, she said, "You must have done some really hard work all these years."

"For the most part," he agreed. "After I left here, I worked on a couple of cattle ranches out west, but it was the horses I loved. Eventually I was seduced by a faster paced world, joining the rodeo circuit. You need to be strong to handle those bucking broncos and bulls."

"That sounds exciting."

"It was."

"And dangerous."

"That, too."

"Do you miss it?" she asked, noting the conflicting emotions that raced through his expression.

"Not enough to go back to it, if that's what you mean. Rodeo is a young man's sport."

Somehow, she didn't believe that was his reason for quitting. "You're only…what?… thirty-two? That's not exactly old."

"No, but I've had my share of injuries and disappointments." He grinned at her, sending her pulse racing. "I had to have knee surgery a couple of times, nothing too serious. I also broke an arm once and a collarbone."

"Hmm, painful."

"Yeah, but there were good things, too. I got my share of wins." He looked down. "I have a collection of belt buckle prizes like this one that could dress up the pants of half the men in this town."

Checking out his silver-and-gold belt buckle decorated with a bucking bronco and 2013 Champion scrawled across it, Priscilla laughed. "I'm impressed. Maybe you need to keep going so every man in town can wear one of those."

"Nah, I figured it was time for me to settle down, do something a little less stressful than be bucked off a horse or have a bull stomp me. Now if only starting a dude ranch really was less stressful."

It could be if they discovered who was trying to ruin his business and why, Priscilla thought. She didn't want to dwell on the negative, though. They'd reached the edge of the park and the festival was just ahead. A dozen tables were set up in a semicircle, and townspeople were milling around getting their ice cream samples. Sam really did need that time-out. So as they walked on, she turned the conversation into what she hoped was a more positive direction.

"Did you think any more about involving your father in your business?"

"Actually, I talked to Pop before leaving, asked him if he would mind continuing to keep an eye on things, let me know if there was anything that should worry me."

"And he agreed?"

"Surprisingly, yes. I also told him I wasn't a paperwork kind of guy and asked if he could keep track of bills and write out the checks to pay them. He said he could do that, too, so I think you nailed it, Prissy," he said as they got to the back of the crowd. "Pop chose to retire. Or maybe he had to. That didn't mean he liked being left without anything to do."

"Well, good. Problem solved."

"Maybe. And I hate the paperwork part of business, so if he really takes it over, that just might be good for both of us." He looked around at people milling about, ice cream samples in hand. "So where do we start?"

"Over there." Priscilla indicated the South Wisconsin Dairymen's Association table that was stacked with brochures and held the prize trophy in the shape of a big double dip ice cream cone. "We need to get our ballots."

"Let's do it." Sam freed his arm and wound it around her back.

The close contact left her speechless, so Priscilla nodded and let Sam guide her to the table. She said hello to other people, familiar faces, as they passed.

She didn't personally know the men representing the association, but she gave them the best smile she could, considering her nerves were suddenly on edge.

A few minutes later, ballots and pencils in hand, they were in line at the first table. As usual, there was room to make notes about the different ice creams, so everyone could remember which samples they enjoyed and why. There was quite a bit to choose from: cinnamon-peach, old-fashioned strawberry, key lime, chocolate-jalapeno, double vanilla and several more.

"Let's skip the chocolate-jalapeno," Sam said. "Maybe I'm old-fashioned but blackberries sound tastier than hot peppers in ice cream." He steered Priscilla toward one of the tables. "I don't think I've ever tried that before. I had huckleberry ice cream in Idaho one time. Kind of tart if I remember correctly."

"Well, do you like tart?"

He gave her a searching stare. "Depends who I get it from."

Priscilla's breath hitched in her throat. Okay, Sam was flirting with her. Definitely flirting. Glad when they got to the table and collected their samples, she took a small spoonful of blackberry ice cream.

"Soft, creamy and sweet," she decided. "Definitely not tart."

Sam merely grinned in response.

Making a quick note on her ballot, she muttered, "Okay, next table."

Following her, Sam stood a bit too close. Though she was eating ice cream, she was warmer than the weather dictated. Sam was just being friendly. She shouldn't make such a big deal about anything he said or did. Right?

"Ah, look," he said, "caramel with sea salt." He handed her a tasting cup and waited for her to try it.

Nerves making her twitch a little, she didn't quite get her spoonful in her mouth the first time she made the attempt. She got it on the second try.

"Oh, yummy." She raised a hand to wipe away the ice cream smeared above her lip.

Sam caught the hand and stayed it. "Here, let me get that."

Still holding on to her hand, he bent his head. Her eyes widened. What was he doing? A moment later she found out when she felt his tongue flick along her upper lip.

"Mmm, definitely yummy."

Her pulse pounding, Priscilla stared at Sam. She couldn't believe he'd done something so intimate in public. Almost as intimate as a kiss. Maybe more so.

She couldn't be in denial now.

Despite her thoughts to the contrary, she was on a date with Sam Larson.

CHAPTER TEN

ON SUNDAYS, IT WAS usually busy at the cheese shop and Priscilla worked the brunch crowd, along with an employee. Today, she couldn't help smiling as she served customers, thinking about the outing with Sam the night before. Replaying everything he said, everything that happened—his licking the ice cream from her lip, his holding her hand as they explored the festival grounds, his encircling her waist with a possessive arm on the walk home—she was lost in conflicting thoughts. Most of her was happy about it, but there was that little part of her that was reluctant to trust him again. She supposed she should just bite the bullet and ask him. Except she was afraid she might not like the answer. What to do? She was so busy running the pros and cons through her mind that she barely noticed things were finally slowing down.

"Do you want me to take over now?" asked Steve.

Priscilla came to. "Uh, sure." Her nieces would be along soon. And she had things to do upstairs. "I have a closet I need to clean out."

"Looking through your bridesmaid dresses, huh?"

Apparently Steve had heard her discuss Heather's plan for recycled gowns. Priscilla simply smiled and went upstairs. For once she didn't feel badly about digging the dresses out again.

As she did so, she couldn't help but let her thoughts go back to Sam. About what a good time she'd had with him. About how he'd had her in an emotional whirl until he'd left her at her door. Without a good-night kiss. That had been kind of odd, made her question whether she'd misconstrued his interest in her. Surely not. Surely he was simply taking things slow and easy. Which was a good thing...probably.

Priscilla finally settled on slow and easy being good and got back to digging out those dresses. By the time Mia and Alyssa came home an hour or so later, she had located most of the garment bags containing her gowns in the large hall closet and laid them across a chair she'd pulled up for the purpose. They made quite a stack.

Mia merely glanced at the pile but stopped to tell her aunt, "Sam thinks I would be a natural for barrel racing. I already have good balance. I just have to get used to neck reining."

"Just as long as you don't break *your* neck. I have to answer to your dad, you know."

"I told Dad about it and he was okay with my learning some rodeo skills."

This morning Mom had reported that her brother had called the evening before and chatted with his daughters. It seemed that anything the girls wanted to do was all right with Paul.

"Are you going to try barrel racing, too?" Priscilla asked Alyssa who ambled along after Mia.

"I'm fine with regular Western riding."

Whatever had set Alyssa off the other day seemed to be less important now. Or else she'd gotten over it. Priscilla hoped so.

The girls headed for their rooms. Priscilla gazed at the pile of garment bags, considering the fancy, useless dresses within them. She had seven, and except for the last gown, would never wear any of them again. What do you do with old bridesmaid's dresses? she wondered, holding up the plastic bag that contained an elaborately ruffled gold metallic gown.

"Wow, going to Vegas?" asked Alyssa with a snicker from behind her.

Priscilla laughed, not minding the sarcasm. "Looks like Las Vegas, doesn't it? All I need is a feathered headdress and a pair of sparkly platforms." She flipped up the bag to look at the dress more closely. "Actually, I wore this for the first wedding I stood up for. It was New Year's and all the bridesmaids wore gold satin." She explained, "We looked fine in context."

"But where would you wear it now?"

Priscilla shrugged. "Exactly. And I have a lot more where that came from."

"More ugly bridesmaid's dresses?"

Priscilla didn't want to call her friends' choices *ugly*. "I've been popular in the bridesmaid department. Now I'm trying to decide what to do with all these mementos."

Alyssa stepped closer, peering at the stack on the chair. "Let me see them."

"If you insist." Priscilla picked up a garment bag and unzipped it, revealing two dresses, one a long country-looking number in black, printed with bright orange and yellow daisies. "I wore a floppy black straw hat with this one."

"Eww."

"Again, it's all about the context. We were in a small rural church." Priscilla pulled out the second dress, a fuchsia pink strapless mini.

"Wow, and what was that for? A fashion doll wedding?"

"No, but everything was pink." She laid both dresses over the chair.

Alyssa picked up the pink mini. "Actually, this could be a party dress."

"For you maybe. It almost matches your hair. You can have it if you want."

"No thanks." Alyssa chortled and threw the dress back.

Another garment bag contained a full-skirted purple gown complete with a matching built-in bustier, long medieval sleeves, flounces and a train.

"That had to be a costume wedding!"

"Right. At the Renaissance Faire." A well-known event which took place every summer near Kenosha, Wisconsin. Priscilla smiled, remembering. "We wore ribbon and flower circlets on our heads and the groom arrived on horseback."

Alyssa fingered the material. "But the only other use for this would be a costume party."

"Unfortunately. At least the bride made the

gown herself. Otherwise, it would have been very costly."

Alyssa quirked her brows. "How many times were you a bridesmaid anyway?"

"Seven. And I have another wedding coming up this fall—that will be eight."

"Wow." Alyssa seemed thoughtful. "At least you have a lot of friends."

"That's true. I'm grateful for that." Priscilla still had not gotten to the garment she was looking for. She rummaged in the back of the closet to pull it out and peel back its protective plastic covering. "And I won't have to buy another dress if I can shorten this one."

Kristen's choice had been classic, a muted moss-green chiffon gown with a moderate V-neck, short sleeves and a drapey skirt.

"That one's actually not too bad."

Priscilla held the garment against her and hiked up the skirt. "How does that look?"

Alyssa stepped back to get a better look. "It'll probably work."

"Heather Clarke, the bride, told me she would supply new accessories. She's having a recycled wedding, at least for the attendants."

"Recycled?"

"She's merely asking that her bridesmaids

all wear green cocktail dresses or pants outfits."

"That's something new."

"And I won't have yet another dress taking up closet space."

"You always need room for new clothes." Alyssa gestured toward the contents of the overstuffed closet. "You would have even more space if you just got rid of the rest of this stuff."

Priscilla sighed. "I know I should do that but the dresses are almost new. Only worn once." She couldn't help it, she was thrifty like her mother.

"Why not take them to a consignment shop? I saw one downtown."

"Several of the brides are from Sparrow Lake. They might see the dresses in the shop and be insulted."

"Hmm, okay, take them somewhere else then. That medieval type of dress could go to a costume shop."

"Maybe." Priscilla still wasn't willing to throw things out. "I can check around. But for now..." She hung the green dress on the back of the door and started to slip others back into their garment bags to return them to the depths of the closet. "Hand me that last one, will you?" She sighed. "Always a bridesmaid, never a bride." Which came out of her mouth unbidden.

"Not *always*, surely. You've had a serious boyfriend, haven't you?"

"Of course." Priscilla admitted.

Sam immediately came to mind—when had he not been on her mind today?—not that they'd ever had a serious relationship. Now it seemed something was starting up between them again. When she was with him, she was happy. But when she was alone, she remembered the downside. Maybe he did, too, the reason he hadn't kissed her when he'd brought her home from the ice cream festival. She'd thought he would when saying good-night. She'd anticipated it. Had prepared herself for it. And when it hadn't happened, she'd been disappointed. Again she reminded herself that going slow was a good thing. It would give her time to know what kind of a man Sam had really become.

"So what happened with you and the boyfriend?" Alyssa asked, claiming her attention.

Priscilla thought of her whirlwind romance with Jeff back in Madison. "It's just that, well, things didn't work out."

"Did you get rejected?"

"Rejected? Not exactly. I would say it was more like a mutual parting of the ways when we realized the sparkly stuff had worn off, so it was probably for the best." She didn't have any regrets about their breaking off their relationship.

"How did you know it was for the best?"

"The feelings I had when the relationship started didn't last, and I don't want to go through life feeling down about some romance that didn't work out." Though she still felt twinges about her high school crush on Sam, probably because he was her first love, she told herself. And definitely because they seemed to be starting…well, something up again. She simply wasn't sure what exactly. Or what she wanted from him. "There are other things in life."

For a moment, Alyssa didn't respond, making Priscilla think she had finally gotten bored with her aunt's reminiscences.

Then the teenager took a loud, shaky breath. "Love is important!"

Priscilla whirled around, realizing her niece was fighting back tears. Her face contorting, Alyssa burst into sobs and ran down the hall toward the guest room.

"Alyssa!"

Priscilla wasn't sure what to do. She simply followed, half-aware that the shower was running in the bathroom as they passed by—Mia freshening up after riding lessons. When she entered the room where Alyssa had thrown herself on the bed, Priscilla expected a firm "get out of here." But the girl didn't complain about her sitting on the edge of the mattress and gently patting her shoulder.

"How can you be okay about not being loved?" Alyssa's voice was muted by the pillow.

Priscilla rubbed her back. "I didn't say love wasn't important."

"He doesn't love me. He was mean!"

"Who's mean?" asked Priscilla, wondering if she'd missed part of a conversation. Logan?

"Ethan was mean."

"Ethan?"

After another couple of sobs, Alyssa raised her head and grabbed for a tissue on the bedside table so she could blow her nose.

Still trying to catch up, Priscilla made a guess. "Was Ethan a boyfriend of yours?"

"In New York."

When Alyssa pushed herself up to a sitting position, Priscilla slid onto the chair nearby.

"Ethan was in his second year at NYU. We

had coffee. We went to old movies. We went cycling in Central Park. I thought he loved me." Alyssa gave a huge, dramatic sigh. "I loved him!"

"And I guess you broke up," Priscilla surmised.

"He told me we were just friends, that I was too young for a serious relationship. He didn't want to hurt me, so we shouldn't see each other anymore."

So this was where the "older man" remarks had come from.

"That doesn't really sound mean," observed Priscilla gently. And, after all, Alyssa was only sixteen.

"It was the way he said it, like I was a…a little girl or something. He said he saw me more as a younger sister. A sister!" Another tear leaked out and Alyssa caught it with a tissue. "He kissed me…on the cheek!"

The teenager seemed to be truly brokenhearted and Priscilla knew what it was like to be young and passionate about someone. She thought about the way she'd responded to Sam the night before. There definitely was something going on between them. What if she fell as hard for him as she had when they were teenagers, and then he went off and left her again? Not something she wanted to consider, but there it was.

For now, she'd concentrate on Alyssa. She rubbed the girl's arm, trying to comfort her. "I know it's awful, honey. I know how it feels."

"You do?"

"I thought...I fell in love when I was just about your age. And it didn't end well." Which was why she had such mixed-up feelings about Sam now.

"But you said that the breakup was mutual."

"That was someone else. Years later."

Alyssa blew her nose again. "I guess you've had more than one bad experience."

Priscilla nodded. "Not all bad, but relationships that didn't work out. And you will, too, Alyssa. You shouldn't worry about that."

"I thought I found someone else but he was mean, too."

"Another one?"

Alyssa admitted, "Well, you know, I thought that Logan guy was cute."

Right. "I noticed."

"And the other day, well, he told me to get lost."

"Really?"

"When the horses were sick. I saw he was really freaked so I came up to him. I put my hand on his arm."

"And?"

"He pushed me away!"

"What do you mean he pushed you?" Priscilla grew concerned.

"He brushed away my hand, that's all."

Priscilla relaxed. "Maybe he was too upset to even speak to anyone." From what Sam had said anyway.

"But he didn't need to tell me I was some little teenager with too much makeup and not enough sense! Or say that I should just leave him alone!"

"He said that?" Again, though, Priscilla thought it sounded like Logan was distraught. Not to mention, Alyssa had her serious flirt on the first time she and Logan met.

"Then he threw the reins at me and said he was leaving."

Priscilla was surprised at how unlike this Logan was to the one they'd first met. "He was really upset about the horses. Stress like that can make a person touchy."

"It wasn't nice."

"No, it wasn't," she admitted. "But you

shouldn't worry about him. We don't even know that much about him."

"I guess we don't."

"He probably reminded you of the situation with Ethan." Then Priscilla asked, "Was Logan out at the ranch today?" Since Sam had said he'd asked the young man to come back.

Alyssa nodded. "He didn't say anything. He just ignored me."

"In a professional way, I hope."

"He was professional. I expected him to at least say he was sorry, though."

"Well, forget about him," Priscilla said, meaning it. "Love can be painful. Believe me, I know, but we have to go on."

Just as she'd gone on after Sam had left town without saying goodbye.

"Sometimes you wonder if it's even worth it," agreed Alyssa with a big sigh, as if she had all the experience in the world.

"Oh, I think it's definitely worth it." Priscilla believed in happy romantic endings, even if she had yet to experience one. Plus, she was at least sharing real camaraderie with her niece.

"You don't think I wear too much makeup, do you?"

Priscilla looked at the girl, whose makeup was not as noticeable at the moment as her puffy eyes and red nose. She tried to be diplomatic. "Uh, well, you do use more makeup than most girls around here, but that's okay." She brushed back a strand of her niece's magenta hair. "You apply makeup well. You're obviously an expert." She pointed out, "Your eyes aren't even smeared much after crying."

"That's because I use waterproof products."

"Really?" Since they seemed to have such rapport, Priscilla added, "You obviously know a lot about clothes, as well. More than I do." She had noticed the fashion magazines in Alyssa's carry-on.

"Well...thanks." Alyssa actually sounded sincere.

"You're going to find someone one of these days, don't worry," Priscilla told her. "There's plenty of time. Not everyone is out to break your heart."

"Thanks, Aunt Priscilla." Alyssa smiled, her eyes red. She took a shaky breath. "I guess I just needed to talk to someone. I've been so depressed."

"I understand." Priscilla was touched that Alyssa had decided to confide in her. "Why don't we do something fun that *you* want to do tonight? I know riding is more of Mia's thing. A movie? Shopping?" Though she didn't think many stores would be open on Sunday night.

Alyssa was observing her closely. "I know something I would enjoy. Let's do a makeover."

"A new hairstyle?" Priscilla was willing to turn Alyssa's hair yet another color, she supposed.

"A hairstyle for you."

"Me?" Now that was a surprise. One that made Priscilla a little nervous.

"I, uh, I don't mean to be insulting, but you could do a lot more with yourself, Aunt Priscilla. Your clothes are..."

Priscilla grinned. "Not so interesting." She'd been told that more than once.

"You could at least use some colorful accessories to dress them up." Alyssa leaned closer. "And do you ever wear any makeup at all?"

"A little mascara."

"You could also use eyeliner, blush." Alyssa ran her fingers over her aunt's cheek. "You have good bones." Sliding off the bed, the girl fetched her makeup case from the nearby bureau and came back to unzip it. It was full of glittery containers and tiny compacts. "We have plenty to work with."

"Well..." Priscilla didn't want to insult the girl but she also didn't exactly want to go around wearing that much makeup.

As if reading her mind, Alyssa said, "Don't worry, I'll give you a toned-down version. I can tell you like to be more subtle." She examined her aunt's hair. "You could also use some highlights. I brought along a kit to touch up the ends of my hair. There's enough for you."

"Uh, I don't think streaks like that are a good idea for me."

"Highlights, not streaks." Alyssa emphasized, "I'm really good with hair and makeup. Trust me."

Though reluctant, Priscilla said, "Okay."

What could it hurt? If nothing else, she and her difficult niece might finally have a good time together.

CHAPTER ELEVEN

MONDAY MORNING AT the cheese shop found Priscilla with highlighted hair to set off her new eye-linered, blushed, eye-shadowed and lipsticked appearance. Alyssa had found time to do her up again before she and Mia left to spend the day with their grandmother. Every time Priscilla caught her appearance in a mirror, she was startled, but she had to admit Alyssa was as good a stylist as she claimed. Her hair seemed touched with red gold and her eyes looked bigger. Her niece had even loaned her a long, colorful, bespangled scarf to go with her simple black top and jeans. She wondered what Sam would think if he could see her now.

When he arrived for work, Steve did a double take. "Wow!"

Priscilla grinned. "I hope that's a good 'wow,' not a bad one."

He headed for the counter to stack his books underneath. He gazed at her again.

"I'm not used to seeing you…uh, dressed up, I guess."

"My niece decided to give me a makeover."

Though Alyssa had kept her word on being more subtle. If the shadow and liner didn't bother her eyes at the end of the day, Priscilla might even go out and purchase some of her own.

"Well, you look great. Um…even better than usual."

"Thanks."

As soon as he had gotten himself ready, putting on a tan apron with the shop's name embroidered in red across the front, he asked, "Did you get the flyer designs from my friend Carol?"

"She's done them already?"

"I told her to email them to you because you wanted to look them over as soon as possible."

Priscilla went back into her email account. "Here they are." She clicked open the first attachment. It showed an abstract design of a wagon and horses under a full moon, advertising Larson Dude Ranch Hayride. "Nice!" There were two other attachments to click open as well, one that could be triple folded. "Very nice! How did she do all this so fast?"

"She has computer programs that manipulate graphics. She said it wasn't hard."

The price quoted was reasonable, as well, so Priscilla promised, "I'm going to show these to Sam." She could either print the flyers out or let him look at the designs on the computer. Then they'd have to find out how long it would take to get them ready to post and hand out.

When a few customers came in, Steve went to help them. Meanwhile, Priscilla sorted through the papers by the computer—invoices, communication—when she came to a sticky note she'd written a while before: Call Walworth Builders.

Oh, right. From what she'd learned about the company at the quilting workshop, Walworth was no longer at the top of her suspect list, but Priscilla wanted to check them out for herself. After all, there were so many rumors about what the company was up to, she decided as a local businesswoman, she deserved to hear their spiel directly from someone in charge, maybe Henry Huber. She looked up Walworth's number on the computer, grabbed the shop's phone, and punched in the numbers.

A woman answered on the second ring. "Walworth Builders."

"Mr. Huber, please."

"One moment."

"Huber here," came a gruff voice at the other end of the phone.

"Mr. Huber, I'm Priscilla Ryan—"

He cut her off. "What can I do for you, Ms. Ryan?"

Sitting down on a nearby stool, Priscilla kept her own voice warm and friendly. "As a Sparrow Lake business owner I just wanted to touch base with you—"

"What business? Building supplies?"

"Um, no. I own The Main Street Cheese Shoppe."

"Good for you but I don't eat much cheese."

"I'm not trying to sell you cheese."

"All right, but I don't understand what you want with me then."

She wanted to know if he'd been responsible for trying to ruin Sam's new business, but of course she'd get nowhere if she questioned him directly.

"People in town have been speculating about your plans for building new housing in Sparrow Lake. Everyone has a different opinion about your intentions, and—"

"I'm a busy man, Ms. Ryan. No time for dealing with local gossip. For information about our plans, you need to talk to my daughter."

And with that, he hung up on her, leaving Priscilla aghast at his rudeness. Well, if Huber was representative of community interaction, Walworth Builders weren't always nice.

By noon, Priscilla had finished with the computer and put the Walworth call behind her. She decided she shouldn't waste any time getting started on the hayride flyers. She should either drop by the ranch or call Sam now and invite him over. Either way, the thought of seeing him made her heart beat faster and her stomach flutter with tiny butterflies.

Nearby, the phone rang and she picked it up. "Main Street Cheese Shoppe."

"Is this Ms. Ryan?" inquired a smooth, feminine voice.

"Yes. May I help you?"

"I think it's me who can help you," the woman went on. "You called my father, Henry Huber earlier today. As is too often the case, he was rude."

Priscilla tried to be diplomatic. "Well, he was businesslike."

"I'm sorry about that. This is Grace Huber,

Henry's daughter. I'm in charge of community relations for Walworth Builders. My father's handling the business end." Grace went on, "Dad said you're a business owner in Sparrow Lake. I'll be happy to talk to you."

Priscilla agreed, "I'd love to learn more about your plans."

"And I'd love to tell you about them in person. Why don't we meet for coffee this afternoon. You know where The Corner is, right?" She named a casual pancake/hamburger place in the town.

"Today?"

"If you want. If not, we could set another date."

"No, today would be fine."

"Is around three okay?"

"Perfect. I'll meet you there."

Priscilla could find Sam afterward. Not only would she have the flyers to show him but, possibly, even more information about the Huber business and what they were about.

PRISCILLA ARRIVED AT The Corner before three and ordered an iced coffee. It tasted good on a warm day. She slid the folder containing printouts of Sam's brochure on the booth's tabletop, intending to take one last look. She planned to call Sam and drive out to talk to him after she and Grace Huber had finished their meeting.

When the café door opened, Priscilla looked up expectantly, but it wasn't a woman who entered the establishment. Instead, Cooper Peterson sauntered inside, followed closely by some friend, a shorter young man wearing a dirty cap pulled low, nearly covering his eyes, and a fatigue vest over a bare chest.

Very classy, Priscilla thought, and returned to the printouts.

But Cooper wasn't about to ignore her. He stepped over to her table. "Hey, Prissy, can't you even say hello?"

Hating hearing the nickname from his lips, she met his impudent gaze. "Hello, Cooper."

"Looking good, I must say." He winked at her.

She almost choked on her coffee, "Thanks."

Cooper raked his gaze over her, but settled on her eyes. "I didn't know you had such long lashes. Good for batting them at a man, huh?"

Flushing, Priscilla refused to respond to the rude comment and looked down at the printout on the table.

But Cooper wasn't going anywhere. "Maybe I can join you."

Though she hated that the situation was uncomfortable for her, Priscilla remained polite. "I'm waiting for someone."

"I'll bet you are," said Cooper. "Who? Old Sammy boy?"

Unable to help herself, she said, "Actually, it's none of your business."

Cooper grinned. "My, my. Aren't we touchy? Hey, I thought we were friends."

He sidled closer, bringing a sour scent with him. Priscilla thought it smelled like stale beer. She hated his standing right next to the table, demanding her attention.

"We're friendly acquaintances, I guess."

"You guess? Well, you don't seem very friendly."

How to get out of this? Priscilla tried to smile but her lips felt frozen. She hated any kind of confrontation. What did he want from her? She gazed toward the café's door, hopeful when movement appeared outside.

"Seriously, I'm meeting a business associate." She reluctantly added, "Um, nice to see you."

Cooper put his hands on the table and loomed over her. He lowered his voice to a husky whisper, "It would be nicer if you asked me to sit down."

He was so close that Priscilla leaned to one side in alarm. Her eyes wide on him, she couldn't see who'd entered the café, but the next thing she knew, Cooper was jerked backward by his collar.

"What do you think you're doing?" Sam glared at Cooper.

"What the..." Cooper balled up his fists. "Let go of me, Larson!"

As the other startled occupants of the café looked on, fearing a brawl was about to start, Priscilla slid out of the booth and stood. The atmosphere felt electric, but she couldn't stand violence.

"It's okay, Sam! Really. Cooper and I were just talking."

Sam let go of the other man.

Cooper gave Sam one last dirty look before lumbering off to join his friend at the counter.

Sam's brow pulled into a frown. "You came here to talk to Peterson?"

Priscilla gaped at him, then was relieved when she saw that a pleasant-looking brunette had entered the café.

Priscilla took a deep breath and forced a smile she really wasn't feeling. "Ms. Huber?" she called. "Looking for me? I'm Priscilla Ryan."

The woman nodded and stepped forward.

Realizing Sam was staring at them in confusion, Priscilla offered the other woman her hand. "Is it all right if another business owner joins us, Ms. Huber?"

"Certainly." Her bright blue eyes lit up. "And please call me Grace."

Priscilla slid into the booth, leaving room for Sam. "Grace came here to talk about Walworth Builders," she informed him. "She's the community outreach for the company."

"Okay." Looking a bit sheepish, Sam sat down beside her. He took a deep breath and swept his gaze to Cooper, who was making his way out of the café with his friend. Then he turned his attention to Grace Huber. "Nice to meet you. I'm Sam Larson."

Priscilla relaxed as things quickly settled down. Grace ordered iced coffee, too, while Sam, saying he'd skipped lunch, wanted a hamburger.

Grace opened her briefcase to produce several plans for the "green community" Walworth Builders hoped to construct. Sam and Priscilla looked over the plans for a few minutes.

"I understand you had your eye on my family's farm for your new project," Sam said.

Grace nodded. "We did. But it isn't really close enough to the town. We want residents to be able to walk to grocery stores and other places if they wish." She pointed at a drawing. "As you can see, the housing is actually only a small portion of the land we plan to develop, the percentage recommended by the ecological planning commission. The rest of the site will be open prairie, pathways, and water reserves."

Sam had to admit, "That sounds pretty good."

"A green community conserves its land, offers multiple options for transportation, provides open space for recreation and cultivation, and uses its natural and cultural resources wisely," Grace explained. "And one of the most important resources is the town itself. A lot of these ecologically-oriented communities are being built near cities. I got my father to agree a planned community near a small town like Sparrow Lake would also be nice. The ecological planning commission was agreeable about using a federal grant for such an enterprise, plus we will have the support of a foundation that encourages and funds these kinds of environmental initiatives."

"Very ambitious," said Priscilla, genuinely impressed.

"We hope to have some of Sparrow Lake's current residents move into the complex when it's ready," Grace said. "They will have beautiful surroundings, a home created with sustainable materials, and as much heating and cooling as possible from solar and other natural energy sources." She showed Sam and Priscilla an architectural drawing of an interior. "There will be both condos and single-family duplexes available for purchase. Plus we're adding a small rental complex, as well."

"You'll have to be looking at other places for residents," said Sam. "Not everyone around here will be itching to move in."

"Of course," agreed Grace. "We think there will be interested parties who are retired, people who work in nearby areas, others from Chicago or Milwaukee who want an affordable second home in a scenic, laid-back area. There should be a mix of age groups for a real community." She went on, "We're barely getting these plans off the ground at this point, but I wanted to show you what was possible. We can't do everything at once, of course. We would have to make a more modest start and add to the area as we get residents."

Priscilla said, "That sounds like a reasonable plan."

Grace winced. "And I wanted to apologize again for my dad. I was the one who talked him into this. He was in the construction and building industry his whole life, but he's never dealt with anything as grandiose as a planned community. He's used to dealing with workmen and contractors. He can be pretty abrupt."

"Understood."

Sam laughed. "You aren't the only one dealing with a grumpy father, Ms. Huber, uh... Grace."

Grace smiled at them both. "Generational conflict is inevitable."

"I guess," said Sam.

By the time Grace took her leave, saying to please call her with any other questions, Sam had finished his hamburger and fries and ordered coffee. He thought about having pie. "You want a slice of lemon meringue?" he asked Priscilla.

"No, thanks. I have to go over to my mom's for supper. I don't want to fill up on sweets."

He and Priscilla remained seated on the

same side of the booth, but he didn't want to move. He liked her warmth against him.

Deciding he didn't need dessert when his coffee came, he paid the waitress before turning his full attention on Priscilla, who looked exceptionally attractive today. "How're things going with your nieces? They seemed fine when they came for their riding lesson yesterday."

"I think I've turned a corner, especially with Alyssa." She put a finger to her cheek and made a silly face. "Like the makeover she gave me?"

He gazed into the green depths of her eyes. "You look beautiful," he told her, "but you always look beautiful in my opinion."

She blushed. "Thank you."

Sobering, he said, "But probably your new makeover is the reason that jerk Coop hassled you."

"I didn't ask for his attentions."

"I'm sure you didn't." Wanting to get closer, to stake his claim on her, so to speak, Sam slid his arm across the back of the booth. "But I'm glad to hear it."

Priscilla's face pinkened as she scrambled for a folder lying on the table. Sam loved the effect he had on her. She was so easily flustered that it always made him smile, and he hadn't had enough to smile about in far too long.

She cleared her throat and opened the folder. "After the meeting with Grace Huber, I was going to call you and drop by the ranch. Steve's art school friend made these brochure samples for you to look at."

Though Sam preferred keeping his attention on Priscilla, he glanced at the papers she slipped in front of him. "Wow!" He had to admit he was impressed. "Looks good! Very professional."

"Do you have any preference?"

"Any of these designs would be great."

"Choose one and decide on a date. I'll tell the designer to get them printed."

"By when?"

"Overnight. We could post them and put them around town tomorrow. There's still time to put an announcement in the local paper, too."

"Okay. Let's use this one." Sam thought fast. "I looked at the old hay wagon. It's not in as bad a shape as I thought. I can borrow a couple of draft horses from a friend of my dad's. He has several."

"So you can drive a team of horses yourself."

"I used to drive an old stagecoach in the rodeo parades."

"It sounds like you can get everything together pretty quickly," Priscilla said. "What about having the hayride next weekend?"

"Sure. Let's make it Saturday at eight."

"Sounds perfect."

Almost perfect, Sam thought, staring at Priscilla. Though he wanted to ask her out, he hesitated.

Instead, he stood. "I guess I should be going." Not that he wanted to leave her, but he had to get at that wagon. "I have some work ahead of me."

"Me, too," she said, getting to her feet.

He let her lead the way to the door, then once outside, he realized she'd probably walked from her shop. "Can I offer you a ride?"

"It's not really that far..." Her voice faded off and she stared at him for a moment, then said, "Why yes, that would be nice."

His truck was parked practically in front of the place. He opened the passenger door for her and placed a hand on her arm to help her in. She was soft and sweet-smelling, and when she smiled at him her whole face lit, making him want to kiss her.

She settled into her seat, her lips still smiling at him, and Sam's heart thundered as he closed the door and walked around to the driver's side. He'd been wanting to kiss those lips ever since he'd picked her up the other night—well, even before that, to tell the truth—but he'd been trying to bide his time. Heading for her shop, he thought about it. As much as he wanted to get closer to Priscilla, he knew he should first make sure his business was a real go. If it tanked, he had no idea what he was going to do to make a living. Or where. He wanted to be a man she could count on.

As he was stopping in front of The Main Street Cheese Shoppe he said, "I was thinking the hayride is not only a great opportunity to add a nice layer to my operation and attract new customers, but a fun one, as well. And I have you to thank for it."

"It wasn't my idea. You need to thank Margaret."

"But you're the one who got me to consider diversifying in the first place. And you helped me turn the idea into a reality. Thank you."

Getting out of the truck, he rushed around

to the other side to get her door and took her hand to help her out. She landed lightly but made no effort to pull her hand free from his.

"I'm just glad you're so enthusiastic," she said. "I think enthusiasm is a great deal of what makes a business succeed."

Priscilla's smile transferred to her voice, making her both look and sound happy. She was practically glowing, and Sam had to hold himself back from taking her into his arms right there. In front of her shop. In broad daylight.

"Easy to be enthusiastic when there's fun involved." Especially if he was able to spend some personal time with her. "Once we get the hay wagon on the road, the sun will be setting, and that area is real pretty at twilight." Romantic, too, he thought, staring at Priscilla. He knew he should wait until he was settled for sure, but he couldn't stop himself from asking, "Would you like to go?"

"I was planning on it. The girls will love it."

He let go of her hand and cleared his throat. "I meant you with me. I could use some company in the driver's seat…um, unless you'd rather sit in the wagon with your nieces in the hay."

Priscilla's eyes widened. Because she was surprised? Shocked? His throat tightened as he waited for her answer.

"I love the smell of hay, but I can do without the itching," Priscilla admitted. "Sure, I would love to keep you company."

Taking a big breath, Sam couldn't keep from grinning. "Good. That's settled, then. I only hope I have more customers than the girls."

"Give it some time and you will. You've started a business that has all kinds of possibilities. And you're willing to try new things to make it work." She placed a hand on his chest and beamed at him. "You're definitely on the right road. I just know you'll pull it off, Sam."

He covered her hand with his and their gazes locked. At that moment, he knew he wanted nothing more than to prove her trust in him.

And to kiss her.

"I appreciate your confidence in me, Priscilla Ryan."

"It's what you deserve."

He slipped his hand from hers and cupped her cheek, mesmerized by the softness of her skin against his calloused fingers. Her face flushed with color and her lips opened slightly, reminding him of how much he wanted to kiss them. He'd had a taste the night before when he'd licked away the ice cream…but a taste just wasn't enough. He needed more, so he swooped in closer and brushed her mouth with his. Her eyes widened more, if that was possible, but she didn't move. Just stood there, lips still parted, looking absolutely irresistible.

Without so much as thinking about what he was doing, he pulled her into his arms, crushed her to him and kissed her properly, the way he had the night before he'd left town.

CHAPTER TWELVE

ALYSSA STILL MISSED the city but she had to admit the country could be beautiful. After the sun went down on the night of the hayride, the sky blazed with a full moon and thousands of stars. There were no bright city lights to dim them. Instead of wailing sirens and beeping taxis, the soft chirp of night insects filled the air. Alyssa leaned back against one of the blankets thrown over the hay bales and enjoyed a balmy breeze full of green scent—alfalfa, her aunt had said on the car ride over.

"Gorgeous, isn't it?" said Sabrina. "This is a perfect night for a hayride."

Both of Gloria's daughters had come for the event, along with their cousin, Marco, and one of his guy friends. Alyssa had to admit Marco was really cute, in spite of his being only one grade beyond her in high school. He was so polite and attentive that he made her feel special.

"Would you like another cola?" He indicated the cooler on the wagon. "Or some lemonade?"

She smiled. "I'm good."

The wagon hit a big bump, jerking her forward, but he caught her arm and steadied her. "Are you all right?"

Alyssa laughed. "I'm fine."

She was more than fine. She was enjoying herself despite Logan's presence. Sitting apart from the paying customers, he strummed a guitar and sounded like he could be a professional musician.

"Your aunt really looks nice," Sabrina said. "So you gave her a makeover?"

She was staring at Aunt Priscilla, up front, perched next to Sam, who was driving the horses.

"Mmm, hmm." Her aunt seemed to be getting involved with her old boyfriend. Alyssa liked to think she had something to do with that. "We still have to buy her some new clothes. We're going shopping next week in Kenosha. At the big outlet mall."

Shopping was one of Alyssa's favorite activities, whether it was for herself or for a friend. She always had lots of ideas. In fact, the makeover on Aunt Priscilla had made her think once again about becoming a stylist. Or a makeup artist. There were plenty of places she could study those professions in New York. She didn't want to be a lawyer like her dad or a socialite like her mom, who had given up being a lawyer herself to support her husband's ambitions.

"That woman is your aunt?" Marco asked. "She's really pretty." Then, catching Alyssa's eye, he flashed a mischievous killer smile. "For an *older* woman, that is."

The group gathered around Alyssa laughed, even Mia. For once, Alyssa didn't mind her little sister's presence, since Mia liked chattering with Jackie, Gloria's youngest daughter, leaving the older teens to converse and joke among themselves.

"Do you girls know any of the other people here?" Marco asked.

"That's Heather Clarke and her fiancé Rick Scofield." Sabrina nodded toward a blonde woman and her attractive, clean-cut escort. She indicated an older pair. "And that's Heather's Aunt Margaret and her boyfriend John. He owns the fish and bait store in Sparrow Lake. I don't know the other couple."

The young woman and man who looked as if they were in their twenties seemed lost in each other's company. Arms around each other, they gazed up at the stars. Alyssa imagined they might be newlyweds.

Marco stared at Logan. "How about him?"

"He just works for the ranch."

"He seems to be pretty good with a guitar," said Marco.

Alyssa stated, "I like the sound of an electric guitar better."

Which launched the group into discussing the newest songs they'd downloaded onto their phones. Alyssa was pleased to find that Marco liked her favorite group, and he knew some other music she might be interested in, as well.

She had felt only a twinge about Logan when they'd come face-to-face earlier. The talk she'd had with her aunt had really helped. For once, she'd been able to express her emotions and be taken seriously, something her mother felt uncomfortable with and her dad wasn't around enough to hear about. Aunt Priscilla seemed to know what suffering from unrequited love was like, and she hadn't told Alyssa she was too young for such things.

After the summer was over, Alyssa wondered if her aunt would mind if she called her once in a while.

THE JINGLE OF a harness and the thudding of the draft horses' giant hooves made comfortable rhythmic sounds. Priscilla moved closer to Sam on the driver's bench as the soft summer night surrounded them. She couldn't help but be filled with happiness. She and Sam were actually on a real date.

After admiring his rugged profile in the moonlight, she looked down at his strong hands. "It amazes me that two horses that size can be controlled by one person."

Sam laughed. "These old girls don't want to go anywhere, unless it's back to the barn for some hay. They'll probably speed up on the return trip." He pointed out, "The reins aren't the only thing anyway. Maud and Bess respond to voice commands."

Which was good, considering how big the horses were. According to Sam, when he introduced them to Mia before they set out, the two bays were eighteen hands tall, a mix of Percheron and Shire. They were also surprisingly gentle and laid-back for their size.

Heather leaned closer on the hay bale behind them to ask, "Is this pasture your family's land, Sam?"

"Yup. And the next field, too," he said.

"We've always had this dirt road out here for farm equipment."

Which circled up and down softly rounded hills. Priscilla hadn't realized how pretty the land was. This was a whole different view from the paved roads she usually drove.

"I'm really enjoying the ride," Heather said. "And we're looking forward to the bonfire."

"That's the best part." Priscilla knew that Sam had cleared space for the bonfire in a wooded area up ahead. "It's been years since I had a chance to sit by a crackling fire." And thinking about doing so with Sam at her side filled her with anticipation.

Rick asked, "Are the motion lights on the barn working?"

Sam nodded. "The lights work great. As soon as I get a new laptop, you can put in the security cameras."

Sam had told Priscilla that his old computer had pretty much given up the ghost and that his father didn't own one of the "confounded" things. To see digital security footage, however, one needed a monitor and software. Luckily, the cost of a computer nowadays was fairly reasonable. And part of Rick's pay for helping install the motion detectors was the hayride for him and Heather, so Priscilla hoped word of the fun evening would give his business a boost, which would help Sam pay for the rest.

"I hear we've got marshmallows!" Margaret said enthusiastically.

"It gets better," said Mia. "We have all the makings for s'mores."

"Yum," said Jackie.

"They still won't be as sweet as you." John McClintock slid his arm around Margaret and drew her closer.

How sweet indeed, Priscilla thought, to see that love could blossom at any age.

And hearts could be mended. Alyssa seemed engaged by the small group of teenagers on the ride, probably because of Marco's courtly interest. However, she noted something was missing as she gazed at the kids seated on the tail end of the big hay wagon.

"Where are their phones?" She realized she'd expected to see flashing small screens.

"They probably don't work out here," Sam told her. "These hills cut off reception for a lot of phone packages. Some phones won't even work on the main part of the farm."

Priscilla nodded. "Oh, right. I remember Alyssa complaining about that. Besides, hayrides seem to appeal to every generation.

Maybe they're just having too much fun to ruin it with technology."

Heather added, "There are some youngsters who'd rather play in the hay than ride in it, though."

"Like Addison and Taylor." Referring to Heather's young twin girls, who had too early a bedtime for the hayride, Rick laughed. "If they were around, they'd probably be up on those horses by now."

"Or maybe they'd take over the reins," added Heather. "The other day, I found they'd hooked up a harness for the dog so he could pull them in the laundry cart like a chariot."

The adults chortled.

"Poor dog," joked Sam.

Rick assured him, "Don't worry about Kirby. He's game for anything as far as those girls are concerned."

Tales about the twins, who were adorable but incredibly energetic, always amused Priscilla. "How young do you take riders for lessons?" she asked Sam.

"With parental supervision, any time they're ready," he told her. "We have horses that are gentle enough to lead around with a child on their back. Depends on the kid. Depends on the parent."

"I'm not telling the twins about riding out here," Heather said. "I'd rather wait until they're older."

"Parents might feel safer about small ponies," observed Priscilla.

"I suppose I could pick up a pony or two at the sale barn if I had enough people asking about lessons for their younger kids."

There were many possibilities, if he could only get his business on more solid ground, Priscilla thought. She was thrilled there had been a lot of interest in the hayride with such short notice. A few people who couldn't make this one asked if there was another scheduled. If hayrides were organized once a month or so, there would be even more customers who would be interested in the dude ranch and its offerings. She also had another idea she was going to discuss with Sam—selling refreshments and a couple of small tables for the patrons who wanted something to eat or drink after they rode. She realized part of the reason for such thoughts, of course, as well as the entire goal of helping his business be successful, was to get Sam to stay in Sparrow Lake.

With her?

Priscilla pushed that question away and took a deep breath. Just because they were on a date didn't mean...well, anything, in particular. Except that she could too easily fall in love all over again with Sam. Did she want to? And if she did, would she have reason for regret?

Over the next rise, a grove of trees appeared, charcoal gray in the moonlight. What a pretty picture that would make, she thought. Pretty romantic, too. By the time the wagon reached the trees, slivers of red and gold gleamed through the darkness.

Sam slowed the team of horses and told Logan, "Go on ahead and start up the fire."

Logan put aside his guitar and leaped off the wagon.

Sam pulled the horses off the road into a small clearing. "Whoa!" Then he put what he called the pole brake into action and leaped down, grabbing one of the battery-powered lanterns attached to the wagon. He asked Priscilla, "Can you take the other lamp?"

She did so and turned to the others. "Follow me. Don't fall."

"No problem." John McClintock switched on a large, blindingly brilliant flashlight. "We'll be able to see with this baby."

"Wow, now we're probably visible from

space," joked Rick, who helped Heather, then the other couples off the wagon.

The teenagers had spilled off on their own from the rear and were headed for the campfire that Logan had started.

Soon the group had gathered around, and the fire was blazing away, creating a circle of flickering, dancing light. Sam had dragged some logs from the nearby woods for seating, and he and Logan brought the cooler from the wagon. Besides drinks, it held the chocolate and marshmallows. Boxes of graham crackers and other snacks had been stored beneath the wagon driver's seat, along with paper plates and plastic flatware.

"Now, we're going to try this the old-fashioned way," Sam said, holding up a fistful of sharpened sticks. "I whittled these branches down a bit to use for roasting the marshmallows."

"Cool!" Mia said. "I'll take one."

Heather and Priscilla laid out a plastic tablecloth and started breaking graham crackers into squares and sizing pieces of chocolate bars to match them.

Everyone got their sticks and loaded them with marshmallows. It didn't take long for a couple of packages to disappear, though a few marshmallows got burned to a blackened oozing mess and others dropped into the fire entirely. Priscilla noted that Marco was putting together a s'more for Alyssa, so she "wouldn't burn her fingers," and that her niece appeared very happy about that.

The group helped themselves to more soft drinks as they ate, and Logan brought out his guitar again.

John called across the campfire, "Can you sing, Logan?"

"A little."

"We promise to be a good audience," Margaret told him.

Which launched Logan into playing a soft rock tune and singing along with it. He had a surprisingly good voice. When he finished one song and started another, there was a round of applause.

Priscilla and Sam sat on a log a little farther away, near the wagon, so he could keep an eye on the horses. That also gave them a little distance from the others. She liked the feeling of privacy, could almost imagine that they were alone on their date.

"Did you know that Logan could entertain, as well as lead trail rides and take care of animals?" she asked softly.

"I did not. I was going to bring along a radio tonight when he told me he'd be happy to play the guitar for us. I'm going to give him a bonus." Then he added, "Logan is a good kid, you know, in spite of some of the things he's done."

"I believe you. But how did you figure that out?"

"Part of it was my gut feeling. Part of it was because when I checked up on his misdeeds, none were that serious. Plus I think Logan was even blamed for things he didn't do. That happened to me, too, when I was younger."

Priscilla hadn't known that. "What were you blamed for that you didn't do?"

"Anything and everything. For a while, if vandalism happened anywhere in town, the police came to the farm to find me. I was accused of letting air out of tires, throwing eggs at houses, breaking windows, stealing things. I never stole anything, Priscilla."

"I wouldn't think you would."

"I did drive crazy sometimes. My recklessness caused that motorcycle accident. And I admit to a little vandalism, though nothing that did serious harm. I pulled my share of pranks." He sighed. "But my reputation far exceeded my real actions. I just liked playing the part of a rebel. You didn't believe all that bad stuff about me, did you?"

Though she hadn't been sure, she said, "Of course not."

"As far as Logan is concerned, he came out here to apply for a job, and when I checked up on him, he had an excellent reputation with the Sparrow Lake Animal Shelter. He was very good with just about every kind of creature. Anybody who is kind to an animal can't be all bad…and anyone who isn't kind, well…"

Thinking about the sick horses, Priscilla agreed. "Watch out for them."

"I haven't gotten to the bottom of why the kid was so upset when the horses got colic, but I'm sure I'll find out one of these days."

They gazed toward the crackling fire, warmth that wasn't needed for the balmy night, though its bright colors were dazzling against the darkness. And romantic when one was on a real date.

Sam leaned closer, his breath feathering her cheek. "Let's take a walk."

Priscilla's pulse sped up, and when he rose and offered his hand, she took it, her own hand tingling at his touch. His hand was strong and calloused. He was obviously a man who worked hard, and he deserved to be rewarded for that by having a successful business. When he put an arm around her as they moved out past the wagon and the shadow of the trees, she leaned against him. Their being together—her being so close to Sam—felt so right. And as they got farther away from the noisy chatter of the group and traded the glow of the fire for the dark, her pulse skittered and jolted her nerves. As if he sensed it—or perhaps he was feeling it, as well—Sam hugged her to him and stroked her arm, filling Priscilla with growing anticipation.

In the open, the fields and pastures stretched out around them, silver in the moonlight. So beautiful. She glanced up at Sam's face. A breeze ruffled his hair, making her want to reach up and brush it back. But he was concentrating on something in the distance. She followed his gaze to see the yard light on the Larson farm was visible, and one of the farmhouse's windows glowed.

"Pop is watching the barn and farmyard tonight. I'm glad you suggested getting him involved in the business," said Sam. "He's taking it seriously."

"Good."

"He told me he liked the brochures for the hayride. I wasn't sure he'd even notice them."

"So retirement probably is an issue for him then. He needs something to do to feel useful again."

"Well, it's more than that...but giving him work is helping."

Priscilla was curious about what the "more" was, but she wasn't sure if she should ask. She skirted around the topic. "You said the two of you were at each other's throats back when you were in high school."

"Even before that, actually. I think he blames me for my mom's accident."

Mrs. Larson had been killed when her car spun out on her way to town one afternoon. Priscilla remembered Sam being in middle school then.

"But you weren't even with her."

"No, I was just in trouble at school, as too often happened. My mom was called in and she was upset." Sam admitted, "As an only child, I probably was a little spoiled. And I had a lot of energy and derring-do."

"I recall."

"I wasn't a rebel yet, though. That came about later."

Priscilla hadn't known Sam that well, but

in high school, he'd had a reputation as a kid who would take on anybody or anything. "Surely your dad doesn't blame you for a car accident."

"Unfortunately, he did...does. Things were never the same between us. On top of an empty house, without my mother, I had to deal with a broken man. He yelled and took everything out on me. I had no one to talk to about it. I felt all alone. No wonder I became a crazy daredevil."

"Oh, Sam." Priscilla hugged him gently.

He hugged her back. "You've always been a sweet and loving person. I never want to hurt you."

Why would he hurt her? Priscilla wondered. Maybe he meant he had never meant to hurt her in the past by leaving her. When he broke the hug, she reluctantly let go, though she longed for more.

To relieve the growing tension, she asked, "Did you and your dad have a fight the night of the prom? Is that why you left the next day?"

"I don't know what his problem was. He was worse than usual. Maybe it was because he saw I was growing up. We had a big argument. He said that I was good for nothing, and that he wished I'd never been born."

"Sam, I'm so sorry." She put a hand on his chest as if she could comfort him. "How hurtful."

"So I got on my motorcycle and left the next morning. I just drove. I got as far as Nebraska, where my bike broke down, and I didn't have the cash to get it repaired properly."

He'd left town without saying goodbye. He'd broken her heart. And though she'd thought she'd gotten over him, apparently she really hadn't. Hearing why he'd left so unexpectedly broke her heart all over again. For him. If only she'd had some idea of what he'd gone through. The disappointment and distrust she'd felt melted away as if it had never existed. He'd been in such pain and had suffered it alone. He hadn't gotten into serious trouble like she'd feared and she felt guilty for harboring that thought.

"Did you call home to ask for help?" she asked.

"Nope. I just couldn't do it. I assumed Pop would just get on my case even more. I hitched rides after that. Got myself into a stock car and slept with cattle on a train one night. I just kept going west where I started a new life."

"Didn't your dad ever try to find you?"

"Who knows? Maybe. He's never said. But I was nearly eighteen. Maybe he assumed I would come to my senses and return on my own. Or maybe he thought I'd join the army. We'd talked about that." He paused. "Whatever, it's over and done with."

She truly felt badly for him. "Your relationship is better now, right?"

"Hard to say."

"When you came back to Sparrow Lake, didn't you talk about the big fight that made you leave in the first place?"

"Pop's never brought up the subject. When I phoned him after so many years before I came home, he sounded halfway friendly. I choose to think he wasn't in his right mind that night that made me leave. I wanted to let bygones be bygones."

Priscilla thought it would be best to try to work things through, since she believed in honesty in relationships. But she didn't want to interfere in a long-standing problem between him and his father. However, now she knew the problems went beyond Dwayne Larson just being uncomfortable with being retired.

"I've never told anyone but you about all this, Priscilla."

If only he'd told her before. "I'm touched that you trust me."

"I always found you easy to talk to. You really care about other people."

Did he care about her, too? "I'm sure your father is sorry about what happened."

"I think so, too. Most of the time. That's what I told myself or I would never have returned to Wisconsin." He slid his arm around her again, but turned her so that he could look down into her face. "We wouldn't be standing here in the moonlight if I hadn't come home."

Her pulse thrummed. "Then I'm glad you did."

"Me, too." His gaze seared her. "And I was lucky to find you again."

Pulling her into his warmth, he touched her lips softly with his own, then deepened the kiss. As their breaths melded, she wound her arms around his neck. For a moment, time stood still, and she felt as if she could stay like this—in Sam's arms—forever.

CHAPTER THIRTEEN

EVEN WHEN SAM ended the kiss, the feeling stayed with Priscilla.

"We've been gone a while," he murmured, his breath tickling her face. "We probably should get back to the others before they send out a search party."

Priscilla laughed. "They're probably having too good a time to worry about us."

"Unless they ran out of marshmallows, that is."

Not remembering when she'd felt this good, Priscilla laughed again. Hooking an arm loosely around her waist, Sam started retracing their steps back to the group. As they drew closer, she saw the fire had died down, but the logs had turned into glowing embers. No one had moved from the ring. Logan was playing the guitar and singing again. Everyone seemed to be savoring the special evening.

What a lovely night. Too bad it had to end.

But end it did.

"It's time we headed back," Sam said. "Logan, would you make sure the fire is completely out?"

"Sure thing, boss."

Logan set down his guitar and got to work as everyone else joined forces to clean the area of any debris. Sam set the garbage bag behind the driver's seat, and then started helping the others get back up onto the wagon.

As Priscilla watched him work, she realized how much she wanted to be with this man. She'd distrusted him because of what had happened years ago, but now that she knew the truth, her heart had opened to him.

"This was a wonderful evening, Sam," Margaret said, as he helped her up the steps and into the wagon. "I hope you're going to do it again this summer."

"Count on it."

"This is the best time I've had since we got here," Alyssa admitted as Marco assisted her into the back of the wagon.

Various compliments came Sam's way, and everyone was in a positive mood as he and Priscilla got settled up front. The horses were shifting and snorting, waiting for the command to get going. They walked out at a much faster pace than they had coming from the barn. Remembering Sam telling her that horses would take them home faster because they'd want to get to their feed, Priscilla smiled.

The smile stayed in place every step of the journey. Happy murmurs came from the back of the wagon. Obviously everyone had enjoyed themselves as much as she had. Well, almost. Not everyone had had a toe-curling kiss to remember. And then Sam took both reins in one hand and slipped the other around hers. Her smile turned into a grin as she gazed at him so handsome in the moonlight. She couldn't be happier. Nothing could ruin this evening for her.

Nothing until, halfway home, a shot rang out, shattering the night.

THE SOUND JARRED through Sam, sending his heart pumping, and he brought the team to a stop with a growled, "Whoa!"

Looking around wildly, Priscilla asked, "What in the world was that?"

"A shotgun," Rick said. When nearly everyone gasped, he added, "Probably just some farmer scaring off coyotes."

Sam hoped he was correct, but he couldn't

take that chance. He was certain the sound had come from somewhere near the farmhouse. "Probably is nothing, but I need to go check on Pop. He's by himself." He'd never thought about danger to his father. Standing, he waved Logan forward. "Take over the team. I'm going to cut through the field to get back to the house faster."

Hopping over the bench back, Logan took the reins from him and switched into the driver's seat as Sam dropped to the ground.

"Be careful, Sam!" The worry ripe in Priscilla's voice matched her expression.

Regretting seeing her lose that happy smile, he tried to reassure her. "Don't worry, I'll be real careful." He also didn't want to turn off customers so he said, "Enjoy yourselves. This is probably no big deal."

"Hey, maybe I should come with you," Rick said.

Sam was already backing off the trail in the direction of the house. "Better you stay with the wagon. Keep an eye on everyone on the ride."

"Will do."

Sam turned and ran, excited chatter following him as he cut through the field. His focus quickly shifted to what lay ahead of him. No more gun shots. He listened hard for something like a struggle or an engine running, but the only sound filling his head as he leaped the fence to the pasture was his own heartbeat.

He ran as fast as he could, terrified that something horrible had gone down.

Pop…if anything happened to Pop because of him…he would never forgive himself.

He leaped over the fence on the other side of the pasture and made for the house. As soon as he reached the clearing, he could see his father sitting out there, in a chair, shotgun across his lap. Not only was he alive, he was on watch.

"Who's there?" Pop demanded, shifting the shotgun into both hands.

"It's only me, Pop!" Relieved, Sam slowed and struggled to catch his breath. "You okay?" he asked, approaching the porch. "Were you shooting at something?"

"I sure was. Some skulker who shouldn't be here. He was sneaking around the barn and those motion lights you just put up went on."

Sam glanced back. They were off now. "So you saw him? Who was it?"

Pop shook his head "Can't say."

"What did he look like?"

"Couldn't really tell other than his being tall and bulky. It was too dark and my eyes aren't what they used to be. Maybe it's me they're after. I've had my own enemies over the years, but you'd think everyone's too old to seek revenge now."

Enemies? "Who are you talking about?"

"Martin Harris, for one."

Sam remembered the neighboring farmer who'd always gotten riled up when the Larson cows got the fence down and wandered into his pasture. Harris and Pop had always been at odds, but not the violent kind.

"And Will Berger, of course," Pop said, "because of that motorcycle accident you had with his kid Tim."

That didn't make any sense. If Berger was angry with anyone for the motorcycle accident, it would be with him, not Pop. And that accident had been nearly two decades ago.

Not wanting to get into that conversation with his father, Sam said, "I think I'd better take a look for myself. Did you see which way the intruder went?"

"Disappeared on the north side of the barn."

Sam backed away. Though he thought about taking the shotgun from Pop, he decided the old man could use the protection. Just in case. Besides, guns were bad business that he could do without.

"You'll be all right alone?"

"I been taking care of myself for more than seven decades! Just go!"

Whipping around, Sam jogged toward the barn, his gaze scanning the area in every direction. The only thing moving were the horses in the nearby pasture. And in the distance, he caught a glimpse of the hay wagon heading in. At the barn, he slowed when the motion sensors turned on the lights. One of the horses inside protested being disturbed.

Those lights were golden. Sam could clearly see fresh footprints made by someone wearing large work boots. No one on the hay wagon was wearing anything like that. They had to have come from the intruder. He circled around the barn to the north. Those same boots had both come and gone from this direction. He followed the footprints but quickly lost them where the weeds had grown in practically to the building. A well-worn path cut through the scrub and then along the pasture fence. Some of the horses caught sight of him out there and raised their heads, shadows in the darkness. But they weren't jumpy. Everything looked okay.

Sam's pulse thrummed with anticipation. The intruder had to be out there somewhere, and it was likely he'd followed that path back the way he'd obviously come. He couldn't have gone far in a matter of minutes.

Unwilling to give up so easily when he might be on the verge of catching whoever had been trying to wreck his business, Sam pulled out his flashlight and headed into the dark.

PRISCILLA COULD HARDLY breathe when Logan pulled the hay wagon into the area next to the parking lot, so people could access their cars. She was determined to keep her wits about her, however. She didn't want the people on the hayride to be turned off visiting the dude ranch.

Sam, where was he? She didn't see him anywhere. But his father was still on the porch, shotgun on his lap.

"I'm going to talk to Mr. Larson," she told Logan, who was helping Margaret off the hay wagon.

"Okay. After everyone is off, I'm going to put up the horses in the far pasture for the night." Logan added, "Thanks for your business, everybody. Come again."

Nodding, Priscilla told the girls, "Wait for me here."

"I'm going to help Logan with the horses," Mia said.

Priscilla was too concerned about Sam to object. Besides, as she'd learned, Mia was a natural with horses. Starting for the house, she realized Rick had joined her, which made her feel better. A former soldier who'd served in special forces, he would know what to do if there was trouble. Sam's father got off the porch and met them halfway.

"Mr. Larson, what happened to Sam?" she asked.

"He went off after the trespasser who was messing around the barn."

"There was someone sneaking around here, then," Priscilla stated, rather than questioned.

"Someone who didn't belong here," Mr. Larson agreed.

"Which way did he go?" Rick asked.

The old man pointed. "Over to the north. That's where I saw the intruder go. Sam went after him and disappeared into the dark."

"I'm going to go after him in case he needs help," Rick told Priscilla.

Grateful, she nodded. "Thank you."

Rick ran off, and though Priscilla wanted to follow, she kept pace with Mr. Larson to the parking lot where everyone was milling and chatting except for the young couple that was just driving off. Margaret and Heather were talking in low voices. Alyssa was in a knot with the other teenagers. Mia was going off with Logan, leading one of the horses to the pasture. Priscilla resisted calling after her niece.

Mia would be okay, and Priscilla wasn't about to leave until she was certain Sam was okay, too.

"Is everything all right?" John asked.

"Just some snooper messing around the barn," Dwayne Larson told him, adding, "I was just thinking...maybe it's someone working for that Walworth guy who's got everyone up in arms."

Priscilla shook her head. "It can't be Walworth Builders. They aren't even interested in the ranch. Sam and I talked to the daughter."

"You never know if rich people are telling the truth or what they're hiding."

"Or maybe they're honest," John said.

"Could be right," Sam's father said. "No

reason for gossip when there isn't a need." Then he asked how the hayride had gone.

"Wonderful!" enthused John. "You get an idea of what things were like before electricity and cars. Nature is beautiful."

Dwayne Larson snorted. "Though it probably wasn't all that much fun to the people who had to build farms and work the land."

As the men continued talking about the "old days," Margaret joining in, Priscilla wandered away from the group. After talking to Grace Huber, she trusted her own instincts. In lieu of a greedy company after the land, she could only think it was either someone who hated the idea of the dude ranch or someone with a personal grudge. Suddenly realizing she was heading straight for the barn, she stopped dead in her tracks when she thought she saw a shadow flit inside the partially open door.

"Sam?"

Suddenly, she heard a noise inside the barn, as if someone was looking for something. Sam must be in there, rooting around, seeking a clue to the identity of the intruder.

Sighing, she called "Sam" again as she entered the barn, which was dark for the night. The motion detector lights came on but she couldn't see into the shadowy corners. Not knowing where to find a main light switch, she kept going. The door on the other side was open and she thought she heard the sound of footsteps coming from that direction.

Heading for the opposite door, she asked, "Sam, did you find anything?" then faltered when she didn't get an answer.

A horse to her left snorted and kicked the stall wall, making her jump. Her heart skipped a beat and her breath caught in her throat. She stood unmoving in the dark. Someone was there. And they were close. Close enough that she could hear whoever it was breathing. Her skin pebbled.

Swallowing hard, she backed up. She had to get out of there and now!

Before she could turn to run, something billowy and rough came down over her, encasing her, head to waist. She choked out a scream, but before she could do anything to free herself, rough hands shoved her hard, and she ended up flat on the ground. She felt the impact but was too stunned for the fall to hurt. Then she heard feet racing out of the barn.

"Help! Sam!" she wailed, fighting whatever

the intruder had pulled over her...something like a pillowcase made of rough material.

Before she could free herself, she heard Sam's voice.

"Prissy, what happened?"

The next thing she knew, she was freed and in Sam's arms. The lights in the barn were on. Outside, the motion sensor lights were all on, as well. She saw the others gathering at the door. Mia and Logan weren't there, so they must still be tending the horses, but Alyssa was at the front of the group and came running to her.

"Aunt Priscilla! Are you hurt?"

"No, just scared." Still frightened, she was trembling, and her legs felt like rubber. Thankfully, Sam hung on to her. He held her close to him, as if he would never let her go.

"Honey, are you all right?" Heather asked.

Sam helped Priscilla to her feet with her still clinging to him. Everyone circled around them in support.

She said, "I'm a little shaky is all." And she'd probably have bruises tomorrow. She'd hit one elbow pretty hard.

Margaret made a sound of distress. "You're white as a ghost."

"Maybe you ought to sit down somewhere," John suggested.

"No, I'm fine." She'd rather stay right here, in Sam's arms.

"I'm just thankful you weren't hurt," he said softly. "I couldn't stand it if anything happened to you."

The way he was gazing into her face made Priscilla warm all over. She was certain she'd gotten a dose of color in her cheeks.

"Did you see him?" Sam's father demanded, poking his shotgun in the air. "If I knew who it was, I'd go shoot him myself, right now!"

"I didn't see anything. Probably why he put that thing on me." Still trembling, Priscilla kicked the cloth with her toe. "What is that?"

Sam picked it up. "It's a grain sack."

John grinned crookedly. "Wearing a feed sack? I heard that's none too stylish."

Margaret poked him. "Be quiet. She's scared, John."

"Just trying to find the light side of the situation," said the older man.

Sam shook his head. "Here I thought I was following the intruder's tracks along the pasture. Thought I'd catch up to him, but suddenly they disappeared."

"He backtracked this way," Rick said.

"And must've hidden in the barn when the hay wagon pulled in," Sam added.

Just then Mia and Logan entered the barn. Frowning, the girl asked, "What's going on?"

Sam had to explain all over again that someone had been sneaking around the barn but now nothing was wrong. He emphasized the latter and he didn't mention the incidents from the past, though the girls knew about at least one.

In fact, everyone might know everything, Priscilla realized. Thankfully, they didn't go on about it.

In case anyone had a question, she said more firmly than she meant, "I'm okay. Really. We can go home."

"I guess that's enough excitement for one night," said Heather.

"We got extra thrills for our money, especially Priscilla," agreed John, again trying to add a little levity.

Margaret and John continued bantering as usual as they headed back to their car with Heather and Rick, who'd ridden out with them. The teenagers were exchanging numbers and chattering.

Sam stayed with Priscilla, his arm around her shoulders.

Priscilla dug the car keys from her pocket and realized her hand was still shaking a bit. She said quietly, “Um, Alyssa, I need you to do something for me.”

“Sure, Aunt Priscilla.”

“I need you to drive.”

CHAPTER FOURTEEN

EXCEPT FOR A multicolored bruise on her left forearm and a sore elbow, Priscilla was none the worse for wear the day after the hayride. Every time she thought about the unknown assailant who'd grabbed her in the dark, she shivered, so she deliberately tried to put the attack out of her mind. She had to remember that it hadn't been personal, and she hadn't been seriously hurt. It was just another incident in the ongoing mystery of whoever it was that was trying to mess around with Sam's business. Most importantly, she and Sam were going to put a stop to it.

Speaking of Sam, she now allowed herself to believe that their relationship could grow. Their attraction had only become more intense because of the date. Furthermore, Sam's willingness to share private secrets showed that he trusted her. She couldn't help but expect even more good things in their future.

Positive thoughts in the forefront, Priscilla

worked the lunch crowd with Steve in a happy mood. Customers commented on her smile and outgoing personality, saying it made them feel good just to be around her.

"I love what I do," she told two young women who had complimented her as they were leaving. "If you love your work and the people in your life, you're lucky."

"We'll be back," one of the women told her with a big smile.

Returning customers had made her business successful. Now she had to help Sam get his enterprise up and going strong, as well. Thinking about that, Priscilla hummed a little tune to herself as she sorted credit card receipts and knelt to put some cash in the small safe beneath the counter. When she rose, she saw Kristen Lange-Novak coming through the front door of the shop.

"Kristen, how nice to see you!" Priscilla looked forward to a chat with her old friend.

Kristen's smile seemed a bit muted. "How are you doing? Heather told me you got roughed up last night."

Priscilla indicated her bruise. "I wouldn't say roughed up. I took a spill."

"Ooh, that looks sore." Kristen frowned. "Do you have any idea who attacked you?"

"No more than we have about who caused the other problems." Priscilla thought about Alex. "Has anyone else complained to the police about similar incidents?"

Kristen glanced around, looking troubled. Her gaze landed on Steve. "Is there somewhere we can speak privately?"

"We can go upstairs." Her nieces were at their grandparents again. "Is something wrong?"

"I'm not sure."

That didn't sound good, Priscilla noted. "I put the receipts and most of the cash away. Come on." She moved toward the door going to the apartment, gesturing for Kristen to head up the stairs. "We can have some refreshments and chat."

A big tree shaded the window of the apartment's eat-in kitchen, making it comfortable to sit at the big round table, an antique Priscilla had inherited from her grandmother.

Priscilla asked, "Iced tea or lemonade?"

"How about some old-fashioned hot tea?"

"Hot on a summer day?"

"Drinking it that way is more soothing."

Hmm, Kristen must be upset, Priscilla thought, as she prepared a mug of tea using her automatic one-cup-at-a-time machine. As the cup brewed, she poured herself a glass of iced tea from the refrigerator and got a package of cookies from the cupboard and arranged them on a plate. Putting everything on the table, she sat down.

"What's up?" she asked.

"How involved are you with Sam Larson?"

Kristen must have heard about Priscilla and Sam from Heather. Their actions had definitely been romantic the night before. "Sam? Uh, well, I guess you could say we're dating." She could say that with confidence now. "Why?"

"Did he tell you about his past?"

Priscilla didn't like her friend's tone. "I know about the trouble he caused in high school. He was having a hard time with his dad." And he wasn't guilty of everything, from what he'd said.

"But he's been in trouble since then."

Priscilla felt a chill of alarm.

Kristen's look was apologetic. "I'm sorry, being a cop's wife is not always the best position to be in."

"What do you mean? What kind of trouble are you talking about?"

Kristen sighed. "Alex checks records when there are problems in town. He wasn't looking for anything about Sam...but, well, he found out that Samuel Larson, your Sam, served some jail time in Wyoming."

"What?" Priscilla's heart beat faster. "Sam was in jail? When?"

"Not long before he returned here, it seems."

"Are you absolutely sure?" She wanted to shout that she didn't believe it, but Kristen wouldn't lie. She managed to choke out, "For what?"

Kristen held her tea cup as if warming her hands. She hadn't yet taken a sip. "Alex said it had something to do with organizing an unlicensed rodeo."

"Is that some kind of fraud or something?" Priscilla asked. Maybe it was all a misunderstanding. Though it made sense that rodeo riders had to have certification.

"It would have to be more serious than that. In Sam's records...there was mention of fraud, and negligence, to the point of criminal responsibility. A rider, not Sam, was badly hurt. Sam was arrested, spent time in jail, and was finally charged with a misdemeanor." Kristen looked at her. "I can tell from your response that you know nothing about any of this."

Priscilla shook her head, her heart still beating too fast. "No."

"I'm not going to spread it around." Kristen reached across the table to stroke her hand. "Don't worry about that. But I think you need to know about a man's past if you're dating him."

"I guess so." Priscilla's whole shining day had collapsed around her. And this came just at the point where she felt that she and Sam could speak heart-to-heart.

"Maybe there's an explanation," Kristen said. "Maybe Sam just got himself involved with the wrong people."

"Maybe."

"Talk to him."

"We'll have to talk all right." But in her heart, Priscilla thought that once again Sam Larson had managed to pull the rug out from under her. "I don't feel good about our level of honesty in communication." Which was an understatement.

"It wouldn't be easy to tell someone you were locked up in jail."

"But it's really important." And if you were going to date someone, even someone you knew in the past, you'd better let them know up front.

"I agree."

For a few minutes, they remained quiet. Kristen took a halfhearted sip of tea and Priscilla stared at her iced tea glass. No one touched the cookies.

Kristen finally said, "This might put a different spin on the incidents that have been happening at the dude ranch, you know."

"What do you mean?"

"What if it's a...bad person from Sam's past? The immediate past, actually."

"Someone we don't even know could be threatening Sam?" And if so, Priscilla realized, she might have been in more danger than she thought when she'd been ambushed in the barn.

"As your friend, I just want you to be careful," Kristen went on, sounding as cautious as she was encouraging Priscilla to be. "You need to find out more details about Sam's past and who he was involved with."

"I guess I do."

Kristen didn't stay much longer. She told Priscilla several times to please keep in touch and to phone her if she just wanted to talk.

When Kristen got ready to leave, she seemed reluctant. "Are you sure you're okay?"

"I'm fine."

"Will you call me later if you decide you're not?"

"I will. I promise."

Priscilla saw Kristen to the door, shut it, and went back to clear the table. The mug of tea was nearly full and the ice had melted in the glass. She should put the cookies back and the dishes in the sink. But she didn't feel like doing any of it.

She stood at the window, trying to sort out her feelings. Disappointment was too mild a word for the churning emotions that surged through her. She was angry, sad and fearful, all at the same time. If she talked to Sam now, she knew she would lose control in about two seconds. She had to take care of herself and her feelings first. She needed someone to talk to, someone who cared about her, understood her, and already knew most of her secrets.

She picked up the phone to call her mom.

LUCKILY, HELEN RYAN was home for the day, since Priscilla's father had driven to Milwaukee to pick up the bathtub they'd ordered months ago, a special custom size for their old bathroom. Alyssa had gone out with her new friends and Mia was holed up in the den watching a boxed set of nature program DVDs from the public broadcasting company.

Sitting under an ornamental tree in the garden with Priscilla, Mom was shocked and disbelieving when she heard about Sam. Someone who always looked for the good in everybody and everything, she was quick to offer comfort and advice.

"He just doesn't seem like the criminal type, honey. He's trying to help a youngster like Logan Keller, give him a chance. And he cares about his father or he wouldn't have come back to Sparrow Lake."

"I know."

"I remember Sam as a teenager. I never heard of him being mean."

Priscilla nodded. "I never saw him being mean, either. Just rebellious."

"I remember the night he showed up for your prom. He was so sweet when he gave you those flowers to match your dress."

"That was a good night." One to remember.

"He assured your dad and me that he'd get you home safe and sound. He told us he wouldn't drive over the speed limit and that he'd borrowed his dad's car so you didn't have to ride on the back of a motorcycle." Mom smiled. "Roger and I were impressed."

"I'm sure, considering all the stuff you must have heard he'd done." Priscilla told her, "He didn't do all the pranks he was accused of...he says."

"I'm sure he didn't. People like to exaggerate. In fact, I know of one particular occasion when the town police found that someone else had broken some windows at the high school. It wasn't Sam."

"Thanks for telling me that." Concrete information.

"I think it was Will Berger who was always accusing Sam of misdoings. Will is so negative and angry. He's always claiming someone is negligent or irresponsible."

Priscilla knew Berger as a grump and a complainer. She stayed away from him if she saw him in town.

Mom continued "From what you say, Sam had a hard time with his dad."

In a phone call that morning, Priscilla had told her mother about most of Sam's disclosures the night of the hayride. "And they were both suffering the loss of Sam's mother."

Helen shook her head sadly. "It's terrible to lose a parent at such a young age."

Priscilla stared at the beds of summer flowers surrounding them, colors tossed by the gentle breeze. Then she sighed. "I just don't know what to do."

"You'll have to talk to him."

"Yes." Not something that would be easy for her.

"Maybe he got involved with the wrong people," Mom said, echoing Kristen's view. "I'm sure there are some rough types hanging around rodeos."

"You'd think he could bother telling me what happened, though."

"I would hope so," Mom agreed. "But perhaps he's embarrassed." She added, "And maybe he's just getting ready to confide in you. You don't know."

"Maybe."

"Talk to him," Mom urged. "I know you don't like to confront people but in this case, you have to."

"You're right," was all Priscilla said, growing restless with the whole situation. She looked at her watch. "It's about five. Shouldn't Dad be home by now?"

"Five?" Helen scowled and pulled her cell out of her pocket. "No messages. He was supposed to call me as soon as he left Milwaukee. That should have been by noon or a little after. He can't have been there this long."

"Might he have called the landline?"

"Mia loaned him her phone and she programmed in my cell number." Mom rose and headed for the house, then called over her shoulder. "You're going to stay for supper, right?"

"Sure." Why not? Priscilla didn't want to go home to be alone with her thoughts.

Inside, Mom checked voice mail on the regular phone but there was nothing from Dad on that one, either.

Priscilla asked, "Why did Dad take Mia's phone anyway?"

"Because it can be voice-activated. Your dad won't use his own cell, though we have a second phone on our plan. He says it's too difficult to use."

Priscilla thought about the complexity of the newer phones with screens and apps. They seemed like mini-computers in comparison to simpler types like her parents preferred.

As if she understood what Priscilla was thinking, Mom explained, "Mia set it up for him. All he had to do was say 'hi' to the phone and ask it to call me. They tried it and it worked. I was there."

"Okay."

"I'm calling him right now and he'd better

answer." Mom determinedly punched in the number and waited. "Oh…voice mail." Mom tried again and again, getting more and more frustrated, so Priscilla suggested they start getting supper ready. "He'll be coming home soon," she told her mother. "Don't worry."

However, it was after six when the truck Dad had borrowed finally pulled up in front of the house. Alyssa had returned and they were all having sloppy joes.

Mom flew out of her chair to meet Dad at the door. "Roger! Why didn't you call? I was ready to call the state troopers and report a missing person."

"I tried to call. The phone wouldn't let me."

"Wouldn't let you?" said Mom disbelievingly.

"I swear. I told it to call Helen Ryan and it kept telling me it didn't know Hello Ryan or Helga Ryan…or Ellen Regan…whatever. It was impossible!"

Mia approached. "Hey, Gramps. Let me see the phone. You shouldn't have had any trouble."

He pulled it out of his pocket. "Here's the dratted thing. You can keep all this new technology!"

"But I called you," Helen went on. "Why didn't you answer?"

"I tried. It rang but when I answered, the phone just kept saying I had a message. I didn't know where the messages were."

Mom shook her head despairingly and Mia started to laugh as she examined the phone.

"What's so funny?" asked Mom.

Mia giggled. "Look at this conversation: the phone says 'I don't have the number for Ellen Regan,' Gramps says 'you stupid phone,' the phone says 'I have to look up stupid,' Gramps says 'you confounded idiot,' the phone says 'I don't know the meaning of confounded.'" Then the girl broke into open peals of laughter. "Gramps! I don't know how you did it, but this is hilarious!"

Alyssa and then Priscilla laughed, too. Soon even her parents joined in.

"I tried to use a pay phone," Dad told them after he'd sat down and helped himself to a sandwich. "I pulled into a rest stop. Wouldn't you know, the phone was broken."

Mom sobered. "But you still should have been here hours ago."

"Uh, well." Dad's expression was sheepish. "I was so frustrated. I bought a soft drink and

I drank it. Then I, uh, well, I climbed up in the bathtub and fell asleep."

"At a rest stop?" said Mom.

"Yeah. There were some trees near the parking lot. I parked in the shade." Dad told her, "It's a good thing some trucker decided to check on me. He saw me lying in there and wondered if I was okay."

That brought more peals of laughter from everyone but Mom. "How could you just fall asleep out in a public place?"

"I was tired." Dad went on, "At least I didn't fall asleep while I was driving. That would have been worse."

"True," Priscilla had to agree.

"You need to have a doctor check you over," said Mom.

"I was already checked by the doctor," said Dad. "I'm fine."

The look her mother gave her told Priscilla things weren't fine at all.

However, Priscilla had more than her father's behavior on her mind. Things weren't fine between her and Sam either.

"I KNOW YOU practiced with Marengo before," Sam told Mia, "But let's walk him through the course again. He doesn't do barrel-racing every day and he has to get used to it."

"Sure," said Mia, guiding the good-looking quarter horse to the starting line Sam had drawn in the dirt with a stick.

Marengo's shiny coat was so dark he looked black except in midday sunlight. He had big bright eyes and a tiny white star in the middle of his forehead. The horse cantered to the starting place, the appropriate amount of yards from three padded barrels set up in a three-leaf clover pattern. There Mia slowed and walked her mount to the right and around the first barrel, circled it, and headed for the second.

"We were too far away from the barrel," Mia complained.

"Don't worry, you're not in a competition." Where seconds mattered. "You're just learning a new skill."

Sam observed the girl take the rest of the course slowly, then speed up to a canter on the drive back to the start and finish line. That was okay. Mia was an excellent rider. He just wanted her to be careful with the barrels—if she wasn't, the horse might go one way and Mia another.

"Wonderful, Mia!" called Priscilla, who

was leaning against the fence railing, her eyes glued on her niece.

"Wait until you see me really go fast!" Mia came back.

"You don't need to be going really fast," Sam put in. "Be careful what you ask of Marengo. He's got acceleration to spare. Now settle down and walk the course again."

"Okay." Reluctantly, Mia again slowed her mount.

Sam gazed toward Priscilla but she kept her face turned as if she didn't want to look at him. Something must be wrong, though he couldn't imagine what it would be. There was a distance between them that he'd felt ever since she and Mia had arrived this morning.

As Mia put the horse through his paces again, Sam approached the fence. "I think she could be a professional if she wanted," he told Priscilla, lowering his voice. He grinned. "But don't tell her that. She'll get even more cocky."

Priscilla smiled tightly. "A professional? In a rodeo?"

"Maybe. But barrel racers also compete at events created for barrel racing alone." And he wasn't sure he liked her tone. "Why not a rodeo?"

"I don't think Mia's parents would approve." She seemed to search for words, then added, "They might not like an atmosphere like that."

"An atmosphere like what?" asked Sam, noting her expression seemed cooler than usual.

"Well, some of the people in rodeos can be rough."

He nodded. "Some, I guess. There are cowboys who've actually worked with cattle and horses all their lives. Hung out with other cowboys. Their language might not be the best."

"Their behavior might not be the best either."

Sam frowned, not liking where the conversation was heading. "Hey, I wasn't really suggesting Mia become a barrel racer. I was just saying she's a good rider."

Priscilla sighed, looking down. "Okay. Sorry."

What on earth was going on? He had felt so close to Priscilla the night of the hayride. He'd even told her about his dad. Now it seemed as though she wanted to maintain her distance and then some. Her remarks about rodeos made it sound as if she didn't approve of his past. Maybe she didn't approve of his present circumstances either. He knew he had little to offer her.

As he mulled over the situation, troubled, he watched Mia put her heels to Marengo at the end of the barrel course. Horse and rider took off for several yards until, with a snap, the saddle suddenly turned and Mia hit the ground.

"Mia!" screamed Priscilla, even as Sam ran toward the fallen girl.

CHAPTER FIFTEEN

MIA STAYED FLAT on the ground. She was conscious, but not moving. A little sob escaped her niece as Priscilla ran to her and got on her knees.

Trying to ignore Sam who stood too close, she asked, "Mia, honey, where does it hurt?"

"My left arm. I—I can't move it."

"Don't try. Just stay like that until we get help." Trying not to panic, Priscilla gave Sam a quick look. "You'd better call an ambulance."

"No, I can get up!" Mia insisted. She tried but, with a whimper, dropped back to the ground.

Seeing the tears gathering in her niece's eyes, Priscilla felt her chest squeeze tight. "We need to get her to the emergency room."

"I'm on it." Sam already had his cell phone out and moved away as he placed the call.

Priscilla found Mia's hand and gave it a soft squeeze. "Stay still." Somehow, she kept her voice even, despite her own racing heart. "Help will be here soon."

"O-okay."

Suddenly she realized Logan was nearby, his face ashen. He looked down at Mia and then at the horse. "What happened?"

Priscilla said, "The saddle slipped."

Logan shook his head. "I must've forgotten to make Marengo let out any air he was holding so the cinch would be tight enough." He walked over to the horse, who'd moved a dozen yards away from them. "I'm so sorry."

Priscilla divided her attention between Mia, who was trying to be brave, Sam, who was still on his cell, and Logan, who was checking over the cockeyed saddle.

When Logan looked up at them, his voice was strained. "The cinch has been cut enough so that the saddle would slide. It's hanging on by a thread."

"Someone cut the cinch?" Sliding his cell back into a pocket, Sam stalked over to the horse to see for himself. He shook his head and looked to Priscilla. "Someone did this on purpose." Then he told Logan, "Get the saddle off and lock it up in the tack room." He grimaced. "Now we're going to have to involve the police."

Which Sam wouldn't like, Priscilla realized. And no wonder he hadn't wanted to involve Alex in his business's troubles, because he'd had recent problems with the law. She knew she had to ask him about that jail time he'd served, just as Mom had urged her to do. But now was neither the time nor the place.

She didn't have long to think on it. A siren's wail suddenly cut through the quiet.

"The ambulance is coming," Sam said, running to the corral gate. "I'll guide them in."

Priscilla looked up and realized she was alone with Mia. Logan had disappeared, undoubtedly having taken the saddle in the tack room as Sam had ordered. She forced a smile for her niece. "Don't worry, a doctor will have you fixed up in no time."

"Promise?"

Priscilla crossed her heart. "I promise."

"Good. I want to be able to get back up on Marengo as soon as possible."

Priscilla bit the inside of her lip so she wouldn't tell her niece that she would never get back on that horse. The fall wasn't Mia's fault. Nor the animal's. Whether or not the girl ever got on a horse again was up to her parents. In the meantime, Priscilla would have to find some other way of coping with her adrenaline-laden niece for the rest of the summer. But she could decide that later because the ambulance was here now. Sam was motioning the vehicle over to the gate.

Promptly, two EMTs—a woman carrying a big case, a man carrying a wooden board—ran into the corral, right behind Sam.

"So she was thrown?" the woman asked as she set down her bag and knelt next to Mia.

"No, someone messed with the cinch of Mia's saddle," Sam explained. "She just slipped off."

Getting down on the other side of the girl, the man asked Priscilla, "You haven't moved her, have you?"

"I can move," Mia protested. "Except for my arm."

Even so, the EMTs checked her over thoroughly, asking questions specifically about whether or not she'd lost consciousness and about whether she'd hurt her neck, but apparently there was nothing dire to worry about. They then secured her arm to her body and turned her slightly to get the board under her. Once she was strapped in, they carried her to the ambulance.

"We're going to take her to the Pleasant

Prairie Hospital," the female EMT told Priscilla. "You and your husband can follow us."

"Sam and I aren't married. Shouldn't I come in the ambulance with you?"

"You can, but it's crowded in the back. I'll be moving around taking care of your daughter."

"Mia is my niece. Let me see what she wants."

It turned out that Mia was thrilled she would get a ride in a real ambulance and didn't seem at all distraught by the idea of doing so alone with the EMT.

"I'll be all right. You can ride with Sam."

Thinking that would give her time to have that frank talk with him, Priscilla reluctantly agreed. "But we'll be there, right behind you," she assured her niece.

Getting into Sam's truck, the weight of responsibility for what had happened to her niece nearly choked her. Several incidents should have been enough to stop her from bringing the girls to the ranch. To stop her from falling for Sam. She was angry at herself and angry at him. Sam had refused to bring in the authorities to find out who was trying to ruin his business, and now Mia was suffering for it.

"Mia's going to be all right," Sam said.

Priscilla couldn't keep the tension from her voice. "Luckily, she wasn't hurt worse. I need to call Mom to tell her what happened."

"Good idea."

"And my brother."

How in the world would she explain this to Paul?

As they sped down the highway behind the ambulance, Priscilla called her mother to tell her what happened, then needed to reassure her that it seemed as if Mia only hurt her arm. Mom said she and Dad would get Alyssa and meet them at the emergency room.

Calling her brother was more difficult. Priscilla held her breath and then only got his voice mail. She'd forgotten the time difference—he was probably asleep. Relieved that she didn't have to explain it all before she knew for certain what exactly was wrong with Mia's arm, she simply asked Paul to call her as soon as he could.

"I just couldn't leave him a message telling him that Mia was hurt," she said, slipping her cell into her purse. "I'll try again later, as soon as I know what the doctors have to say."

Sam didn't say anything, but she sensed his mood had darkened. She gathered herself together to have that talk with him. More than ever, it seemed to her that someone held a grudge against him. Someone from the rodeo? Or someone he'd met in prison?

There was no easy way to start this conversation, so she dived right in. "I know you were in prison before coming home, Sam."

He started. "How do you know that?"

"Alex found out."

His voice tightened. "I thought I told you I didn't want to involve him."

"Now you have no choice. And I didn't involve him. I talked to my best friend Kristen about what was happening. There were already rumors going around. She talked to her husband, and the next thing I knew, she told me what he'd learned. So, an illegal rodeo. Jail time. You didn't tell me about either of those things."

Sam was silent for a moment, but stress poured off him. Priscilla could feel it. She could see it in the way his expression changed, going from dark and angry to disappointed.

"And isn't that great. The one person I thought I could count on…the one person who I thought actually believed in me doesn't trust me…just like everybody else in Sparrow Lake."

"Trust is earned," Priscilla reminded him, "not a given."

"Sorry that I thought I *had* earned it in your eyes."

Priscilla shifted uncomfortably. Sam hadn't done anything to make her think he could be dangerous or reckless. But that didn't mean he didn't know people like that.

She said, "Someone dangerous with a grudge could have followed you here."

"You don't have to worry—no one from the rodeo circuit would have come after me. They have no reason to. And my friend who got me into that mess with the unlicensed rodeo is dead."

Sam's mood had darkened even further. He was staring out the windshield, his mouth in a straight line. She couldn't see his eyes hidden behind his sunglasses, but his features might have been cut out of rock. He was obviously angry with her, and he'd isolated himself against her.

And who could blame him?

Priscilla felt bad that she'd had such an accusatory tone. Sam had obviously gone through something terrible, and rather than giving him the benefit of the doubt, she'd jumped right into that conversation full force.

Sam seemed *so* angry, he might never forgive her.

And she might never forgive herself.

SAM REMAINED SILENT during the rest of the drive to the hospital and was grateful that Priscilla did the same. Poor Mia. His gut knotted again, just as it had when he'd seen the girl hit the ground. She had to be all right. Surely she was. She'd hurt her arm, but it could have been a lot worse. Even so, guilt lodged in his throat, made it difficult for him to swallow. She shouldn't have gotten hurt at all, not on his watch.

He sneaked a glance at Priscilla, who was lost in her own thoughts. Disappointment warred with his guilt. He should have known better than to think anyone in Sparrow Lake would trust him.

He should have known better than to get involved with the one woman whose distrust could drive an invisible knife straight into his heart.

He should have known better than to return to Sparrow Lake in the first place.

But it was done. He was here. What little money he'd had after leaving Wyoming, he'd sunk into his new business. Which meant his options were gone, too. He had to stick around and make his business and this life work somehow. Truth be told, he didn't know how he would stay here with Priscilla against him. Though he was angry with her, he couldn't stand the disappointment in her eyes, and yes, the fear he'd heard in her voice when she'd suggested someone dangerous from his past might be responsible for this mess he was in. What gave her the right to pass judgment on him when she didn't know the facts?

Her getting that information about his doing time cut him to the quick. As did the suggestion that he'd brought trouble with him.

And yet…

Could it be true? Had his recent past followed him home? He just couldn't fathom who would have anything against him to ruin the decent life he was trying to make for himself.

Someone who would go so far as to hurt a child!

Arriving at the hospital, he pulled directly behind the parked ambulance as the rear doors swung open, and the EMTs got set to rush little Mia inside the emergency room.

"Why don't you get out so you can be with

her?" He couldn't help his cool tone with Priscilla, but the words practically stuck in his throat. "I'll park, then come inside."

"Okay." She opened the door, then gave him a stricken look. "Thanks."

What was she thanking him for? Getting her niece hurt? She sounded sincere, though, so Sam knew it was his own gut eating him up. He watched as she closed the passenger door and ran to Mia as the EMTs got the girl onto a gurney. He waited until they'd whisked her inside and then moved the truck into the parking area.

He sat there with the engine off for a few minutes and let the recent past run through his thoughts. His mind searched for someone either from the rodeo circuit or from the prison who might have followed him here.

That led him to thinking about Dan Thompson, the local Wyoming cowboy who'd been severely hurt when the bull had thrown and stomped him. The town Thompson was from had demanded action. The incident had escalated into the rodeo's shutdown, the event organizers taking off with the money and Sam's arrest.

But no one had reason to come after him—

he hadn't done anything wrong. He'd been blindsided by the whole deal.

Someone from that world seeking retribution just didn't compute.

Reluctantly, he traded the safety of his truck for the ER. Priscilla was nowhere in sight, so he just sat and waited. Finally Priscilla was there, looking around as if she expected to see someone else.

She settled for him, saying, "My parents were supposed to meet me here."

"Sorry, haven't seen them. How's Mia?"

"Good news. I mean...I guess. It's only a broken arm, nothing else wrong. They're putting her arm in a cast now. The doctor said she'd have to wear it for about six weeks, but she would be up for activities in a day or two and perfectly fine once the cast is removed."

Sam took a relieved breath. "Good. That is good. Not that I think it's okay she was hurt," he clarified.

Priscilla seemed about to say something when the outer door opened and her parents and Alyssa rushed in. "Oh, there they are. I need to tell them what the doctor said about Mia."

Doubly uncomfortable, expecting the girl's grandparents and sister to blame him, Sam rose. "And I need to take care of things at the ranch. Please let me know how Mia is doing."

Priscilla merely stared at him, speechless for a moment, before turning to the family that instantly surrounded her, pelting her with questions.

Sam felt like a heel leaving, but he had to check that saddle for himself and see what other trouble he could find that had been done to his place. Unfortunately, he also had to make the dreaded call to the authorities. Someone had to figure out what was going on and stop it before anyone else got hurt. He made that call as soon as he reached his truck, speaking to a woman who assured him someone would meet him at the ranch. And then he called Heather's fiance, Rick Scofield, and told the security expert about Mia and the cut cinch.

"Oh, no, Priscilla must be beside herself."

"Pretty much," Sam said glumly. "But the doc said Mia would be good as new when the arm heals. In the meantime, I've alerted the police, but I was wondering if you had any other ideas for security."

"Yeah, those cameras," Rick said. "We need to get them up. They have motion sensors and whatever they catch will go straight to your computer."

Something else he didn't have. "I'll pick a computer up tomorrow." He was low on funds, but he would charge it if he had to. "About your fee—"

"Don't worry about it now. We'll work something out. You can make payments if you have to. In the meantime, I'll sketch out a plan for your place and then pick up the cameras."

Happy to have a friendly person in his corner, Sam said, "Thanks, Rick. You don't know how much your help means to me right now."

"Glad to do it."

Eventually, Sam pulled into the parking lot by the barn. He calculated he'd be broke after putting in the extra security features, but he couldn't take a chance on another person getting injured. He would do whatever it took to safeguard his customers. He only hoped he wouldn't be forced to walk away from his business. And Pop. And the people he now thought of as friends.

Though he was still angry with Priscilla, he didn't want to think about leaving her again, either. Especially not her.

Saddened by the whole idea, he left the truck and went to look for Logan.

The kid was sitting on a bench in front of the shed near the barn that Sam had turned into a tack room. Though he seemed to be guarding it, the kid was hunched over, looking as though he'd been kicked by a mule.

"Hey, you okay?" Sam asked.

"Me?" Logan looked at him wide-eyed. "What about Mia?"

"Broken arm. The doc says she'll be just fine when the cast comes off."

Logan's eyes closed for a second. "She shouldn't have been hurt in the first place!"

Sam was getting an uneasy feeling here. Did the kid know something?

"When you put the saddle back in the tack room, did you see anything suspicious?"

Logan shook his head. "I checked all the equipment to make sure there wasn't anything else wrong with any of it. Just that cut cinch. That was enough! I can't believe he did that."

He?

"Who are you talking about?" Sam demanded. "You have some idea of who's been trying to ruin me?"

"I'm really sorry, Sam, believe me." Logan

appeared stricken. "He said he'd beat me up. I already owe him money..."

Sam was taken aback by the confession. "Wait a minute—*you* cut the cinch?"

"No! But I'm the one who let the horses loose and spread those nails around," Logan said, as a siren blared from somewhere nearby. "I was desperate. And really sorry afterward. I wish I could go back and undo it. But I didn't hurt Mia, and I didn't hurt the horses, either. I would never do anything like that."

But obviously someone had paid him to mess with the business. Sam was outraged. He balled up his fists and stepped toward the kid. "Well, who did do those things? Tell me. Now!"

Before Logan could say anything more, a siren came straight at them. Sam looked around and saw the police car pull into the parking lot in a swirl of dust.

"You can tell your story to the authorities," he said, but when he turned, Logan was gone.

He'd disappeared again.

So Sam was left alone to face the music and tell the man stalking toward him what he knew.

"I'm Sam Larson. I put the call in to your

station about Mia Ryan's cinch being cut. I've had a series of things happen around here over the past week, but this is the first time anyone got hurt."

"I'd be interested in hearing everything from the beginning. I've been meaning to get out here and meet you for myself." When he added, "I'm Police Chief Alex Novak," that knot in Sam's gut grew tighter.

"Because you think I'm guilty of something?"

The other man's gray eyes narrowed. "Because I like to know everyone I serve and protect."

Sam crossed his arms. Sounded like the police chief didn't hold anything against him, but he wasn't convinced. "Is that why you ran a history on me?"

"I heard you were having trouble out here," Alex said. "Trouble is usually caused by someone you know."

"Trouble didn't follow me from Wyoming."

"You're sure about that?"

After talking to Logan, he absolutely was. Still, feeling defensive with the police chief, he insisted, "I didn't make any enemies on the rodeo circuit. But probably you don't want to believe that."

"Why wouldn't I?"

"Because you found out I spent time in prison. For something that I had no part in creating," Sam added.

Alex looked thoughtful for a moment, then asked, "What about enemies here in Sparrow Lake?"

"Yeah, it has to be here, even though I was practically a kid when I left."

"Some people have really long memories and know how to hold a grudge."

Sam shook his head. "But who? What did I do to deserve this? And Mia didn't do anything to anyone! She sure didn't deserve getting hurt. I tried to get it out of Logan Keller. The kid has been working for me. He admitted he let my horses out of the pasture and that he spread nails in the parking lot, but he swears he didn't do anything to hurt anyone."

"Logan Keller, huh? I thought he'd straightened out."

"He said that he owed someone money and whoever it was physically threatened him."

"I want to go over everything from the beginning," Alex said. "First, let's take a look at that cut cinch."

"I've got it locked up here in the shed."

As Sam unlocked the door, the choke hold

on his gut eased. It seemed that, despite Sam's time in prison, Alex Novak was giving him the benefit of doubt. His tone was straightforward, not suspicious or unpleasant. For once he wasn't being judged unfairly.

Which gave him hope.

Maybe for once, the law would be on his side.

Maybe the police chief could even help him save his business.

CHAPTER SIXTEEN

AFTER THE POLICE chief left, Sam called the hospital to see what was going on with Mia. He wasn't too surprised to learn that she was being kept overnight since in addition to a broken arm, she might have a mild concussion. He would drop by and see how she was doing for himself.

And he'd probably run into Priscilla. Still feeling raw after her insinuating questions, he was nonetheless going to have to face her. He'd probably have to face the rest of the Ryans, too. He wondered if Helen and Roger knew about his past.

Later, pulling into the hospital lot, Sam went inside and asked what ward Mia was in. He found the girl surrounded by her family as he guessed she would be. She was sitting up in her bed, her left arm in a sling, but looking far better than he'd last seen her sprawled out on the ground. Best of all, her eyes were bright and she seemed happy to see him.

"These are for you," Sam told her. He offered the bright bouquet of flowers that he'd bought, daisies mixed with wildflowers.

"How pretty!" said Helen Ryan.

"Nice!" Mia grinned.

Roger Ryan smiled, and Alyssa said, "Hi, Sam."

Only Priscilla seemed to be wearing a less-than-friendly expression." And this is for you, too." Sam handed Mia a horseshoe that he'd polished up. "From Marengo. He's sorry you got dumped and he sent along a lock of his mane." Which was inserted through one of the nail holes in the shoe and tied with a ribbon.

Mia's face lit up with a big grin. "Wow, that was nice of him. This is good luck!" She added, "I don't think they'll let me put it up in the hospital but I'm going to hang it above my bed in New York."

"Hopefully, it won't fall on your head and make you even crazier than you already are," said Alyssa, though her tone was warm, rather than sarcastic.

"Do you know any more about who may have done this?" Roger asked Sam.

"Logan Keller knows something about it, I guess," Sam admitted.

Priscilla stirred, looking surprised. "He does?"

"Yeah. He hinted that someone was threatening to beat him up or some such."

"Then Logan did it?" Priscilla jumped on the possibility.

"No, he did not," Sam said decisively. "He pulled a couple of pranks in the beginning but nothing else." He still didn't want Logan to get blamed. The problem was bigger than one scared kid.

"But why hasn't he said anything before now? That's irresponsible," Priscilla said.

There was that word again. "Logan's really afraid," Sam told her. "I knew something was going on with him. And now he's taken off again, possibly left town." He looked at Helen and Roger. "The police are in on this now. They're going to look into Logan's cousin, the one he's been living with, and his lowlife pals. We'll figure it out."

Priscilla said, "So it was Logan's cousin."

"We still don't know who did what," Sam said. "Meanwhile, security cameras are going up tomorrow."

Roger nodded. "That will help, I bet."

Sam watched Mia, who smiled as she examined the horse shoe and stroked the lock of mane, showing it to Alyssa.

Reluctantly, Sam ventured, "I don't think kids should be riding out there right now, though."

"I totally agree. It's too dangerous," said Priscilla. "Mia's horse riding is over for the summer."

Mia looked up, horrified. "What? I'm not going to quit riding!"

Helen patted her. "Honey, you've just broken your arm. You can't ride a horse for a while anyway."

"Yes, I can!" Mia cried. "Maybe not Marengo. Maybe not right away. If I have trouble neck-reining with my left arm, I'll just use my right."

"You can't be riding. If anything happened to you, your parents would kill us," Priscilla put in.

"Let me talk to my dad." Mia's usually sunny face pulled into a frown. She gazed at Sam pleadingly. "He still hasn't returned our call but I know he'll tell me I can ride if I want to."

Sam broke in, "Your aunt has a point. Not only about your being hurt but because of the danger from this jerk who's threatening my business. It seems he's willing to make some serious moves. That fall could have done more than break your arm."

"How will you have a business if you don't let anyone ride? You can't let bullies stop you from doing things in life," Mia insisted. "No one should stop you from doing something you love. Just because Alyssa and I live in New York doesn't mean we bar all the doors and stay in our apartments."

Alyssa interjected, "Though you do have to watch yourself and use common sense. But that goes for anywhere."

"No way I'm letting some country weirdo stop me from learning Western riding," Mia went on. "I'm used to living in a city with eight million people."

"Though there are bad people in the country, just as much as in the city," said Helen. "You need to realize that."

"But there are *more* bad people in a city," Mia insisted. "And we're used to fighting back. If I get a shot at the guy who cut my cinch, I'll kick him!"

Alyssa laughed and her grandparents joined in, though halfheartedly. Even Sam had to grin at the thought of Mia taking on a full-grown intruder. Priscilla's expression remained sober.

"Mia does have a point about not letting bullies stop you from living," Alyssa said. "Our dad believes that. Otherwise, he wouldn't go to troubled places in the world and deal with human rights issues."

"Human rights?" From her surprised expression Priscilla obviously hadn't been aware of that. "Is that part of working for an international law firm?"

"It's part of our dad's job now," said Alyssa. "He told us he knew it could be dangerous and he would be careful for our sakes. But he's really good at what he does and he's tired of big guys beating up on smaller or weaker ones."

Sam could tell the Ryans were impressed. So was he.

Roger cleared his throat. "You know there's no reason I can't go out to the dude ranch with the girls for their lessons. I have plenty of time."

"That would make at least two other adults there," agreed Helen. "You and either Priscilla or me."

Sam put in, "Plus the security cameras are going in. That's extra safety."

"And we can check every inch of the tack before we put it on a horse," Mia said.

"And look all around the barn and the corral area," Alyssa added.

"Okay," Helen said. "We'll run this past Paul when he calls. If he agrees, Mia can keep riding."

"It's a plan," agreed Sam.

He noticed Priscilla didn't say anything.

PAUL FINALLY CALLED his daughters a little after eight in the evening. Since they wanted to talk to their father alone for a bit, Priscilla and Mom left the room. Roger had gone to pick up some take-out food for everyone, including Mia. The girl said the meal the hospital had served her was blah.

"I don't know why I never heard that Paul was working in human rights," Priscilla confessed to her mother. She hadn't realized her brother was so dedicated to the issue.

"He may have told me," said Mom. "And I forgot to mention it. That's not what he was doing when he was first hired by this particular law firm. But then, we see them so seldom, I always want to get caught up on what the family is doing. We don't discuss much about his job." Priscilla tried to understand, but the risks her brother was taking… "Dealing with international human rights demands takes a lot of courage, especially the way the world is these days." She knew Paul had a decent heart, had never been just about money, but she hadn't expected him to add human rights issues to his international practice. She felt proud and admitted, "I don't think I could do it."

"Yes, you could, if you thought it was necessary," her mother told her.

"I chicken out when trying to face someone I've had a disagreement with."

"Hmm, maybe you're not so confrontational," Mom agreed. "But you like to be kind. Kindness isn't a bad trait either."

Priscilla sighed. "Whatever traits I have, I'm lacking something when it comes to Sam."

Mom looked interested. "Did you ask him about his past, dear?"

"He got really mad." Priscilla realized she'd barely had time to even think about it, what with Mia being hospitalized and all the commotion that followed. "He didn't explain a whole lot either, but he insisted that no one from that rodeo would have come after him. There was no reason."

"He seemed sincere tonight."

"Yes. But you'd think if he cared about me,

he would have told me more details, wouldn't you?" Although she had been rather accusatory when asking him questions, too. Still. "He should have told me about it a long time ago."

"Do *you* care about Sam?"

Priscilla opened her mouth as if to answer but nothing came out. She knew she would say "yes" and that would scare her. She cared more than she was willing to admit. She'd always been half in love with Sam, ever since she was a girl. Now those feelings had only intensified.

"You should think about how you feel about Sam, Priscilla," Mom went on. "You two need to have a discussion about everything...his past, the future...your relationship. From how you've been acting, from your expression right now, I can tell it's very important."

Before Priscilla could respond, a loud "Food is here!" caught her and Mom's attention. They both glanced down the hall to see Dad approaching with a couple of bags.

Mom put her hand on Priscilla's arm and squeezed it encouragingly before turning to go back into the hospital room. Mia and Alyssa were waving them in. Mom ended the conversation with, "Talk to him, Prissy. You can't afford to avoid confrontation when your heart is on the line."

Priscilla thought that was good advice but hated thinking about bringing up the sore subject with Sam yet again. Tonight, he'd merely glanced at her a few times when he'd visited the hospital room and she hadn't been able to read his expression.

As they entered the room, Mia handed the phone to Priscilla. "Dad wants to talk to you."

Priscilla took the device from her niece and heard her brother's voice. "I'm very grateful that you agreed to look after the girls this summer," Paul told her.

"Well, I've been sharing the duties with Mom and Dad."

"You've gone out of your way to make them happy. They're having a really good time." Paul added, "Don't blame yourself for Mia's accident. She explained things, and it certainly wasn't your fault."

Priscilla had to be honest. "Did they tell you about the problems the dude ranch is having? I don't want you to feel they're in danger. We don't have to go there if you say so."

"Mia told me that Dad will be out there, too. He'll be serious about protecting his granddaughters." Paul continued, "Besides, Mia is a little daredevil. This isn't the first time she's pushed herself too far. She was probably riding that horse for all he was worth."

Priscilla recalled that Mia had dug her heels into Marengo's sides when she'd finished with the barrel course. "She wanted to go fast."

"A broken arm should slow her down a little."

Priscilla couldn't keep the shock out of her voice when she asked, "Are you really going to allow her to ride?"

"Allow her?" Paul laughed. "I think you mean can I stop her? If the doctor says Mia can ride, it's all right. Put her on a slower horse, if you can, though she'll hate it. I trust you to take care of my girls."

"Okay, then. It's good to talk to you."

"We need to do it more often."

Agreeing, Priscilla then handed the phone back to Alyssa so the girls could say their goodbyes.

Meanwhile, Dad was dividing up the food. He'd brought tacos for Mia and burgers for everyone else. When she'd finished with the phone call, Mia asked him if he'd brought packets of hot sauce.

Dad reached in a bag. "I got plenty."

"Hot sauce?" said Mom. "Is that going to upset your stomach, Mia? They gave you pain medication."

"Only one pill and it didn't do anything to my stomach. I like hot sauce on tacos," said Mia, splatting on several packets before she took a bite. When she did, she grinned. "This is a lot better than macaroni and cheese or whatever that gooey stuff that was on the tray."

"I like their macaroni and cheese."

Priscilla bit the inside of her lip. Dad had been known to stop at the hospital from time to time just to eat in the cafeteria.

Mia laughed. "Too bad I didn't save it for you, Gramps." As soon as she'd gobbled down one taco, she unwrapped and added hot sauce to the other. "What are you going to serve out at the dude ranch, Aunt Priscilla?"

Mom's raised her eyebrows. "Food at the dude ranch?"

Priscilla wasn't certain what she'd do in the future except for making sure her nieces were safe. "Sam and I talked about the Cheese Shoppe selling refreshments a few times. We thought that might be attractive to customers, especially those from out-of-town."

"Refreshments would be a great idea," said Mia.

"There aren't even any soft drinks available out there," agreed Alyssa.

"It would help Sam," added the younger girl. "Part of the profits could go to the ranch."

Mom looked thoughtful. "He's had such a terrible time. He probably can use all the help he can get."

"I'm willing to pitch in," Dad said. "I can sell food. I have plenty of time." He nodded. "I can pitch hay. Fix fences. Round up horses. Whatever."

"Round up horses?" Mom grinned. "You mean with you on a horse, too?"

"Sure, why not?"

Everyone laughed.

Roger Ryan had never been on a horse in his life, as far as Priscilla knew. She teased, "When did you take up riding, Dad?"

"I learned the Zen method where you visualize exactly what you're going to do before you even do it. I saw it on TV."

"Sure you did, Roger," said Mom. "I think all of us will be safer if you stay on your own two feet, not on a horse's four hooves."

"Aw, Gramps can do it," Mia said. "I can teach him."

Mom snorted. "Like you taught him how to use your new-fangled phone? I don't think so."

It had been a while since Priscilla had witnessed Dad joking around. If nothing else, dealing with the problems at the dude ranch was perking up her father.

ALEX NOVAK DROPPED BY the dude ranch the next morning to tell Sam that Logan Keller had been seen trying to catch a ride near the main highway. The state police and local authorities from surrounding towns had been notified to keep a watch out for him.

Meanwhile, Sam racked his brain trying to come up with who he could hire to take Logan's place. If he could get a high school kid who was available for the summer that could tide him over until he could hire someone more permanent. If his business still required another employee, that is. If his business was still in operation. Trying not to think negatively, though admitting such was entirely warranted, Sam called acquaintances and neighbors to see if they knew anyone who needed a part-time job. Several people said they would get back to him.

Sam considered his past again and who might have something against him. He'd been a wild kid but he hadn't been mean or purposely destructive. The old police chief had hated him, had blamed him for all kinds of things he'd never done, but the man had retired and moved to Florida. So it couldn't be him.

Then there was Mayor Auerbach's wife. She'd always had it in for him. Once she'd made a report that he'd run over her mailbox flowerbed with his motorcycle, which of course was not true. She'd always been a little strange and accusatory every chance she got. Still, he didn't see a woman of her age being a viable suspect.

Someone he'd gone to school with?

Coop had been his main competition right through grade school and high school, Sam often the winner. They'd traded barbs, but they'd never actually had any kind of physical altercation.

Then Tim Berger came to mind. Pop had claimed his father Will was an enemy because of the motorcycle accident he'd had when giving Tim a ride. Old Berger seemed to have enemies everywhere, though. He was cranky and rude to everyone. And he was too old and too sick to have been the intruder the day of the hayride. He could hardly get around anymore. Which made Sam think about his son, the person who had actually been hurt all those years ago. Maybe he should check out whether or not Timothy Berger held a grudge. He knew Tim worked for an accounting firm in Milwaukee. He could drop by, just to talk to Tim and see what he had to say.

Pop came into the room, interrupting his thoughts. "Hey, I've been thinking about that Keller kid."

"Yeah?"

"I heard what the cop said about him hitching rides. If you don't mind, I could go out looking for him myself."

"You?" Sam glanced down at Pop's leg.

"I can drive the old Chevy. It only requires one foot," Pop reminded him. "The kid was a good worker. I'll grant him that. And he seemed to be a decent person…in spite of his family."

Pop had no doubt heard gossip about that. "The authorities in this area are already looking for him."

"But they might not find him. He probably knows how to avoid the cops. If he hears there's an old man looking for him, someone who is not connected to any authority, he might be more willing to be found."

Sam hoped so. "You might have to drive a hundred miles." Or more. "It could be tiring."

Pop grimaced. "Hey, I'm not ready to die yet, boy. And driving isn't going to kill me. Besides, I can stop and rest from time to time. I did that when I went looking for you."

This was the first Sam had heard about Pop coming after him. "You searched for me?"

"Yeah, of course I did."

Sam was stunned. "For how long?"

"A few weeks. Followed your trail over into Iowa. Then I lost it when you must have cut off onto secondary roads." Pop said hurriedly, "This boy's not on a motorcycle, though. He should be easier to catch."

Sam just stood there, not knowing what to say.

Pop went on, "I don't want to stand by while another troubled kid messes up his life."

Sam wanted to say he hadn't messed up his life but, in a way, he certainly had messed up his relationship with his father. And he had messed things up with Priscilla.

He finally said, "If you really think you can pick up his trail."

"I know people in almost all of the towns around here. I know who owns a lot of the service stations. I can at least try."

The way Pop glanced at him furtively, then looked away, probably embarrassed, Sam knew this was probably as close to an apology that he would ever get for that horrible night they'd fought so long ago. He felt a lump in his throat.

"Okay. Do what you can. We'd better pack you some food."

"And blankets and extra clothes."

"Don't sleep in the car," Sam told him. "You'll get stiff and sore."

"Don't worry, I know people I can visit," said Pop.

As his father moved away, Sam remembered wanting to talk to Tim Berger. "Pop? Can you wait until later to take off? We don't have any customers this afternoon and I need to drive into Milwaukee."

TO SAM'S SURPRISE, Tim Berger seemed happy to see Sam.

Smiling broadly, he motioned Sam into

his private office. "It must be nearly twenty years."

"Not quite that long."

Sam noticed Tim still had that slight limp as he made his way to a chair, gesturing for Sam to take the seat across from him. The office was professional-looking with a large, polished mahogany desk and bookcases. A painting of a landscape hung on one wall.

Sam looked around. "I'm glad to see you're doing well for yourself."

Tim laughed. "Accounting's pretty boring to some, but I always liked numbers. I'm a partner in the firm now." Then he asked, "What brings you here anyway?"

Sam cleared his throat. "Well…I just wondered if you'd heard about the dude ranch I started up near Sparrow Lake."

"Dude ranch? With horses?"

"And hayrides. All kinds of stuff."

Tim shook his head. "To tell you the truth, I haven't heard about it. A dude ranch isn't my type of thing. My wife would probably like it, though." He quirked his brow. "But you haven't come all the way here to do some personal advertising. Does your business need to be audited?"

"I only wish it was established enough to

need auditing," Sam told him, then launched into the reason he was there. "Actually, I'm sorry if I'm wasting your time but I've come to ask you if you hold any bad feelings over that accident we had."

Tim seemed taken aback. "Sam, this limp is nothing. The leg doesn't even bother me except when it gets really cold." He looked thoughtful. "But whatever I did and did not do was my own problem back then. I take responsibility for my life."

He seemed absolutely sincere, Sam noted. "I know I was hotdogging it that day when we hit the black ice. I always felt bad about what happened."

"And you told me that long ago. Like I said, though, what I did as a kid was my own choice."

Sam took an easy breath. "It's good to hear that."

"Did my dad say something to you?" Tim asked.

Then his throat tightened again. "Your dad?" Pop's *enemy*?

"He's…he's not in a good way, I'm afraid."

"I've seen him walking around town using an oxygen tank."

"There's that. And then there's his attitude. He's been bitter and angry for years."

"About what?" Sam asked, thinking maybe Pop was right.

"About everything and anything." Tim frowned. "I'm afraid some of it might be my fault. He's just so cantankerous, I can hardly stand to be around him anymore."

Sam knew what that was like, though his feelings toward Pop were mostly positive ones now.

"We had a falling-out," Tim went on. "I forget about what. The upshot is my wife won't go to my dad's house," said Tim. "It's gotten so I don't go there either. I guess you could say we're estranged."

"He's still your dad, though." Sam thought about his own fifteen-year estrangement from Pop. "You should try to see if you can't reconnect."

"Yeah, he is my dad, and you sound like the voice of experience. You getting along with your father these days?"

"Better than when I rode out of town on my motorcycle."

And knowing Pop had actually tried to find him softened Sam's resentment a lot. He would make sure they found common ground and had a decent relationship, no matter what happened to his business.

CHAPTER SEVENTEEN

PRISCILLA DIDN'T RETURN to the dude ranch for several days. She had plenty to do at the Cheese Shoppe, and the rest of her family was at the ranch every day, at least for a few hours.

Besides which, she was stalling seeing Sam again. The last time they'd spoken had been awkward. What if she tried to talk to Sam again and he was still angry with her? She just couldn't tolerate the idea of another confrontation with him.

So, when Mom phoned and said that her father had gotten the temporary "café" set up for food sales—some picnic tables under a big, shady tree—Priscilla bit back a moan of uneasiness. She knew she couldn't avoid facing Sam any longer, but she couldn't help being nervous about it. If she wasn't such a coward, she told herself, she would have done so before now.

Taking deep, calming breaths, Priscilla

loaded coolers into her car that contained a selection of sandwiches, salads, cheese trays, and drinks for the first lunch at the ranch. There were going to be three trail rides that day. The ads she'd put up on internet weekender sites had no doubt attracted summer tourists from nearby cities.

Mom was ready for action when she drove in and parked at the ranch. Priscilla was relieved when she didn't see Sam anywhere.

On her way to the trunk to get the food, Mom called over her shoulder. "Marco. Would you help us please?"

"Sure, Mrs. Ryan."

Mom told Priscilla, "That boy is really willing to do whatever you ask, I'll give you that."

Alyssa had said that Marco had been hired temporarily to take Logan's place. He didn't have any experience with horses or riding, but Mom was convinced he was a good kid and a hard worker. Besides, it was none of Priscilla's concern who Sam hired. It wasn't as if he'd consulted her. To her niece's credit, Alyssa gave Marco's inexperience as an excuse to be at the ranch every day herself to help him. Though she wasn't as good a rider as her little sister, Alyssa knew the ins and outs of tack and handling horses.

"We can store some of this stuff in the farmhouse refrigerator," Mom said. "And leave the rest in the coolers for the first customers."

"Are we expecting a lot of orders?" Priscilla asked.

"There were at least six people on the trail ride that will be returning any minute," said Mom. "And another group will be going out after lunch. It's noon and I think everyone will be hungry."

Outside, they set the remaining coolers on a table and Priscilla got out a calculator and metal box for cash. As her mother predicted, when the trail ride returned to the barn, customers made their way over to the shady area to buy food and drinks. It was a gorgeous if warm day, and people seemed to enjoy sitting under a tree and soaking in the atmosphere.

Priscilla glimpsed Sam talking to Marco as they cooled out the horses but he didn't glance in her direction. Her heart beat faster. When was she going to talk to him and what was she going to say? Should she apologize for asking about his time spent in jail, at least in such an abrupt manner? That would be honest because she truly didn't feel she shouldn't have asked at all.

Priscilla was brought back to the present when a customer inquired about credit cards. "No, sorry. We don't take them at the moment."

Luckily, the young man had a few bills stuck in his pocket that he'd forgotten about.

Giving him change, Priscilla suddenly looked up to see Sam standing in front of her. "I'll take a cola," he said, handing her money.

She waved it off. "That's okay."

About to add that they could figure things out at the end of the day, she was interrupted when, with a tight smile, Sam said, "Thanks, but you and your family are already offering enough charity."

Priscilla didn't like his tone. "Selling food isn't charity. The Cheese Shoppe makes money, too."

"Yeah, but I seem to have at least three free workers out here," Sam told her, referring to Mom, Dad, and Alyssa. "Not that I don't appreciate them helping out."

"They're also watching out for Mia." Her youngest niece had been riding Gold Mine up and down the corral...slowly.

Sam frowned. "Hey, seriously, I really appreciate the help. I'm not complaining."

"Then you're welcome." Though it did sound like he was complaining to her.

Priscilla handed him the cola. Their fingers brushed, making her heart beat faster, but her smile felt as forced as his had looked. She sighed as Sam stepped away and she moved on to the next customer.

Would anything break the tension between them?

Her mother stopped in front of the table. "We need a couple more ham and brie sandwiches."

Alyssa and Marco were sitting nearby. The girl flipped back a strand of turquoise hair—her newest color—then rose. "We can get it, Grams."

Chattering happily, the two teenagers headed into the farmhouse.

"I'm glad Alyssa seems to be having a good time these days," Mom said.

Priscilla agreed. "She's got a nice little summer romance going. Exactly what she needed to pull her away from texting all the time."

"I heard Marco tell her he wants to visit her in New York this fall."

Priscilla raised her brows. "Maybe it will get serious."

"Speaking of serious, what's going on with you and…you-know-who?" Mom lowered her voice, her gaze sliding toward the barn.

"It's okay."

"It didn't look okay when you were selling him that cola. I could tell you were both uptight."

Priscilla sighed again. "Well, we still haven't talked things through since Mia got hurt."

"You haven't been out here."

"I had things to do."

"And people to avoid."

It took some prodding to irritate Priscilla but she was nearly there with Mom. "When I get the right opportunity, I'll take care of the situation. Don't worry!"

"You don't have to snap at me."

"I'm not snapping!" Though Priscilla knew her answer had been curt.

Mom just looked at her sideways as, to her relief, another batch of customers appeared, and they got busy again.

"Let's talk about this some other time," Priscilla told her mother.

In reality, she didn't want to talk about it at

all. She had enough to do figuring out how to get back with Sam on her own. Not that he wasn't professionally pleasant but there was little or no warmth to his smile and glances. She wanted more connection with the man she loved…

Priscilla's thoughts suddenly came to a standstill.

She was in love?

Yes, she was in love.

She might as well admit it.

For better or worse, she knew she had lost her heart to a man who couldn't trust her with his secrets.

WHEN THE NEXT GROUP was ready for a trail ride, Sam got on Marengo and led everyone out. Since the last trail ride would be later this afternoon, Sam had told Marco he could come along, too. Part of the kid's pay was free riding lessons. Alyssa, Marco's constant companion, accompanied him as usual. Sam didn't mind—the girl was also teaching Marco the ropes. Like the other Ryans, she was free help for him.

And Sam had to admit he felt a little uncomfortable with that. He appreciated help deeply but part of him also wished he didn't need it. A man who relied on himself, he was the descendent of farmers who valued independence. If you got something from someone, you paid them back in some fashion. He didn't know how he'd ever repay Priscilla and her family.

Waking from his funk, he suddenly realized he had to give the other riders directions when they came to a rough area of the trail, a path that wound down beside a creek, around some patches of trees, and up a hill.

"Slow down. Keep your horses back by pulling on the reins, gently," he told the group. "Don't let your mount step on the heels of the next horse."

The group pretty much followed directions but a couple were having trouble and Sam dropped back to help them. This was the type of situation when he most missed Logan, who would take the lead while Sam brought up the rear. However, Alyssa recognized what was going on and urged her horse to the front, Marco following. The kid had possibilities. He was a quick learner and was doing pretty good for a beginner.

After getting the problem riders straightened out, Sam found himself at the back of the line, as he'd expected. They were going so slow now, he found himself nearly nodding off. No wonder, considering he'd been up half the night walking the rounds outside and checking the computer. Though Helen or Roger always stayed until 8:00 p.m. or so, there was no one but Sam on the property the rest of the night. He would be glad when Pop came home.

Dealing with fatigue wasn't helped by the fact that his heart was so heavy. Today Priscilla had glared at him as if he was a criminal of some sort, which he probably was in her book. While he hoped there was a way he could repair their relationship, logic told him that staying apart might be for the best. He could barely support himself, much less his woman…

His woman?

Sam paused. Where had that thought come from? He knew he had been serious about Priscilla but he guessed he hadn't realized how deep his feelings went. He was in love with the woman.

In love with a beautiful, sweet person.

A beautiful, sweet woman who couldn't trust him.

"WHAT IS WRONG with those idiots?" Alyssa fumed as she and Marco rode at the front of the trail ride.

"What idiots?" Marco sounded puzzled. He glanced back at the other riders. "They seem to be doing pretty well."

"I don't mean the trail riders. I was talking about Aunt Priscilla and Sam Larson."

"Oh." Marco raised his brows.

"They really had something going," Alyssa explained. "Didn't you notice on the hay-ride?"

Marco admitted, "Well, I guess they were holding hands."

"And walking off into the moonlight together." Alyssa gave a frustrated sigh. "But now they won't even speak. They totally avoid each other." Plus Sam looked like a wreck and Aunt Priscilla was a bundle of nerves.

"Do you think they had a disagreement? An argument?"

"My aunt doesn't like to argue."

"Maybe Sam offended her?" Marco speculated.

"Maybe." Alyssa urged her horse up the gentle incline of the hill that rose before them. "Whatever, it all started when Mia got hurt. Aunt Priscilla couldn't even look at Sam when he came to the hospital to see how Mia was doing. I don't get it. Sam didn't hurt her.

Afterward my aunt had some kind of hush-hush conversation with Grams."

Grown-ups didn't always notice but Alyssa paid close attention, observing others even while she did other tasks, like talk with people or check her phone.

"You can't do anything about it though, right?" asked Marco.

"I'm not sure," said Alyssa thoughtfully. "It's good for a person to have romance in life, especially as they get older." She had read that in more than one magazine. "Those two are getting *really* old. I mean they're both over thirty. They *need* each other."

"Romance is important." Marco gazed at Alyssa with warm eyes.

Alyssa instantly forgot about other peoples' romantic problems. Marco was such an adorable guy. Too bad he didn't live in New York. She would be sad to leave him behind at the end of the summer. Maybe she would even be a little heartbroken.

Alyssa sighed. Her having a romance wasn't as important as Aunt Priscilla's having one. At her age, she might not have another chance.

So as they turned the horses to head back home, Alyssa decided she was going to have a talk with her aunt and see if she couldn't fix things between her and Sam.

AFTER THE FINAL trail ride left with another half dozen people, Priscilla and Mom cleaned up and repacked a cooler with the food that was leftover.

"We sold most of it," announced Priscilla. "That's good."

"It surely is. I definitely think you should have refreshments available every weekend," said Mom. "Can you work it into your schedule?"

"I'm not sure."

"Well, I can sell food if you're too busy at the shop."

"If you did, I should pay you."

"I'm doing this for love, honey, not money."

"But I won't have you working yourself to death," Priscilla pointed out.

Mom laughed. "Work won't kill me."

"You should be retiring in a few years."

"I'm not retired yet." Mom looked around, then quickly changed the subject. "Speaking of retired, where on earth is your father?"

"I haven't seen him. Was he out doing something before I arrived?"

"I think he said he was going through some tools in the barn."

Their eyes met, both no doubt thinking the same thing.

Mom said it out loud, "He fell asleep."

With that, Mom stomped off toward the barn, Priscilla soon following. They entered the building which smelled like hay. A bird flew above them in the rafters.

"Roger!" Mom called. She looked up at the hayloft on one side which could be reached with the sturdy-looking ladder propped against it. "Maybe he's up there."

Before she could start to climb, Priscilla grabbed her. "I'll go up and look."

"Thanks, dear."

Priscilla ascended, not gazing down so she wouldn't get dizzy. But the hayloft was empty. There also was no sign of Dad anywhere below.

Mom made a disgusted noise. "I'd call him but he probably doesn't have his phone with him, as usual."

"Could he have gone into the house?"

They looked there, as well, but the farmhouse seemed empty.

Mom complained, "Honestly, I think that

man has narcolepsy or something. He can fall asleep on a dime."

"Has he been sleeping while he's been at the dude ranch?"

"Not until today."

Priscilla assumed her dad was okay but she could understand her mother's frustration with him. Walking back to the corral, they met up with Mia on foot.

"Have you seen your grandfather?" Mom asked the girl.

"I saw him heading for the pasture about an hour ago."

Mom frowned. "Hmm, maybe there's a nice shady tree out there."

"He was carrying a toolbox and a roll of wire," said Mia, who had stopped using the sling for her casted arm just that morning. "Hey, did you notice how well I'm riding? I know I could canter and even gallop if I tried."

"It won't be long," Priscilla assured her. "Meanwhile, the doctor said to be patient."

"Aw, I'm getting bored with walking a horse."

"Which way did Gramps go?" asked Mom.

Mia waved toward the horse pasture with her good arm. "Over there."

The three of them made their way past the barn. On the other side, some distance away, they sighted Dad banging on a fencepost with a hammer.

"My heavens," said Mom, sounding surprised. "He's actually awake."

Priscilla had to admit she was a bit surprised herself. She waved at her father as they approached. "How long have you been out here, Dad?"

"I don't know—two or three hours."

"Fixing fence for two or three hours?" asked Mom.

Dad indicated a post. "There were a lot of loose brackets holding the wire and some of the wire itself had to be replaced." He lifted his straw hat to mop his brow with a shirtsleeve. "You didn't happen to bring any cold drinks with you, did you?"

"No, but you're very welcome to come back to our little café and have one," Priscilla told him. She inspected the fence, which appeared fine to her. Then again, she didn't know much about fixing fences. "Honestly, you've been fixing fence for hours?"

"Not sleeping…er, resting in the grass?" added Mom.

Dad raised one hand like he was taking an

oath for a jury. "Honestly, I've been working. I didn't forget how. I was raised on a farm, you know."

"I'm impressed," said Priscilla.

"So am I," said Mom. "Why didn't you work like that on our bathroom?" In which the tub and shower had only been installed the previous weekend.

"It's a long story," Dad said, wincing. "Why don't we talk about it over that cold drink?"

They headed back to the farmhouse. Sitting at one of the picnic tables, Dad was on his second small bottle of lemonade before Mom brought up the topic again.

"Why are you so energetic all of a sudden?" she asked.

"I wouldn't say energetic. I'd say interested."

"You're interested in fences?" Mom looked disbelieving.

"I like to be around other people, doing something someone needs. I guess the idea of retirement kind of got me down."

"You were depressed?" asked Priscilla.

"Something like that."

"Doing something someone needs—we *needed* a bathtub," said Mom.

"I know. I know," said Dad, appearing a bit uncomfortable. "But I had to work on the bathroom by myself and...well, home improvement is something that would be expected of any retired person." He went on, "I mean, I keep thinking I've got twenty good years left. Well, at least ten."

"Hopefully, longer," Priscilla put in, not wanting to think about the loss of a parent.

"So make whatever years you have meaningful, Roger," said Mom.

"That's what I've been trying to do." Dad explained, "But I've come to the conclusion that *meaningful* means having something important to do. I worked for forty years. I had to be there or the mail wouldn't get delivered. People had questions I needed to answer. I had to oversee other employees who needed to be there or else. Then, all of sudden, I didn't have to be anywhere and do anything...well, it's been stressful."

Priscilla nodded. "Dad, a lot of people experience the same feelings after they've stopped working. It's not uncommon."

"But you've got family, Roger, tasks around the home. That's important. And you could take up a hobby..." Mom was saying.

Priscilla cut in, "But he likes to feel useful outside the home."

"Sam really needs us out here," Dad explained. "His business is on the line. I'm going to do everything I can to help him."

"I think I understand." Priscilla had been mulling over what her father was saying. "You need to be needed." She looked at Mom. "Above and beyond the family. He should volunteer or work with other people."

"I always felt I was serving the community to some extent at the post office, even if I received a wage."

Priscilla wondered how Mom would take this but she saw that her mother's expression had changed. Slowly she smiled, then reached across the table to take her husband's hand.

"Oh, Roger, if you want to help others… well, how can I object?"

"Don't worry, I'll finish the home improvement, too."

"I'm sure you will. And if you don't, well… you just keep working at something you love and we'll hire someone else to work on our house." Mom smiled. "It's really nice to see you with a light in your eyes." Then she stood and leaned over to kiss him as Priscilla hugged them both.

Beyond her parents, Priscilla could see the trail ride coming in. As he had before, Sam stayed in the corral to cool out and check the horses. Alyssa and Marco walked toward the area set up as the café. Once there, Marco said something to his companion and went up the steps into the farmhouse.

Alyssa skirted the table to join her aunt. "Everything okay?"

"We nearly sold out," Priscilla told her, thinking the teenager was referring to Cheese Shoppe business.

"No, I mean is everything okay between you and Sam?" Before her aunt could even answer, Alyssa noted, "I realize it's not. Not okay, that is. You both look pretty tragic."

Priscilla curbed her surprise and cleared her throat. "Uh, we kind of had a falling-out."

"I won't ask over what, since it's not my business," Alyssa said. "But unless he did something really bad—in which case, Mia and I will deal with him—you should make up."

"Um..."

"You both seemed so happy on the hayride. And he, well, for an older guy, he's not too bad-looking," said Alyssa.

"No, he's not," Priscilla admitted. "I just

haven't had the chance to talk to him for days..."

"You probably avoided him on purpose. I know what that's like. I played hard-to-get plenty of times myself."

"I'm not playing hard-to-get." There were deeper trust issues that Priscilla didn't want to discuss with her niece.

"Get him alone. Tell him how you feel. Either he'll be okay or he won't be. It's worth a shot." Looking over her shoulder, Alyssa saw Marco approaching. "Got to go." She turned back to her aunt. "Unless, as I said, Sam did something really bad. In which case, Mia and I—"

"You won't have to deal with him!"

"Who's getting dealt with?" asked Sam, who'd somehow managed to sneak up on the two of them. He stood near the table with a couple of dollars in his hand.

"Bye!" Alyssa took off with a smirky little smile.

And Priscilla snapped about, saying hurriedly, "We were just joking."

"Have you still got cold drinks?"

"Only orange soda, lemonade and iced tea."

"Give me a tea, please."

"Sure." Priscilla used her perkiest tone. While she was giving Sam change, she noticed he really looked tired. "Been staying up late?"

"I'm up most of the night, checking the computer, jumping at every noise."

"You could use a watchman." She glanced toward her dad.

"No." Sam frowned. "You are not going to volunteer any more work out of him. I already saw him fixing fence."

Priscilla frowned. "So? What's wrong with repairing fence?"

"I've had enough help from your family."

"How much is 'enough'?"

"More than I can ever pay back." Sam opened the tea and took a big sip.

Priscilla was about to tell him that some things in life couldn't be paid for, one of which was letting someone help, when Mia ran up, nearly out of breath.

"Wow, have I got a great idea!" the girl said. "I talked to some of the other kids who went on the trail rides and some said they can do amateur barrel racing and roping, that kind of thing. Why don't we have a rodeo?"

"A rodeo?" Priscilla and Sam said together.

"Sure, we can sell tickets and put on a show. It'll be great!"

"That would give the business more exposure," Sam confirmed. "But we won't call it a rodeo."

"Why not?"

"For one, we don't have any broncs to ride. Or bulls."

"Farmers around here have bulls," Mia argued.

Sam ignored the claim. "We'll call it a Western Riding Exhibition."

"So we can't barrel race or rope?"

"We can. We can get all the students together and rehearse a drill, using all your Western skills. And we can have a couple of other competitions, as well."

"Like what?" Priscilla asked. Sam actually sounded positive. Even a little enthusiastic. While he had some new students, especially since the hayride, they hadn't had more than a few lessons yet, but he figured they would enjoy a little competition.

"First of all, you would be surprised at how much they've already learned. I can set up an obstacle course—the riders will have to open, pass through and close a gate. Then they can ride over several logs or poles. And finally, they'll have to back their horses over an obstacle. It will be fun to watch for the audience."

Priscilla could picture it, especially how the kids who were taking lessons would love it. "And they can practice doing all of those things at their next lessons."

"Exactly."

Sam's lips started to curve into a smile, but they quickly faded back into the tight-lipped expression he'd been wearing for days.

He looked away from her. "Lots of work to do," he said. "Better get busy."

With that, he walked off, leaving Priscilla with the sinking feeling that she might never see him smile at her again.

CHAPTER EIGHTEEN

THINKING ABOUT THE LONG, profitable day at Larson Dude Ranch, Sam finally relaxed out on the farmhouse porch. He'd taught a beginners' group for kids, another semiprivate class for an adult couple, a tack workshop for students of various ages. And he'd finished the afternoon by taking a bunch of noisy teenagers on a trail ride. Being tired from a full day felt good. Crickets chirped and leaves whispered in the light breeze. He took another swig of lemonade and put his feet up on the porch railing.

He could look forward to being able to relax even more tomorrow since he'd just got off the phone with Pop who'd picked up Logan and was on his way home. Pop hadn't gone into details about how he'd found the kid or what Logan had to say but he'd told Sam they were staying the night in a motel merely six hours away.

Pop's return couldn't be too soon. Sam was

bone-tired and could use a break, but he simply couldn't let down his guard until whoever was trying to ruin him was caught. He should probably walk the rounds again, out to the barn and tack shed, then beyond to the horse pasture and back. He should also check the computer. But sitting felt so good, he was reluctant to move.

He'd been resting for a while when a pair of headlights appeared out on the highway. The car slowed when it reached the Larson gate, then turned in, crunching gravel as it pulled into the parking area.

Sam immediately recognized the car as Priscilla's, but he wasn't sure whether he should feel excited or not. He hated that the arrival of the woman he cared for filled him with such mixed emotions. Torn about how he should feel, he stood up.

"Hey, forget something?" He tried to sound pleasant as Priscilla got out of the car and headed for the porch. "Your dad left about an hour ago."

"I'm aware of that. I'm not looking for him," she told him. "I'm looking for you."

"Something wrong?"

Priscilla started up the steps to the porch, then hesitated and took a deep breath. Her brow furrowed and she was standing so straight, her spine seemed to be made of steel. "Something's been wrong ever since we talked about your arrest background."

Well, that was on the mark, Sam thought. And rather than the soft, lovely woman he'd grown to care for, tonight she looked like one ready for a fight. Had she driven out here to tell him off again, just to torture him?

"I know you have a problem with what happened to me." And it *had* happened *to* him, not of his own making, but he was reluctant to explain anything when she was being so close-minded. "Frankly, I'm surprised you and your family have continued to keep coming out here. Mia must really want riding lessons."

She stepped on the porch, her lovely face half in shadow, half-lit by the yard light beyond them. "We aren't coming out here for Mia alone. The whole family wants to help you."

Her tone didn't sound helpful at all. Stilted. Upset. Maybe even angry.

"Oh, you want to help me in spite of my being an ex-convict?"

"Only Mom and I know about that."

"And the police chief, and anyone else he

told." Sam realized he sounded bitter but he couldn't help it.

"Alex and his wife, that's it. And they're very discreet."

"I guess I should be thankful for that."

"Sam, you can't spend time in jail and expect no one to ever find out."

"I would have shared the information when the time was right."

"The right time?" Priscilla took a deep breath. "How involved did you want me to get before you told me the truth?"

Sam's pulse picked up. "What do you mean involved?"

Priscilla went silent. Then, her voice softening, she said, "I really care about you, Sam."

Her whole being had gone soft. Vulnerable. Even her expression reflected the change. So maybe she didn't want to fight, after all.

"I care about you, too," Sam confessed.

"No, I meant care *for* you."

Did she mean what he thought she did?

Before he could get to the heart of the matter, Sam was distracted. From the corner of his eye, Sam saw a light blip on at the side of the barn, meaning it had detected motion. Then he heard a distinct ping from the laptop sitting on the table inside the farmhouse door, beyond the screen door.

He froze, his focus changing immediately. "Somebody's out there."

"Oh, no..."

He turned to fling open the door and stare in the direction of the computer where one of the four quadrants—indicating four security cameras visible in the grid onscreen—had disappeared, leaving a black space.

"They knocked out a security camera!" Immediately taking action, he whipped around and took the steps in one leap, yelling to Priscilla, "Stay here!"

The running footsteps behind Sam told him she hadn't obeyed his order. But he couldn't stop and make her go back to the house. Heading for the barn, he heard a series of whinnies from Gold Mine. The horse had been stabled inside for the night after Sam had bandaged a cut on her foreleg. Her scream terrified him.

Sliding the door open, he caught sight of absolute horror. In one corner, flames leaped from a pile of straw, climbing up the wall. The acrid smell of smoke filled his nostrils, along with another sharp scent.

Gasoline!

"Gold Mine! We have to save her!" shouted Priscilla who'd come up behind him.

Sam didn't answer, but he motioned for Priscilla to stay put as he made his way to the stall and clipped a lead to Gold Mine's halter. As he did so, he saw a shadowy figure slip out the door on the corral side.

"Hey! You!" Sam yelled. He stopped Gold Mine and launched himself onto her back.

"Sam, what are you doing?" Priscilla cried.

"Going after whoever set this fire. Get away from the barn now!"

He hesitated only long enough to see that she did as he'd ordered.

Even so, the delay gave the intruder a head start. Gold Mine was prancing and squealing in fear, and without reins, Sam had to work to control her and use his hands and legs and words of encouragement to get her to move past the flames and out of the barn after the intruder. By the time he got the mare beyond the corral door, the blaze had grown larger, and whoever had started the fire must have gotten as far as the horse pasture.

Adrenaline surging in his veins, Sam sped Gold Mine after the arsonist, who was making a beeline for the fence. When the man reached it, he hoisted himself up and half-way over.

"No, you don't!" Catching up to him, Sam slowed Gold Mine as best he could and launched himself forward to tackle the guy. He hit the bigger man hard, his arms circling around the other man's middle.

Both men fell back onto the ground, the arsonist on top. The mare danced around them, squealed again, then sped off. Sam had the breath knocked out of him. The other man turned and punched him in the face. Though Sam saw stars, he wouldn't let go. They rolled over each other on the dusty earth.

"You're gonna pay for this!" Sam shouted, dust-filled eyes unable to focus on the identity of the arsonist.

The other man just grunted and hit him again. He was strong, with a lot of power behind his fist. He obviously wasn't going to give in without a fight.

Well, let it come. Sam had a lot of anger he needed to shed, and he wouldn't mind sharing that with the man who'd been trying to destroy him.

PRISCILLA CAUGHT GOLD MINE as she circled away from the burning barn. Taking the lead, her eyes stinging from the smoke, she led the mare toward the farmhouse. She coughed repeatedly, then tried to quiet Gold Mine, who continued to be freaked out. The horse's flesh quivered and her eyes rolled.

"There, there, poor girl. Poor baby," Priscilla murmured, petting the palomino's neck, trying to reassure her.

Then, not knowing where else to go, she took Gold Mine into the café area and tied the lead around a sturdy picnic table leg. She looked back to see smoke billowing from the barn.

"I've got to call the fire department!" She ran to the porch where she'd left her purse and punched in the emergency number. When someone answered, she cried, "Fire! At the Larson farm. Come quick!"

Then she dropped the phone and glanced around. Was there a hose somewhere on the farm? Not that a garden hose would have much chance against a burning building. If so, she had no idea of where to look for it. As Priscilla stood and watched, flames shot out of the hayloft's opening while burning wood crackled and popped.

Sam was nowhere in sight. Where was he? Fear raced up her spine. Priscilla knew he'd ridden after the intruder, but the mare had come back alone. For all she knew, Sam might be hurt or worse.

Making sure the horse was safe, she ran off again, skirting the burning barn. Ahead, out by the pasture, she caught sight of the silhouettes of two men struggling. Without thinking, she picked up a board propped against a tree and brandished it as a weapon. Even as she drew closer, she could see the other man hit Sam, hard, and knock him to the ground. As she drew within yards of them, the intruder stood over the man she loved and hit him again.

"Sam!"

The attacker turned toward her in surprise. Dancing red flames reflected over him, but she could see his face clearly. To her shock, she recognized Cooper Peterson.

Rage flowed through Priscilla as quickly as the fire, heating her to her fingertips. "Cooper!" she screamed, and lunged forward, hitting him with the board as hard as she could. He went down. "You no-good creep!"

As Sam struggled to his feet, he caught the board before Priscilla could whack Cooper again. "That's good enough, Prissy!"

Cooper was stunned but not out and, moaning, he scrambled to his feet and grabbed Sam around the chest like he was going to squeeze the air out of him. Sam flailed his arms and tried to get a grip on Cooper to make him let go, but he couldn't seem to manage it.

Despite Sam's warning, Priscilla waved the board, looking for another opportunity to use it on the despicable man. But Cooper and Sam were now struggling in a bizarre dance, whirling this way and that. If she swung out again, she might hit the wrong man. Despair filled her. Cooper was bigger and stronger. And Sam seemed to be losing ground. Then, unexpectedly, Sam spread his arms upward and smashed the heels of his hands into Cooper's head hard enough that the man jerked and loosened his grip. Sam shoved him away and punched him hard, knocking him flat again. Then he turned him over, grabbed one wrist and jerked Cooper's arm in an awkward position behind him, then put a knee in his back, police-style.

"Move, and it'll break your arm," he said.

Sirens sounded through the night. Priscilla spotted a parade of vehicles speeding down the highway, a police car in front, followed by the Sparrow Lake fire trucks, one of them a tanker with water.

"Help is here," she told Sam.

The farmyard soon was a blur of motion with firemen, volunteers, and police.

Alex Novak was the first to find Sam and his prisoner and put the cuffs on Cooper. He and another policeman got him to his feet. "So this was your midnight visitor, huh?"

"Seems so."

"Sam's just lucky he only had one horse in the barn," Priscilla said. The fight had given him a split lip and what looked like a bruised eye. "Luckily, he was able to get the mare out without her being hurt." She held herself back from fussing over Sam as she longed to do. He faced Cooper. "I know we were always trying to out-do each other whether it was on the playing field or on the road, but I can't believe you'd hate me enough to do this, Coop!" He shoved the other man hard in the chest.

"I never did like you," growled Cooper. "But I'm not alone in this. Will Berger is the one who paid me to bring you down."

"Will Berger wanted to burn my barn? Kill my horses?"

"Paid or not, you did the deeds, Peterson," said Alex. "Trespass. Destruction of property. Then you hurt Priscilla's niece, could've killed her. Now arson."

"Blame Berger!" Cooper cried.

"If he's responsible for hiring you, you'll both pay." With that, Alex pushed Cooper toward the police car.

"Oh, Sam." Priscilla couldn't resist any longer. She reached out to touch his face with one finger. "You're hurt!"

Her chest went tight when Sam swept her into his arms and said, "Don't worry, Prissy. It's not that bad."

He held her as firemen ran back and forth. It gave her hope that she and Sam could settle things between them. Pick up where they'd left off before the fire.

When more volunteers arrived from town, Sam let her go. "I have to help."

"Certainly."

Watching him run to the new arrivals, Priscilla wanted to help, too. She strode toward the pasture where the other horses were whinnying loudly, obviously disturbed by the loud noises and bright lights. As she calmed the animals, she couldn't help staring at the orange flames and the firefighters who sprayed not only the barn with water from the tanker but the fences and other buildings, as well. Unfortunately, it appeared that the barn would be a complete loss.

What would Sam do now?

WHAT WAS HE going to do now? It was still middle-of-the-night dark as Sam stared at the blackened shell of a barn. The fire trucks and cars filled with the townspeople who'd come to help pulled away, and Sam knew this was the end of his dream.

At least he hadn't lost the horses. And not the saddles and bridles—luckily the wind had kept the fire from the tack shed, so it was still untouched.

But the barn and the hay and the feed and tools he needed were all gone. As was his money after putting in the security system. Knowing Pop was a little tight, he might have insurance, but who knew if he'd kept up with inflation. There might not even be enough to cover rebuilding the barn. How long would it take to settle a claim? Sam didn't even have enough leftover to buy feed for his small herd, and the pasture grass wouldn't last long.

He would have to sell them to make sure they didn't starve to death.

Sam felt empty and hopeless, and when Priscilla tried to put an arm around him, he pulled away. "You'd better get going, too."

She seemed startled. Eyes wide, lips trembling, she said, "I don't think you should be alone."

"I *am* alone." He looked around at the devastation. "And I'm done here."

Though he had no idea of where he would go or what he would do. His life spread out before him, crushingly empty.

"You're not alone," Priscilla argued. "People here care about you. *I* care about you."

She'd said that earlier. That she cared *for* him. And the way she was looking at him with cautious longing told him that she wanted him to return the sentiment. He'd cared for her since prom night. He'd never forgotten her. Now he'd fallen for her, just as he'd known he shouldn't. He'd had nothing to offer a woman but hope. And now that was gone, too.

"Sometimes caring just isn't enough. Go home, Prissy."

"You can't really want me to leave now."

He took a step farther back from her. "I do. There's nothing here for you."

Her expression of disbelief and hurt was enough to break his heart. She opened her mouth and he thought she was going to argue with him, but she said, "I guess you're right. No doubt you'll be gone by morning without saying goodbye. Again."

With that, she spun on her heel and made for her car.

His insides in knots, his heart feeling as if it had been crushed under the hooves of a bull that had thrown him, Sam watched the woman he loved run out of his life.

CHAPTER NINETEEN

Sam had no idea how long he'd slept but when he woke, the morning sun was blazing through the farmhouse windows. He straightened in the easy chair he'd nearly passed out in and groaned as he got to his feet. He was sore all over, even his brain. He had to force his groggy thoughts back to what he'd been doing in the wee hours of the night before, after putting Gold Mine back in the horse pasture. He guessed he'd planned to inspect the tack shed, still in good form if charred by smoke on one side. Instead, he'd gone into the farmhouse and collapsed.

Today he went outside on the porch and took a deep breath. The farmyard still smelled like smoke. And his spirits were just about as sodden as the remains of the barn. Only a few posts still stood, blackened like a burnt-out forest. The building had been totaled. The hay and grain inside had been destroyed, as well as tools and who knew what else.

He mourned the life he'd worked so hard to build and had lost, but more than anything he mourned losing the woman he loved.

Though losing Priscilla had been his own fault. Feeling demoralized, he'd sent her away, despite her usual upbeat attitude. It had killed him to do it, but he just couldn't saddle her with his problems any longer. She and her family had done enough for him, and he would never be able to make it up to them.

His future had never been so grim.

Sam glanced toward the highway where a car sped toward the farm. Immediately, he thought it might be Priscilla coming back. His chest tightened and a wisp of hope teased him. But when the car slowed down and turned into the drive, he realized it wasn't her. Deflated, he took a better look but didn't recognize the car, nor the woman who got out after she parked. She was carrying a big bowl with plastic wrap crimped over the top.

"Sam Larson?" The woman was middle-aged with light brown hair and a friendly face. "I heard about your fire last night and I thought I'd bring you a casserole to help get you through the mess."

His mouth dropped open in amazement, but he took the bowl from her. "Well…thanks."

"Is your father around?"

"Not yet. He should get back this morning."

The woman smiled, no doubt recognizing the confusion on his face. "I'm your neighbor, Cecelia Patterson, in case you're wondering. I've known your family since you were a boy." She glanced toward the remnants of the barn. "What a tragedy! Hope it won't be too hard to rebuild."

Sam didn't say he had little money and no intention to do so. "Thank you for your concern. Really nice of you. Thanks again."

She nodded. "Of course. Well, I have to get off to work. That's why I dropped this by so early. Please call us if you need anything else. Your dad has our number."

As she drove away, Sam peeked inside the bowl at what appeared to be a macaroni dish. He'd forgotten about the way small town and country folks reacted to a neighbor's misfortune. After a death or a fire or a flood, neighbors and friends always came by with foodstuffs. He went back inside to put the bowl in the refrigerator.

Then he returned to the porch again to survey the barn. He decided he should inspect that tack shed as soon as he got the chance.

Before he could do so, another car, an old

Chevy, turned into the drive. Pop. To his surprise, Logan was driving with his dad in the passenger seat.

As soon as they parked, Pop got out of the car as fast as a man with a bum leg could possibly move. "What on earth!" He stared at the barn, then at Sam. "What happened?"

Sam stated the obvious. "The barn burned to the ground last night. I didn't want to call you and get you worried." Pop couldn't do anything about it anyway.

"You seem to be a little worse-for-wear yourself."

Sam glanced down at his smoke-stained clothing. "Yeah, well, I was helping the firemen."

"And what about your face?"

Sam touched his sore jaw where, he guessed, a big bruise was spreading. One of his eyes was swollen, as well.

"Cooper Peterson tried to put me in my place," Sam told him. "He had some trouble doing it, though. Coop's the one who set the barn on fire. He's been the one sneaking around here. He said he was paid to do it."

"By who?"

"Will Berger. I guess he never forgave me for that motorcycle accident."

"Berger? That old coot!" Pop's face reddened with anger. "I'll have his head on a plate!"

"Don't worry," Sam told him. "The police are going to take care of him and Coop, too."

Looking shame-faced, Logan came around the car to hand Pop his cane.

"I never dealt with Berger," Logan said. "But Cooper threatened to beat me up if I didn't pull the first couple of stunts. I owed him money from a poker game. After that, when I told him I wouldn't do anything else, I just tried to keep out of his way. I was always afraid, though." He gazed at Sam. "I'm really sorry."

"Kids make mistakes," said Pop, adding, "though it would have been nice if you'd come clean a few weeks ago."

"Cooper said he'd make sure the police knew I was responsible," said Logan. "I would've been blamed for the other stuff, too. I know that's probably not a good enough excuse."

Sam shrugged. "It's all water under the bridge now. I'm ruined. I'm going to sell the horses and the tack and get on the road again." Not that he had a clue as to where he was going to go.

"What?" Pop exclaimed. "You're gonna take the coward's way out?"

Sam wasn't in the mood to dispute the comment. "I'm not afraid, Pop. It's the logistics. I have no more money. I don't even have enough to feed my horses."

"I have some money."

"I'm not taking your savings," Sam told him, surprised the older man was even offering. Despite his dark mood, he was touched. "I wanted to contribute to your retirement, not take it away."

Logan put in, "And I'll work for free, Sam. I owe you that and more."

Pop cleared his throat. "I told the kid he could stay in the farmhouse with me. He'll have room and board taken care of. I could use some help anyway."

Sam merely nodded. That was another surprise, a plus for Logan, who didn't have a supportive family. There was a recognizable rapport going on between the old man and the kid—Pop was obviously treating Logan as more than a stranger. He wondered if his father was trying to make up for how he'd handled his own wayward son.

Still. Sam gave a big sigh. "That's all well and good. I'm happy you two get along, but it would take more than the three of us and a little money to get this enterprise started again."

"What about insurance?" Pop asked. "Did you call the agent?"

"Not yet. And insurance might cover the materials for the barn, but not the labor." Sam warned, "Don't tell me that the two of you can put up a building. None of us is that kind of carpenter."

"There's gotta be a way," grumbled Pop.

All three turned to look when yet another car pulled in from the highway. This time it was Roger Ryan with Mia. Sam looked to see if anyone else was in the car.

No Priscilla.

So she had finally given up on him.

He couldn't blame her.

"How terrible!" cried Mia as she scrambled out of the car. She ran to Sam. "Aunt Priscilla called us this morning and told us about the fire. Are the horses okay?"

"I think so," Sam told her. "They're safe out in the pasture."

"Let's go check them over," Logan suggested to the girl.

They headed off together.

"Have you called your insurance company?" Roger asked, repeating Pop's question.

"You need to do that right away," said Pop. "And take photos as documentation. They'll send out a claims adjustor."

"I'll get to it."

"In the meantime, we could start cleaning up," offered Roger. "That's why I came out here."

Sam objected, "You've done enough. Your whole family has done their part trying to dig me out of the hole." No doubt because they saw he and Prissy had something good going on. Surely they knew he'd sent her away last night.

Roger said, "But I've enjoyed the work. And the company. I haven't felt this good since my last day working for the post office."

"Don't try to stop a man from doing something he likes," said Pop. "That's why you shouldn't stop either. Get back on the horse that threw you." He stepped closer and lowered his voice so only Sam could hear. "Otherwise you'll become a stupid old fool like me."

Sam reeled. That was probably as close to an apology as Pop would ever make.

"Go on, Roger." Pop turned to Priscilla's

father. "Lead the way. I'm not as much use as I once was, but I can lend a hand."

Which left Sam standing alone, rethinking his plans. He didn't have to take off right away, leave Pop in a mess, and he could at least take care of calling the insurance agent. He strode back to his cabin to clean up and came back to find some telephone numbers.

More than anything, he wanted to call Priscilla, to make certain she was all right. It took a strong will not to do so. To do the right thing and not involve her further.

By noon, Sam had taken photos of the ruined barn and checked out the tack shed where he found all the equipment safe, if in need of airing because of the smoke. After that, he called the insurance agent, who said she would come by that very afternoon.

Meanwhile, a steady stream of vehicles dropped by the farm delivering more casseroles and jello molds and other food items. Some people tried to give Sam blankets and clothing but he assured them the farm hadn't suffered a house fire. However, he had to admit he truly appreciated the hay and grain that some nearby farmers donated for the horses.

And he thanked everyone profusely and

sincerely. He supposed Pop's advice was good as far as not giving up entirely, but his dad's example, a stubborn man who'd often refused to let anyone "in," affected him even more. He remembered his mother chiding Pop for not acknowledging emotion and not expressing his true thoughts and feelings. Both he and Pop had suffered from the loss of not only her presence but of her influence on their lives.

The reason he'd sent Priscilla away even when she'd been trying to keep up his spirits?

He had to think about that one. But what good would it do when he didn't even know that he'd have enough money to start over? He couldn't ask a woman to take him on without offering her a future. If she even wanted to take him on anymore.

Forcing Priscilla from his thoughts, he got to work.

A while later, he spotted Mia returning to the farmhouse, no doubt having thoroughly checked over and comforted every single one of the horses. Logan joined the others, cleaning up the debris. There were at least half a dozen neighbors outside who'd stuck around to help.

"Wow, you're going to need another refrigerator," Mia told Sam as he entered the kitchen. She was surveying the extra casseroles, roasts and various dishes on the kitchen table. "A whole ham. Homemade bread. Yum." She opened a large foil-wrapped package. "And here's a big batch of chocolate chip cookies."

"The least I can do is to offer potluck to the people out there working," Sam said. "We'll still have plenty left."

"Good idea." Mia finished the cookie, then stuck a fork into what appeared to be a bowl of meatballs.

"You might want to get a plate." Sam grinned. "Unless you're going to eat all the meatballs yourself."

Outside the kitchen window, Sam saw a big SUV drive in. A group of women exited the vehicle and gathered around the back to lift out baskets and bundles.

"It's the quilting group from town," Mia told him. "Gloria Vega. That woman called Nellie—that's the older woman with big glasses—and others from Sew Fine."

"I met Gloria," said Sam as yet another big SUV pulled in, this one loaded with men.

Carrying a whole cooked turkey, Gloria came up the porch steps and smiled at Sam as he opened the door for her. "I figured you could use this." Since her hands were full, she gestured with her chin toward the others sorting the burnt remnants of the barn. "I see you've got some fine folks already hard at it."

"Are they going to rebuild the barn?" asked Mia.

As if they could. Sam said, "We don't have the materials yet."

Yet. He realized he'd made half a promise when he didn't intend to. But how to tell Mia?

"We'll need somewhere to store stuff, at least another shed, if we're going to have the rodeo. I heard the tack made it through the fire okay." Then Mia saw Sam's disapproving gaze, misinterpreting it. She corrected herself, "I mean 'Western Riding Exhibition.'"

Gloria pounced on that piece of information. "You're having a riding show? That sounds wonderful!"

Before Sam could get a word in edgewise, Mia was telling Gloria and the other women all about the roping and barrel-racing they planned, as well as how the sale of tickets would help fund the dude ranch.

"I'll buy some tickets," Gloria offered, as did just about everyone else within hearing distance.

"Whoa." Sam had to slow things down. "There's been no final decision or plan about any of this stuff. For starters, where would so many people sit?"

"I bet you could borrow the high school football bleachers," said Gloria. "I have the number of someone you can call."

Sam took a deep breath, he knew everyone meant well. "Let's just hold on here for a moment. I'm kind of exhausted." And confused about what to do. What was possible.

Gloria looked empathetic. "You sure look beat up all right. Why don't you just sit down and the rest of us will put together a nice big lunch for the crowd out there."

In the end, Sam couldn't sit, however, since the insurance claim adjustor arrived. As they made their way to the burned-out barn, he saw that the farm was crawling with people. Everybody wanted to help. Some individuals Sam knew, such as a couple of kids who'd taken lessons and their parents. Others were strangers, like the young married couple who'd gone on the hayride. Sam was speechless. He didn't know that he and Pop had so many friends in Sparrow Lake.

By the time he came back to the house, Gloria and Nellie and the rest of the quilting group had put food out on the picnic tables as a buffet. Someone had even brought a huge stack of paper plates and cups and plastic flatware. A large jug of lemonade had appeared, along with bags of ice. Neighbors and townspeople sat on the porch, the steps, and anywhere else they could find. Many just stood under the shady trees to eat turkey or ham sandwiches, along with potato salad and cookies.

Sam found that he was ravenous himself, having not eaten anything since yesterday afternoon. He sampled everything on the tables and came back for seconds. Spotting an opening on a picnic bench, he sat down to make conversation. Before he could do so, a Sparrow Lake police car turned off the highway.

Alex Novak parked and got out to give him a wave.

Sam rose, wondering what Alex had to say.

"Can we speak privately somewhere?" Alex surveyed the crowded farmyard. "Some party you're having here."

"I didn't send out invitations, but everyone seems to want to help." And Sam planned to thank them all again, though words only went so far.

"Well, that's good," said Alex. "Come on. I have things to tell you."

"Let's go this way." Sam led the other man away from the crowd, toward the horse pasture. "Do you know more about Will Berger's part in all this?"

Alex nodded. "We picked him up this morning. Old guy can hardly walk and he's on oxygen. He admitted he paid Peterson to mess with your business."

"All because he's still angry over an accident I had with his son? He really knows how to hold a grudge."

"I don't think that's all of it," Alex said. "Berger claims Peterson went beyond what he originally wanted to do...bother you, harass you a little...not ruin you. But once he had the money, Peterson did what Peterson wanted to do, then threatened to tell the police it was all the old man's idea. He extorted even more money out of Berger." He looked thoughtful. "And I believe him. Cooper Peterson is a real criminal."

"Yeah, he is," Sam said, thinking of the things the man had done to ruin him, including hurting an innocent kid.

"Berger's son came back today to see to him. His dad's under house arrest."

"Probably too frail to lock up."

Sam wondered how Tim was taking the state of events. Despite the situation, he kind of hoped they'd grow less estranged. Reestablishing contact with his dad might make the elderly man less volatile.

"Berger's always been a mouthy, angry type," Alex said. "One time he paid a kid to take a bat to a mailbox he didn't fancy that was too close to his house. I can't see him wanting to burn a barn, though."

"So what's going to happen?"

"Well, that's why I wanted to talk to you. Even if Berger didn't want Peterson doing things like burning a barn to the ground, he paid the man to mess with your business. He'll still be brought up on charges."

Sam merely nodded.

"But I didn't see how we could put a sick old man like that in prison," said Alex, "especially since he was being threatened himself. I talked to the DA this morning. He already offered Berger a deal, and the old man agreed."

"Which is what?"

"Wearing an ankle bracelet and being confined to his own property for six months if he makes amends. The man's got quite a bit of money. Berger agreed he'll pay for the barn."

Sam's mouth dropped open. Everyone knew the Bergers had inherited money from the days when a railroad was built in the county. And Will Berger had been a savvy businessman.

"I would suggest you agree to take the money," Alex added.

"How much are we talking about?"

"Whatever it costs to rebuild it."

"There will be some insurance coming in."

"Then you can have it built bigger and better than before."

What could Sam say? He was stunned, not to mention grateful.

"So it's okay with you?" Alex asked.

"Uh...yeah. Yeah. It sure is okay."

In a way, he felt like he'd escaped a death sentence. He had another chance to rebuild his life.

He could have something to offer a woman.

If she still wanted him...

"Great." Alex clapped him on the back. "This mess won't turn out to be a complete disaster after all." He said, "Of course, you're going to need to drop by the police station and give a statement." He glanced about. "Is

Logan Keller around? Peterson put the blame on him for some incidents."

"Those incidents were nothing important. No loss involved. And he's apologized up one side and down the other. I don't want to press charges against Logan."

"That should go a long way with the district attorney." Alex looked around at the people milling about the farmyard. "Seems like you have all the backup you need here today. I have to get going."

"Thanks for your help in this, Alex."

As the chief headed for his police car, Sam caught sight of Helen Ryan serving food. And she wasn't alone. Priscilla glanced his way. Their gazes locked for a split second before she quickly turned away. Sam swallowed, wondering how he was going to talk to her alone with so many people around.

And when he got the chance, what was he going to say?

PRISCILLA TRIED NOT to think about Sam as she helped feed the crowd that had turned out to clear away what remained of the barn. He'd told her there was nothing here for her. Apparently not even him. Apparently, he saw her wanting to help him as some kind of charity.

Did he believe that about her feelings for him, too?

Everything had been great between them until she'd tried to question him about the jail time he'd served. She'd come back last night to have it out with him. To clear the air. To see if he would talk about what had happened so that it wasn't some big question constantly tormenting her. But most of all, she'd wanted to put her biggest fear at rest. Fear of confrontation had been a constant in her life, but Mia's courage had inspired her. She'd found the courage to tell Sam that she loved him.

Unfortunately, the fire had been the ultimate interruption.

Sometimes caring just isn't enough. Go home, Prissy.

You can't really want me to leave now.

I do. There's nothing here for you.

Sam's rejection had haunted her all night. She'd barely slept.

"We're out of ham," Mom said, cutting into her thoughts. "Could you go back to the kitchen and get more?"

"Okay."

Though reluctant to leave her safe place, Priscilla headed for the house. Focusing on the back door, she hoped that when she opened it, Sam wouldn't be there. If he was, what would she say to him? Part of her had wanted to stay away, to not have to face him, but she'd decided she was no coward. Her coming to do her part had been the right thing to do. She would have done so for anyone in trouble. Only coming back for Sam had been more difficult than she'd imagined.

"Prissy..."

Stopping dead in her tracks just feet from the door, she froze, at least on the outside.

"Aren't you ever going to look at me again?"

She shook her head as she turned to see Sam, who'd just come around the side of the house. "Well?"

"Well, I want to apologize."

"For last night?"

"For everything. Can we talk?"

"I'm supposed to get more ham."

"The ham can wait. This can't." Sam's brow furrowed. "Let's get away from the crowd for a few minutes. Please."

With trepidation, she followed him to the backyard, the only place that was empty of people. What exactly was the apology for? He indicated she should take a seat in one of the lawn chairs but there was no way she could sit. Instead, she leaned against a tree, arms crossed protectively over her chest.

Sam looked her straight in the eyes and said, "You were right, Prissy. When I realized I felt more than friendship for you, I should have told you everything about my past."

"You mean about your serving time?" Something she hadn't expected.

Sam nodded. "You deserve to know what happened. Some promoters came to my buddy Jackson and me, and asked if we would lend our names to their rodeo. It was a small rodeo that played in a different town every night. Being off season, we agreed. We weren't going to turn down work, and the contract made us part owners, so we would get profits."

"Sounds reasonable," she agreed.

"But we made a mistake. Turned out the promoters were a couple of shady guys with expired licenses. We might not have found that out if a local cowboy hadn't nearly died when he got run over by a bull that never should have been used. He'd already maimed a couple cowboys and had been taken off the circuit because he was too dangerous."

"And you were blamed personally when you didn't know?"

Again, he nodded. "The promoters disappeared overnight with all the money, so Jackson went after them. I tried to convince him we should take the loss and walk away, but he wouldn't listen. They found his body the next day."

"How horrible."

"That it was. And when the local rider didn't regain consciousness for days, the town was in an uproar. With the promoters and Jackson gone, there was only me left to blame."

It suddenly became clear to her. "So you served time for something that wasn't even your fault." No wonder Sam had been so testy when she'd tried to talk to him about it.

"I'm guilty of a lack of due diligence." He sighed. "I didn't know this particular rodeo, but I foolishly signed that contract without consulting a lawyer or having the promoters or their license or the animals they were using checked out, so in that respect, I *was* to blame." He rubbed the back of his neck. "I might have spent years in prison if I hadn't finally wised up and gotten a good lawyer to get me out of that mess. He pleaded the charges down to a misdemeanor with time served."

"So you paid for being so trusting." And she hadn't trusted him at all.

"Something I would never do again. Businesswise, I mean." Sam stepped closer, reached out and cupped her cheek. "But I want to trust you, Prissy, and I want you to trust me. I've always cared for you, even in high school."

Her pulse raced at his touch. "I know you asked me to the prom on a bet."

"A bet I was glad to take. That was the best night of my life. So far." He slid his hands up her arms and grasped her shoulders, pulling her closer. "I'm hoping for better in the future."

"W-what are you saying?"

"That I not only care for you, Priscilla Ryan, I *love* you. That's why I tried to send you away last night. Because I didn't think I had a future to offer the woman I wanted in my life."

"You love me?"

He nodded. "Can you trust me after what I put you through?"

She wanted to cry for happiness, but she wouldn't allow it. "I think I can trust you, but I want something cleared up first."

"More?"

"If I want to be with someone, I don't care if he's poor or rich. And I don't want him making my decisions for me," she stated. "You can be a proud man, Sam Larson."

"Like father, like son." Sam gave her a rueful smile. "I think things are going to change in that quarter."

"They'd better, because I'm going to be up front about it. I've recently gone looking for the courage it takes to get what I want. And I want you, Sam Larson, because I love you, too."

With a whoop, Sam tightened his arms around her and kissed her soundly. Good thing he was holding her, because her knees turned to butter. When the kiss ended, she tucked her head against his shoulder and reveled in his warmth, knowing that being with the man she loved opened possibilities for her future that she couldn't even imagine.

EPILOGUE

A FEW WEEKS LATER, the first Western Riding Exhibition at Larson Dude Ranch was a resounding success. Sitting in the audience with her parents, surrounded by friends, Priscilla yelled encouragement to the youngsters showing off their best in categories ranging from the simple opening and closing of a gate on horseback to difficult tasks such as roping "calves" constructed of sawhorses with horns, and riding barrel races. Mia excelled in the latter, putting Marengo through his paces, and winning a first place blue ribbon handed out by Sam.

"I knew she could do it," Mom said.

"I never doubted her." Priscilla watched the other participants receive awards in the middle of the corral. "Not even a broken arm can stop that girl."

"Yay, Mia!" yelled Dad, along with the crowd.

They had cheered for every single winner,

as well as those who got red, yellow or white ribbons. And there was quite a gathering of people seated on the bleachers a local trucker from Sparrow Lake had hauled over from the high school's football field. So many were attending the event that the overflow of cars was parked on the grassy sides of the highway, and Alex Novak had assigned a deputy to direct traffic in front of the dude ranch.

Speaking of the dude ranch, there were many improvements in only a few weeks. A huge, fancy new gate stood at the entrance featuring a tall wrought iron arch decorated with running horses. The new and bigger barn rose beyond the corral, its pristine lumber glistening in the sun. Though Sam said he could pay for construction workers, many of the townspeople had volunteered to help, as well.

The last ribbon given out, Sam stepped forward in the corral, a wireless microphone in his hand. "Are you ready for a parade?"

The crowd roared in return. Though the exhibition had started with a procession of young riders and the ranch's horses, Sam had put together a bigger, real parade to end the event with many outside participants. The corral was too small to hold it, so part of the fence had been opened up on one side and a gate put in, which a couple of young men now opened. A dirt road had been graded that led from the corral into the nearest pasture, circled and came back. The parade had lined up out there.

"Let 'em come on in!" yelled Sam.

First in line was Alyssa wearing sparkly purple pants with a fancy T-shirt and equally sparkly Western vest and hat. The gray horse she was riding, borrowed from the county's saddle club, pranced, obviously knowing he was the center of attention and enjoying it. Coming through the gate, Alyssa took her mount around the arena ring and out the other side.

Next came the members of the saddle club themselves, twenty-two strong, riding everything from quarter horses to American saddlebreds and a couple of mules. The kids from the exhibition followed, getting cheers again as they passed family and neighbors. Bringing up the rear were a miniature stagecoach and a "chuck wagon" drawn by teams of small ponies that had arrived from a farm near Milwaukee.

"This is as good a show as the county fair!" exclaimed a man in the crowd.

Nearby, Priscilla saw Taylor, one of Heather's twins pointing at the ponies. "Those are small enough for me to ride, Mom."

Heather merely nodded, her gaze meeting Priscilla's over the tops of people's heads. Priscilla nodded back, knowing she would have to remind Sam to buy a couple of those ponies for little kids to ride.

The tail end of the parade was composed of larger horses drawing wagons and carriages. The very last was a fancy little black buggy that had been refurbished and was being driven by Logan. It stopped next to Sam. Logan handed him the reins and jumped down.

Before he got in the vehicle, Sam put the microphone to his mouth. "This is a buggy for two, just enough room for me and my lady." He gestured. "Priscilla Ryan. How about joining me?"

The crowd applauded.

"Go on." Mom gave her a little push in the right direction.

Apprehensive, Priscilla walked out into the arena where Sam was waiting.

He took her hand and leaned closer. "I love you."

"I love you, too," she told him, before realizing that the microphone had amplified what they'd said.

Sam hadn't turned it off!

"Whoo, hoo!" yelled more than one voice, as the crowd cheered and clapped.

A woman called, "What's a horse opera without a romance?"

Sam just shrugged and leaned in to kiss Priscilla, his lips both firm and soft.

"Way to go, Aunt Priscilla!" Alyssa hollered over the noise.

Priscilla looked around to see her nieces and parents and friends and townspeople and even people she didn't know cheering for her and Sam. A smile of pure happiness filled her as she wrapped her arms around his neck and kissed him again.

* * * * *